The Legacy Collection

Book 1: Maid for the Billionaire

Book 2: For Love or Legacy

Book 3: Bedding the Billionaire

Book 4: Saving the Sheikh

Book 5: Rise of the Billionaire

Book 6: Breaching the Billionaire

Sign up for the mailing list at RuthCardello.com to be notified as soon as Breaching the Billionaire is available.

Breaching the Billionaire:

Alethea's Redemption

By Ruth Cardello
Copyright © 2014 Ruth Cardello

First Printing, 2014, Paperback edition 1.0
ISBN: 978-1495367335

This book or any portion thereof may not be reproduced or used in any manner whatsoever without the express written permission of the copyright owner except for the use of brief quotations in a book review.

This is a work of fiction. Any resemblance to actual persons, places, event, business establishments or locales is entirely coincidental.

Print cover by Calista Taylor

Author Contact
Website: RuthCardello.com
Email: Minouri@aol.com
Facebook: Author Ruth Cardello
Twitter: RuthieCardello

Dedication:

I am so grateful to everyone who was part of the process of creating Alethea's Redemption. Thank you to:

Calista Taylor for designing the covers for my series.

My very patient beta readers: Karen Lawson, Heather Bell, Lucy Wright.

My editors: Karen Lawson, Janet Hitchcock, Marion Archer and Nina Pearlman.

My three year old daughter who feels that she's helping when she sits on my lap while I review edits. Although she doesn't understand a comma's function, she's sure I need more of them.

Melanie Hanna, for helping me organize the business side of publishing.

My Roadies for making me smile each day when I log on my computer.

Merci C. for naming Alethea's hero.

Anita Schnegg for lending me her name for a cameo as a secretary.

Thank you to my husband, Tony, who listens to the story so many times he dreams about the characters.

To my niece, Danielle Stewart, for joining me in self-publishing. It's amazing to watch your own journey! As Abby would say – Always better together!

And special thanks to:

As with many of my characters, I based Alethea on someone I admire. No, the real Alethea doesn't break into places, but she is an outspoken local advocate for education in her community. She'll go nose to nose with anyone she thinks isn't protecting the best interests of the children.

So, Alethea, thank you for lending me your name and for not being offended when I rounded your character out with flaws. The world needs people who are willing to stand up for what they believe in. Thank you for being one of those people.

A note to my readers:

I thought I could end this series with six books, but I'm leaving the door open for more. I have outlines of novellas I'd like to add to the series and I get requests for more characters to find love in the series.

You'll see glimpses of the characters from the Legacy Collection in my new series, The Andrades.

CHAPTER *One*

EMBRACE IT OR fight it until your last breath; change is life's only constant.

Or more succinctly:

Change sucks.

Pacing her uptown Manhattan apartment, Alethea paused to look out the window at the busy street below. It was one of her many homes, but since her New York-based company was doing well, it had been a natural choice for her to settle in the city. It was also where Lil Dartley, her best friend, spent most of her time. A friend whose sister was about to have a baby. Today or tomorrow, if the doctor's predictions were correct.

A second Dartley having a baby.

The first time, I was needed.

This time, I'm not even welcome.

Still, Alethea felt she had to be nearby, in case Lil or her family needed her. No, they hadn't forgiven her yet, for what, even she had to admit, had been poor handling of "the Jeremy situation." *Is there anything worse than someone telling you how horrible you are and realizing they're right?*

I've hurt people I cared about.

I've been selfish.

Being sorry isn't enough to make things right. I have to remove the stain of my mistakes. If that's even possible.

Some mistakes are unforgiveable.

Alethea scowled. *Especially if Saint Abby declares them so.*

Alethea gave herself a silent lecture. *Shake it off. Don't hate her. Be glad she and Lil have each other again. She's a part of Lil's life. Don't give up. For Lil.*

1

The ringing of her cell phone pulled Alethea out of her dark thoughts. She smiled when she saw the caller ID. *Speak of the imp.*

"Al, Abby called." Lil's voice vibrated with excitement. "She just went into labor. She and Dominic are heading to Mount Sinai Hospital right now. This is it."

"Do you need someone to watch Colby?" A smile spread across her face as she mentioned the little girl she considered her niece.

"No, she's coming with me. There is a whole suite for us. You know Dominic, only the best. I'm sorry I didn't call you earlier. Things have been crazy the last couple of days. The press is everywhere. They really want a picture of this baby. I'll tell you, I almost miss the calm of no one knowing me. They literally block you in sometimes. No wonder Dominic has so much security. I used to think he went overboard, but I would be worried about how they'd get to the hospital without it."

Instinctively Alethea asked, "What's the security plan for the hospital?"

Lil said, "I have no idea, but I'm sure it's top-notch."

By whose standards? Alethea frowned. "I hope so. People take advantage of chaos."

"You worry too much, Al. There'll probably be a swat team guarding the door. It'll be like Fort Knox. No one is more paranoid than Dominic." Lil laughed. "Well, maybe just you."

Alethea cast her eyes heavenward. *Vigilance isn't a suggestion; it's a necessity for survival.* "It's *not* paranoia if people are actually out to get you. You know as well as I do that something is brewing." With an exasperated wave of her hand, she added, "I know you don't think I have enough proof yet, but my gut tells me that trouble for Corisi Enterprises is only just beginning. The glitches in their system. The rumors that there's someone working on the inside. Now a lull in the software issues while Abby has her baby. It doesn't feel right. The two shouldn't be related."

"Because they *aren't*." Lil sighed. "Listen, Al, I love you, but I can't talk about this right now. Everyone is heading to the hospital. Let me simply enjoy this time. I don't want to talk about conspiracy theories or computer glitches. I want you to tell me that my sister is going to have a healthy baby and an easy birth. That's all. Be happy for Abby. Be happy for me."

Alethea shifted her attention to her new Jimmy Choos—stylish, with four-inch heels that could double as a weapon. "I am happy for Abby... and you."

"Are you? Are you really?"

"Yes," Alethea said defensively. *I sent a shower present. A password-protected, close-range, encrypted, recording-enabled teddy bear nanny cam. I bet it's still in the box. I wouldn't know since I wasn't invited to the shower, nor to Abby's home since.*

When will they give me credit for trying to save Corisi Enterprises? How long will I have to pay for losing my temper at Jeisa?

Instantly contrite, Lil gushed, "I'm sorry, Al. You know I wish I could bring you with me today. Everyone is going to be there today. Everyone, but you. If you would just tone it down a bit, they'd see the you I love. It's your intensity they don't understand."

"Intensity? You mean because I won't accept the fantasy that nothing bad could ever happen to us again? I can't pretend everything is okay when it isn't." Her gut clenched painfully. *Don't you think I want to be like you? You probably still forget to lock your door at night because you think bad things only happen to other people.*

"Nothing is ever okay for you, Al. That's the problem. You always find an issue because you always look for one. Always. You never let yourself believe that things can be good. Abby found her happily ever after. I found mine. Why can't you simply be happy for us?"

Alethea blinked back the emotion that welled within her. *You have to fight for that kind of happiness. You have to protect it every day or someone will rip it away from you.* "The truth is your best defense."

"Against what, Al?" Lil took a deep breath, then said quietly, "Please, stop. You have nothing but a gut instinct and some glitches to go by. Just stop. I can't do this right now. I have to go."

Swallowing her frustration, Alethea looked out the window again. "Call me if you need me."

Lil hesitated, obviously torn. "I'll call when it's over."

Unable to stop herself, Alethea snapped, "Why would I care about the news if I'm not happy for either of you?"

"I didn't mean it that way, Al. I know you care. I just..."

"I know. Go... go be with your sister. She needs you."

After Lil hung up, Alethea laid her phone down on her glass coffee table. She flipped on the television. Every channel she checked showed live feed of the hospital where Abby and Dominic were headed. The press was indeed everywhere. Men in dark suits were scattered through the crowd, evidence that Dominic's security was already in place.

Chaos always leaves an opening to slip in unseen. She'd tested enough event security plans to know that. *All it takes is determination and a good lie. Those who would do the most harm rarely walk in the front door. They come in through crevices, like cockroaches. Does Dominic have the laundry room covered? The kitchen? How about the locker room? Is someone counting uniforms?*

I'd ask Dominic or Marc Stone, his head of security, but they don't want to hear from me. If they did, they would have asked me to look over the security plan before it was implemented.

Lil wants me to back off and give them time to get over our last encounter.

As the news continued to stream images of the crowd gathering around the hospital, one video showed the building's back entrance. No one was stationed at the door near the trash. *Maybe someone is inside.*

Or maybe anyone could walk in that door. As the camera panned away, she saw a brief flash of movement that looked like a kitchen staffer exiting the door and lighting a cigarette. *Smoker breaks. Did anyone consider how often people prop otherwise secure doors open?*

Unable to watch the television a minute longer, Alethea strode to her bedroom, changed into casual street clothes, and brushed her long red hair up into a bun, which she concealed beneath a brunette wig. She wiped off most of her makeup. The tennis shoes she chose were necessary to her mission, regardless of how much she disliked wearing anything but heels.

Her stomach was churning—always a sign that she needed to act. Anyone could walk in that back door. She'd never be able to forgive herself if something happened to Abby or her baby.

No, they don't want me there, but they just may need me.

Dressed in his usual black Brooks Brothers suit, Marc Stone listened to the chatter in his earpiece as his security team spread throughout the hospital. They were on the street, in the alley, in the hallways—everywhere someone might lurk. Some were dressed in suits, ready to form an impressive wall of defense when Dominic and Abby pulled up to the hospital's emergency entrance. Some were dressed casually, to blend into the crowd and observe.

Years of working for Dominic Corisi had not only made Marc quite wealthy, but had also taught him to prepare for anything when it came to dealing with the public. The fairy-tale version of Dominic and Abby's whirlwind romance had made them instant celebrities in a way that wealth alone wouldn't have. As loved as he'd once been hated, Dominic was now practically American royalty, and that came with a different set of challenges. Abby's popularity made her a sought-after photo op and attracted a fair amount of unwanted attention from overzealous admirers of both sexes. *Icing on the cake? The baby.* The paparazzi were locked in a wild competition to produce the first photo.

Keeping them at bay was his responsibility.

And his privilege.

"The stork is in view," his point man, Craig, announced from the emergency entrance. Marc rolled his eyes. The young man was full of drama and flair. His training was extensive and admirable. He was intelligent and dedicated, which was why he'd been hired, even though he'd never shot his gun outside of a practice range. He was the best set of eyes Marc had, but his enthusiasm for his job was sometimes exhausting.

"I'm at the east door."

"Roger that," Craig said.

With a wave of his right hand, Marc sent a line of men outside to flank the couple's walk from the limo to the hospital entrance. Presidents moved with less security than had been hired for this big day.

Dominic stepped from the limo and turned to help his wife out. A nurse rushed forward with a wheelchair. Dominic leaned down and kissed his wife on the cheek. In the distance a flash went off. Marc looked up and saw that someone had climbed into a tree across the street. He nodded his head toward it and two of his men took off after the photographer.

That picture will never see the tabloids.

Not on my watch.

How they'd erase the photo might not be entirely ethical, but, simply by working for Dominic, Marc had made enough influential friends that a complaint would never go public. If resolved correctly, the photographer would either leave happy with some extra money in his pocket, or scared that he'd never sell another photo. The choice would be his, but the result was not in question. There would be no photos of the baby until Dominic and Abby released one.

Taking his place beside Dominic as they entered the building, Marc smiled for the first time that day as he spoke to Abby. "You look ready to have this baby."

She smiled up at him and winced. "I am. Anything you can do to help the next phase of this along?"

"Not part of my job, ma'am. Thankfully."

He turned to Dominic. "Everything is in place upstairs. Your suite is secure. The doctor is here. Your family is gathering along with the Andrades in an adjoining private sitting area."

"Good," Dominic said, not letting go of his wife's hand as the nurse pushed her wheelchair along.

Marc lowered his voice and said, "Piece of advice?" Dominic raised one eyebrow—enough of a show of interest for Marc to continue. "Follow the baby. I know you want to see your daughter born. I hear it's one of the most amazing experiences in life. However, once she's out, keep your eyes on her. Everything after her arrival is like a gory car crash and will leave you with memories that will haunt you. Look away, especially if you want more kids."

Although Dominic still had a worried, protective look on his face, he spared Marc half a smile. "I didn't realize you had children."

"I don't," Marc said. "Just a hoard of nephews, nieces, and sisters who overshare."

Dominic chuckled. "Understood."

They rode up the elevator together. Just before the door opened, Marc reiterated, "Follow the baby."

Abby looked up and over her shoulder at her husband. "What does that mean?"

Dominic kissed her forehead. "It means Marc is worried that he'll be carrying my sorry ass out of the delivery room if I pass out."

Abby smiled up at Marc.

He winked. "Exactly."

When the family came rushing toward Dominic and Abby, Marc retreated to a nearby position. He pressed a button on his earpiece and ordered, "Close off the entrances and stairways leading up to the suite. No one but cleared staff gets in."

Craig relayed the message to the rest of the men. "The stork is perched. Repeat. The stork is perched. Make a nest."

CHAPTER *Two*

"GET OUT," LIL said in her sternest voice. "You are making things worse instead of better. Please don't make me call Marc."

Dominic roared, "I'm not going anywhere."

His sister-in-law didn't back down. In fact, his refusal brought an angry red heat to her cheeks. "You're scaring the nurses. The doctor can't get the information he needs. You need to take a walk and cool off."

Arms folded across his chest and feet planted, Dominic held his ground. "I will not miss the birth of my daughter."

From the bed beside them, Abby said softly, "We have plenty of time. I'm not fully dilated."

Lil continued her reprimand. "At least, we don't think she is. We'd know if you hadn't just threatened the doctor's license and sent him scurrying."

Remembering the arrogance of the doctor, Dominic didn't regret his outburst. "He brought interns with him. I said no students. Abby is not a case study."

Her expression softening, Lil touched his arm. "It's common, Dom. It's how new doctors learn. I'm sure Abby doesn't care as long as the baby comes out today. Trust me, when I had Colby, I didn't care if ten people were standing around me. All I cared about was getting her out and getting the right painkillers. Which won't happen if you don't let anyone help her." With a shake of her head, she looked at the door that led to the attached suite. "Where is Jake? Maybe he can talk some sense into you." With that, she stepped out of the delivery room to find her fiancé.

Dominic turned to his wife, who was flushed and struggling to look brave. Nothing. Absolutely nothing would ever make him leave her side.

Her next words rocked him back on his heels. "She's right, Dom. Take a short walk."

"No."

Abby held out her hand to him. He closed the distance between them in one stride and took it in his, bending to kiss her fingers lightly. Abby smiled despite the pain of a contraction. "You won't miss anything. I'm okay. But you—you look like you're going to have a stroke. The doctor said it could be hours still. Get a soda with Jake. Give Marie a hug. Nicole is probably dying to see you, too. You'll feel better, and I can get the epidural I thought I didn't want but which I'm quickly changing my mind about."

Jake poked his head in, covering his eyes. "Is it safe to come in?"

Abby laughed. "I'm all covered."

With a flash of a smile, he was beside Dominic. "No offense, Abby, but there are some things I'd prefer remain a mystery for as long as possible."

Abby grimaced as another contraction hit. "None taken. You'll have your turn soon enough. For now, can you take Dominic for a walk? I want to meet with the doctor before Dominic drives him to quit his profession."

Dominic shrugged. "I'm sure there are others here. Better ones who follow instructions."

Abby made a face and her grip on his hand tightened. "I'm not using another doctor. I like the one I have. I trust him. Now, get out of here for a few minutes and send him in."

"Abby—" Dominic started to say.

She dropped his hand and pointed at the door. "If I have to get up and get him myself, no one in this room is leaving with the testicles they came in with." She glared at Jake. "That includes you."

If he hadn't been sick with worry, Dominic would have enjoyed the fire in his wife's eyes and the way she ordered him about. He normally loved her strength and respected her opinion, but this time he didn't budge. He searched for the words that would convince her he should stay.

Jake surprised him by giving him a none-too-gentle shove toward the door. Dominic spun angrily on him, but Jake met his glare with his infuriatingly calm stare. "She means it, Dom. Come on. I'm sure she'll be happier if you let her get properly medicated."

Growling under his breath, Dominic walked with Jake toward the door. He stopped just before stepping outside. "I love you, Abby."

She wiped a hand across her red cheek. "I know. I love you, too. Now send in Lil and the doctor. It'll only be a few minutes. Go for a quick walk. Calm down, then come right back. I need you, Dom, but I need the doctor, too."

Feeling slightly ashamed that his wife was reduced to scolding him like a child for impeding the process, Dominic nodded and left the room. The waiting room was overflowing with flowers, friends, and family. Marie was playing with Colby and her blocks on the floor while Rosella watched and cooed. Victor and Alessandro were chatting with their wives.

Nicole came rushing forward with her fiancé, Stephan, in tow. She wrapped her arms around Dominic's waist. "How is Abby? Is she okay? You look awful."

Dominic hugged his sister to his chest and admitted, "She threw me out."

Nicole patted her brother's cheek sympathetically. "Oh, she'll let you back in. Just remember that no matter what she says, she loves you. Even if she stands on the table and screams that she hates you, she doesn't mean it."

Dominic looked at Jake in concern. "Is she going to do that?"

Jake shrugged. "How would I know?"

Nicole continued, "The most important thing is that you made it to the hospital."

For once, Stephan wasn't sarcastic. "That's true. Nicole delivered my nephew, Joey, with none of this, in a limo. Don't worry. Abby will be fine." Then a wicked smile spread across his face. "Next time will be easier. I hear Abby wants a big family."

Dominic paled and swayed.

Nicole swatted Stephan's arm. "Play nice today."

Jake took Dominic by the arm and said, "Let's go get you something to eat."

Dominic walked away, shaking his head. "I don't know if I can do this again."

Lil overheard his comment and, her tone thick with sarcasm, said, "I'm pretty sure it's tougher on Abby than it is on you, Dom."

The joke was a painful reminder of how he was failing to give Abby what she needed. She was right to throw him out. He couldn't remember a time in his adult life when he'd felt so emotionally on edge. "You think I don't know that?" he growled, then instantly regretted his harsh words.

He was used to being in control.

Used to being willing to fight for the outcome he wanted.

Here he felt a bit helpless, and that wasn't an emotion he dealt with well.

Obviously.

I'm a selfish ass. Abby needs me, but I can't control myself enough to be there for her. And now I'm taking out my anger with myself on Lil.

She walked over and put a hand on his forearm. "It's going to be okay, Dom. Delivering a baby is stressful and painful, but it's also beautiful and completely natural. Abby is at the best hospital in the country and she's got the best care possible. All you have to do is hold her hand and be there for her."

He put his hand over his sister-in-law's in a show of gratitude. "I would do anything for her."

With a teary smile, Lil said, "I know you would. So, have something to eat with Victor and Alessandro. Call Jeremy and

Jeisa and update them. I'll come out and tell you as soon as Abby wants you in there."

Dominic nodded and headed toward the Andrades.

Jake chuckled.

Lil waved a finger at him. "Don't you dare laugh at him. You're going to be just as much a wreck when we have ours."

A humbled Jake joined Dominic.

In a low tone, Dominic growled to him as Lil walked away. "If I see that doctor going in there with anyone who looks like they are not a nurse, I will hang him out the window by his feet."

Jake gave the room a quick scan and motioned for Marie to come over. She handed Colby to another woman and stood slowly. Her age didn't stop her from sitting on the floor, but it did slow her ability to stand quickly afterward.

Marie looked back and forth between the two men and said, "Did she throw you out?"

Dominic gave a small quick nod and frowned.

Marie led them both toward a food-laden table that took up an entire wall of the private waiting room. "Didn't I warn you to be nice to the doctor? What did she say to you?"

"She told me to get something to eat and calm down."

"Then that's exactly what you're going to do."

Dominic picked up a croissant and took a bite. For Abby, he would eat. For Abby, he would stay outside while she spoke to the doctor. He would even work on keeping his temper in check. But remain calm?

That was asking the impossible.

The rear door near the hospital's dumpster was still unmanned when Alethea arrived. The door was locked. She sat in one of the nearby chairs, took out a cigarette, and lit it, even though she didn't smoke. Smokers were seen but unseen. She let the cigarette burn in her hand, tapping off the excess and posing as if bored. When someone came through the back door dressed in a kitchen uniform, Alethea stubbed out her cigarette and entered the building before the door closed.

The narrow hallway led to a small break room and then a locker room. There she found a white kitchen-staff uniform and a hairnet. She hunted through the lockers until she found a staffer's badge at the bottom of one of them. It was always a risk to use someone else's ID, but most people didn't read the name on the badge.

One hospital kitchen was pretty much like any other. Orders were generated via a computer. Luckily there was a computer and printer in the corner of the room. Even though it was early afternoon, Alethea typed in an order for pancakes. She needed something that would be a special order.

She went over to the grill station and handed the cook the printed order. "I need this ASAP."

"Pancakes?" the frazzled cook snarled. "Breakfast is over."

"Hey, don't bite my head off," Alethea said in a thicker New York accent than normal. "This is a VIP order. Nursing says they have a child up there and this is what she wants."

"Nursing? Do they understand that my grill is prepped for lunch items? No, to them it's one quick item. It's a royal pain, that's what this is."

"Can you do it?" Alethea asked, doing her best to sound worried.

The cook shook his head in disgust but agreed. "Give me five minutes. But tell them I'm not happy. Once dinner rush starts, I don't care who they are, they can order from the menu or they can wait."

"Thanks." Alethea shot him a small smile. She didn't look him straight in the eye. Connections made interactions memorable. They opened the door for people to ask questions. She kept her eyes down and her red locks hidden beneath the dull brown wig.

Meek.

Average.

Easily forgotten.

When she had the order in hand, she carried the tray to the service elevator and went up to the maternity ward. Just outside the door she faced her first set of suited security. She explained that she was delivering food to the nurse's station. They called downstairs to the kitchen to confirm. With a curt nod after confirming her story, they used their badges to let her through.

The nurses at the private station didn't look past her name tag and uniform. Alethea guessed hers wasn't the first food delivery that day. She flashed the printed order and stated what was on the tray, explaining that the order had been called down by the family. The nurse nodded impatiently and said, "You can take it in. Hard to believe they forgot anything after seeing what was already delivered."

Alethea explained that it was for one of the young children.

The nurse nodded. "They brought their whole family with them. Unbelievable, huh? A lot of fuss over something that happens here every day."

The other nurse leaned against her station and sighed dreamily. "Don't even try to pretend you're not excited that the Corisis are having their baby here. I'd ask to take a photo with them if I wasn't sure it would get me fired."

Alethea nodded and smiled blandly in agreement. Nothing out of the ordinary. Nothing to question. One of the nurses walked Alethea to the outer door of the suite, where two more security men where standing. "It's okay, she works here. Just more food being delivered."

The nurse had her hand on the suite door and was swinging it open when the hair on Alethea's neck rose and she turned her head to see why. Steel blue eyes clashed with hers and she knew she'd get no farther.

Marc Stone strode forward and shut the door firmly. He took the tray in one hand and grabbed her arm with the other. "You don't belong here," he ground out.

The nurse waved her hands nervously in the air. Her high-pitched voice carried. "What do you mean? They cleared her at the door."

Not letting go of Alethea's arm, Marc addressed the nurse. He handed the tray to her and said, "You're not in trouble. I'll handle this."

Alethea struggled to free her arm, but his grip was ironclad. She tried not to enjoy it. There was something about Marc—perhaps his imposing height, the expansive breath of his muscular shoulders, or the cool steel in his eyes—that never failed to set her libido running. What would it be like to be with a man she wasn't entirely certain she could control?

And why was that image so damn enticing?

He pulled her around the corner into a quieter hallway. "I should have known you would show up today."

"Let go of my arm," Alethea ordered between clenched teeth.

"Not likely. Not until I throw your cute little ass back out the door you came in."

Cute little ass? She fought the bolt of pleasure that his comment sent through her. With a slight curl to her lip, she pushed back at him verbally. "You should be thanking me. I could have been anyone. Now you know that you need to cover all back entrances and issue specific photo security badges to enter this area. Take your Neanderthal hands off me and I won't even tell anyone about the hole in your security."

"There was no hole. You never made it into the suite."

"Because you recognized me. But what if you hadn't? Or what if you'd looked away for just a moment?" Her rebuttal came out huskier than she would have liked. "That's all it takes. One opportunity."

Something we had the night we met, before I blew it. I could have achieved my goal without testing if I could distract you from your duties that night. And, having discovered how wonderfully easy it was, I could have reaped the benefits of our mutual attraction instead of documenting your lapse in judgment in a report to Dominic.

So I may have earned the bite in your grip, but I don't have to accept it. She glared at him and assessed the likelihood that a well-placed kick would loosen his hold long enough for her to break free.

"Oh, my God, Al." Lil came rushing toward them. "Why are you here?"

Marc dropped Alethea's arm and swore beneath his breath.

Alethea took off her wig, shook out her long mane, and faced her friend proudly. "I had a feeling Marc had failed to cover all access points, and I was right."

A less observant person would have thought her barb didn't bother him. Marc's expression remained coldly professional, but his pupils dilated and his nostrils flared ever so slightly. Without an audience, Alethea was certain his response would not have been so well concealed.

Lil turned to Marc and said, "Can you give us a moment?"

He nodded abruptly and moved a few yards away but kept his eyes on them. He'd moved out of respect for Lil's request, but his nearness declared that the reprieve was only temporary.

Lil threw up both hands and paced in front of Alethea, her tone high from emotion. "I can't do this right now. I can't deal with you and your crazy need to test everything. The nurses are upset. We heard someone tried to break in." She shot her friend a furious look. "Do you know what that did to the mood in the waiting room? Thank God Dominic is back with Abby. Jake calmed everyone down. He didn't have to come out here with me—you know why? Because we both knew as soon as we heard what happened that it was you. Only you would do this."

Contrition was slow in coming. No, she didn't like upsetting Lil, but how upset would everyone have been if something had happened to Abby or the baby? Lil's anger was acceptable collateral damage. "Be grateful it was only me. Anyone could have come in that back door. Anyone."

Lil covered her face with her hands. "I know you mean well, Al, but you took it too far today. I don't know what to do with you anymore. I thought it would get better as we got older. I thought you would calm down once you knew Jake and Dominic. I keep putting off my damn wedding waiting for you and Abby to make up. It's never going to happen unless you change."

Alethea folded her arms in frustration. "So, you'd prefer to have your family in danger than be annoyed by me?"

With a frustrated sigh, Lil said, "No. Of course not. But was there danger today? Really? Or did you need an excuse to come here?"

Arms falling to her side, Alethea rocked back on her heels beneath the accusation. "That's what you think?"

Hugging herself around the waist, Lil said, "I don't know what I think, Al. But I know you can't stay here. Go home. Wait for me to call you and tell you how everything went. Just like I asked you to do. Like any other friend would."

Suddenly torn between believing she was right and regretting the pain she was causing her friend, Alethea offered what was close to an apology. "I didn't mean to upset anyone."

Lil's bottom lip quivered, a sure sign that she was holding back tears. "I know, Al." She shook her head and walked away. "Please, just go home."

As Lil departed, Marc started toward Alethea, but halted when Jake called to him from the suite door. "Marc, we need to talk."

Alethea was about to take advantage of the distraction when Marc pinned her with an angry glare from across the hall. There was heat as well as anger in his gaze, and her breath caught in her chest as she reeled beneath the intensity of their attraction. The desire to cross the distance between them was almost irresistible. What would he do if she boldly walked over, not stopping until her breasts were pressed against the solid wall of his chest? She imagined winding her arms around his neck, pulling his stern mouth down, and kissing him until he groaned and lost control.

All that anger would only flame his hunger for her.

Just as it had the first night they'd met.

She was saved from herself when Marc spoke into his earpiece and two of his men instantly flanked her. Yet he held her eyes, and she held her breath. Was he also remembering their first encounter?

"Please come with us, ma'am," one guard said. "We're to escort you out."

"Of course," Alethea said with forced politeness, but she didn't look away from Marc. He was listening to Jake and nodding. Unable to stop herself, she winked at him.

A red flush spread up his face and he turned away, but not before she saw the truth in his eyes. No matter how cool he tried to appear, he was just as drawn to her as she was to him.

Not that either of us can act on it. Alethea lectured herself the whole way to the elevator. *It doesn't matter if he's attracted to me. It doesn't matter that his kiss shook me as none had before. He's off limits. Focus on why you came here today.* As she rode down the service elevator with the two security men, Alethea said, "Check that someone is watching the morgue. People hesitate to question a person who is wheeling a corpse." She looked at the other operative and said, "It wouldn't hurt to have one of you in the laundry room either."

One of the men wordlessly put her out the back door, ironically the same one she'd used earlier. The other followed her out and stationed himself outside the door, acting as a physical barrier to her reentry.

Walking away, head held high, Alethea glanced back with satisfaction. *I wouldn't win a popularity contest, but the kitchen entrance is now secure. Going home alone is a small price to pay for achieving that objective.*

Marc walked with Jake down a side corridor until they were out of everyone's earshot. Normally composed, Marc was more than a little frustrated with Alethea's invasion and how it had left him wanting what he'd successfully denied himself thus far.

"She shouldn't have been able to get as close as she did," Jake said.

Pulling himself out of a fantasy—in which Alethea writhed beneath him and called his name as he pounded a year of pent-up frustration into her sweet wetness—Marc met Jake Walton's eyes. "No, sir."

"Don't go all formal on me, Marc. I didn't pull you aside to chastise you. Alethea's good at what she does. She may be the best I've ever seen. That's why she's in high demand. She always gets in. But seeing her made me think I can't wait any longer to make you aware of something that's been going on."

"Today? Here?"

Jake shook his head. "No, at Corisi's main headquarters. I haven't said anything to anyone because it may be nothing. Right now it's a series of computer glitches and a rumor that someone is doing it deliberately."

Marc frowned. "The kind of technology you're talking about is not my area of expertise."

"I know that, but if this isn't a series of minor code errors, then someone is sabotaging our software again—but the firewall that Jeremy designed should be impenetrable."

"So do you think it's an inside job?"

Looking a bit grim, Jake said, "It would have to be. I've had our people on it, but so far they believe the errors are unrelated."

"And the rumor?"

"Unknown source of initiation. I don't know what to think, but I want you to keep your eyes open. Watch for anything out of the ordinary. Don't bother Dominic with this. He's in Daddyland right now. It may be nothing. I don't want to bring this to him unless we find evidence of tampering."

If the saboteur was good enough to circumvent Dominic's pet hacker, getting evidence wasn't going to be easy. "I'll beef up the physical security at the main building and at the satellite offices. I can have additional cameras installed discretely. We'll comb through the security clearances and background checks. If someone is where they don't belong, I'll find them."

Jake nodded. "I have every confidence that you will."

Marc looked down the hallway at the service elevator. Coding errors that did nothing more than reveal a weakness in a firewall. He didn't want to believe that his late-night fantasy woman would go that far, but he had to admit it fit her pattern. "You don't think..."

Rubbing the back of his neck tiredly, Jake said, "I hope not. She means well, but there isn't a line she won't cross when she thinks she's right."

"A bit like someone else we both know." Marc referenced his boss, who had made his fortune living by his own code of ethics.

"Dominic has me to keep him in check, though. Alethea listens to no one." Lowering his voice, Jake said, "I want you to watch her closely. It would break Lil's heart if she found out Alethea was causing more trouble. No matter what you discover, bring it to me first."

"Understood."

Business done, Jake smiled. "Time for me to head back in there and see if Dominic still has his manhood."

Marc almost asked what Jake meant, but decided he didn't want to know.

CHAPTER *Three*

"THIS ISN'T GOOD," the doctor said, watching the monitor. "The baby is in position but she's not moving as much as I'd like. The heartbeat is still steady." He wheeled a small machine closer. "We'll need another ultrasound."

Abby put a protective hand over her stomach. "What's wrong?"

"I don't know yet," the doctor grumbled, and pulled more equipment into the room. He ran a wand over Abby's stomach.

"That's not good enough," Dominic snarled.

The doctor looked from Abby to Dominic and said, "I will have you removed from the room, Mr. Corisi, if I believe your presence in any way inhibits me from saving the life of your child or her mother. Do you understand me? You may bark orders in your boardroom, but this is my world. My patient."

Deflating a bit, Dominic said, "What can I do?"

"Hold your wife's hand, talk to her, and let me do my job."

Dominic nodded and went to look down at his wife's worried face. He sought the words to comfort her. In all of his life he'd never felt as terrified as he was right then. "The doctor said everything is normal. He's just being cautious."

Abby smiled bravely. "I heard him, Dom." She squeezed his hand. "He's right. Something's different. I can feel it."

Talking around them instead of to them, the doctor started barking orders. "The baby's heartbeat is slowing. It looks like a potential umbilical prolapse."

"What does that mean?" Abby asked, gripping Dominic's hand tighter.

"We have to act now. If the umbilical cord drops out before the baby we risk compression, which means blood and oxygen may be cut off."

"Do what you need to," Dominic said harshly. He held his wife's cold hand to his face. "I'm here, Abby. Right where I'll always be. Right beside you."

She gripped his hand and said, "I'm scared."

As the doctor worked, Dominic took his advice and kept his attention on the only place he could help. He said, "Do you remember backing your car deliberately into mine the first day we met?"

Some of the fear left her eyes as she defended her actions of that day. "You were an arrogant ass. I couldn't believe you'd offered me money to spend the night with you. You're lucky your car was the only thing I hit."

He smiled down at her, using those memories to soothe her. "I didn't know it at the time, but I fell for you the moment I laid eyes on you. No one had ever stood up to me the caring way you did. You made me want to be a better man."

Abby's eyes filled with tears. "You were a good man before you met me, you just didn't know it."

The doctor said, "Looks like we can stay here. She shifted. What a smart little girl you have. And impatient. She's coming out fast."

Dominic looked at the doctor and then back to Abby. She said, "Go meet her."

Watching his daughter come into the world filled Dominic with a rush of feelings. Shock held him immobile even as the doctor caught her and cleaned her off quickly. The nurse said, "Time to meet Mommy," and laid her down on Abby's chest.

Ever so gently, Dominic touched the tiniest fingers he'd ever seen. He met the doctor's eyes across the bed. "Thank you," he said quietly.

The doctor merely nodded and started giving instructions to the nurses again.

Abby kissed her crying daughter's forehead and said, "She's so beautiful."

"Is her head going to stay that shape?" he asked without thinking.

Abby smiled down at the baby with love. "If you'd read the baby book I gave you, you'd know they all look like that."

"I read some of it," Dominic said. When she raised her eyebrows in disbelief, he said, "Okay, I had Jake read it. He was supposed to give me the bulleted notes. Knowing him, he's cross-referencing everything in it against medical journals. I'll be briefed before she comes home, I promise."

Abby laughed and shook her head. "Briefed? Like she's a new project?"

He leaned down and kissed Abby's cheek, then the back of his daughter's head. "The most important project of my life. One we need to name. I know we came up with a list and said we'd choose when we met her, but I've been thinking. What about Judith Rosella?"

"Judith for my mother and Rosella for yours. I like it." Abby tipped her head to one side. "What do you think, Judy? Do you like the name?"

At the sound of her mother's voice, the baby stopped crying. Abby smiled up at her husband. "Judith Rosella Corisi it is. We'll name the next one after Marie."

Dominic swayed on his feet. "Next one?"

The doctor said, "Mr. Corisi, would you like to cut the cord?"

Feeling a bit queasy at the idea, Dominic nodded once with authority and took the scissors with shaky hands. "Of course." This was his wife, his baby. Refusing was not an option he considered.

He returned to Abby's side with relief.

"Just a few more contractions and we're done, Abby. How are you feeling?" the doctor asked.

Abby looked down at her baby and then up at Dominic. The love in her eyes clogged Dominic's throat with emotion. He prayed the doctor wouldn't ask him a question. He doubted he was capable in that moment of saying anything that would make sense.

With a few adjustments to the bed, Abby was comfortably covered again and propped in a semi-seated position. Dominic nodded and sank into the chair beside Abby's bed. The nurse took the baby for a moment to tag her with a wristband and run some routine diagnostic tests.

In hardly enough time for Dominic to catch his breath, Judy was back. This time the nurse handed her to him. He held her in the crook of his arm, looked down into the most beautiful blue eyes he'd ever seen—a smaller version of Abby's—and fell even deeper in love with his wife and the child they'd made together.

A few moments later, Lil burst into the room, stopping at the sink to wash her hands, and then rushed to where Dominic sat. "I'm so sorry I was... I had to... forget it. Where's my niece?" Jake was on her heels, the love he had for Lil evident in his eyes, as he watched her wiggling with excitement beside Dominic until he handed Judy over to her. With Judy in her arms, Lil went to Abby's side. "She's perfect, Abby. Just perfect." Then she looked over her shoulder at Jake and said, "Jake, I want another baby. Colby needs a sister. And maybe a brother."

Dominic stood and offered his chair to a suddenly pale Jake. "You look like you need this more than I do." Jake shook his head, but he wasn't fooling anyone with his brave face.

Walking over to Lil's side, Dominic said, "Abby, tell me if this is too much for you. I can clear the room."

Lil hugged little Judy to her and laughed up at him. "You could try."

Abby held out her hand to Dominic. He took it in his, loving the strength and love in her eyes. "I'd love it if you brought Nicole, Rosella, and Marie in. I'm sure they're dying out there."

He bent down and kissed the cheek of the most generous woman he'd ever met. "I didn't want to invite my family until you were ready."

"Our family," Abby said softly, looking over at their new baby with so much love that Dominic had to clear his throat of the emotion welling there.

It wasn't difficult to gather the three Abby requested; they practically fell in the door that led to the outer room of the suite. Nicole and Rosella were crying happy tears and—for the first time Dominic had seen—embracing. Marie's eyes were shining with emotion, but she was attempting to remain composed.

"Abby is asking to see you," Dominic said.

Nicole gave Dominic a kiss on the cheek and flew past him into the room. Marie cocked her head to the side in question, and it didn't take more than a slight nod from him to send her in with equal haste.

Rosella stood before Dominic, tears on her cheeks, hands clenched so tightly in front of her that her knuckles were white. "You, too," he said gently.

Fresh tears flooded her eyes. "Are you sure? I'll understand if you want me to wait."

He cleared his throat. "Abby is asking for you." When she still looked uncertain, he instinctively held his arms open and his mother flew into them, hugging him so tightly he could barely breathe. He wiped a betraying bit of moisture away from the corner of one eye, and felt a bit uncomfortable when he looked up and realized all eyes were on them. That feeling quickly faded when he met Victor Andrade's eyes across the room. He and his brother, Alessandro, were nodding with approval. Having grown up with a cruel and judgmental father, he was not used to the warm feeling their approval filled him with.

Some of his apprehension about being a good father lessened in that moment. No, he might not have been raised by a good man, but that didn't determine what kind of father he would be. Judy's birth had erased the last of his bitterness about the past.

His life was no longer about what he didn't have. His wife, his daughter, and the family they'd made together—that was his future. "Come inside, Mom. Judith Rosella Corisi needs to meet her nonna."

CHAPTER *Four*

A WEEK LATER, Lil and Alethea sat at a West Village restaurant whose touted brick walls were accented with spicy wallpaper depicting nude women. As requested, they were seated in a corner table, away from the other diners.

"Do you mind taking the battery out of your phone, Lil?"

"Are you serious?"

"Unless you have it protected with anti-spyware, it's pathetically easy to upload a virus to a phone that allows people to listen in to your conversations, even if the phone's turned off."

"I'm not dismantling my phone because you're feeling paranoid today."

Alethea simply met her friend's eyes and waited. Friends since middle school, she knew curiosity would change Lil's mind.

"Oh, fine." Lil opened the back of her phone and removed the battery, placing it on the table between them. "Now can you tell me? Or are you going to ask me twenty questions to make sure it's me? What if I've been abducted by aliens and replaced with an exact replica? They may have uploaded all of my memories, so I'd also suggest a blood test."

"Laugh all you want, Lil. Just because it's not probable doesn't mean it's impossible." She met Lil's eyes as she tried to drive her point home. "I'm not talking about alien abduction and you know it. I'm talking about the rumors that something's going on at Corisi Enterprises. No, don't give me that look. You're living in a fantasy. Safety requires diligence. You have a niece today because the doctor didn't blindly trust that everything would go smoothly. He watched for problems. He acted quickly."

Lil slumped against the back of the booth. "Do we have to do this today, Al? I was hoping to have a nice lunch with you. You know, one where you ask me how Abby and my new niece are doing and I get to gush about them and show you pictures. Normal stuff."

If that's the game I need to play to get you to listen to me, sure. It wasn't that she didn't care about Abby or the stories Lil had to share—she did. It was just that what she had asked Lil to meet her to discuss was urgent. "How is Abby?"

Lil looked like she wanted to say something else, but she decided to play along instead. "She's good. She's home. They named their baby Judith Rosella. You should see how beautiful she is. And when she wants something she has a cry you can hear throughout the whole house. Not like the soft cry Colby started with. This girl has lungs."

Corisi lungs, Alethea thought but kept it to herself. Lil wasn't in the mood for her cutting humor. "Is Dominic back at work?"

"He hasn't left Abby's side. I'm pretty sure she's ready for him to go, though. He's such a mother hen. Who would have guessed it?"

"He knows how easy it is to lose something that's unprotected."

Lil shook her head in defeat. "I give up. Let's talk about something else. Was it my imagination or did I break up something between you and Marc at the hospital?"

"Marc, the security guy?"

"You know which Marc I'm talking about. The one who looks like a cross between a gladiator and the Secret Service. I could have sworn you were getting all moony-eyed over him."

Damn it, she could feel herself flushing. Lil knew her too well. "You're crazy. I was pissed because he couldn't see that I was doing him a favor."

"Pissed? No. That wasn't the expression on your face. I think it was more like, 'Oh, baby, take me now, you big hot stud.'"

Alethea threw a crouton at Lil's head. Lil ducked and chuckled. "That was definitely not what I was thinking." *Liar, liar, pants on fire.*

Lil raised an eyebrow in disbelief. She lifted her phone in one hand and the battery in another. "No one is listening but me. You don't have to lie."

Alethea denied the truth to even herself for a moment, then caved as a grin spread across her face. She bent forward across the table. "I have the hottest dreams about that man." She shivered. "I don't know what it is about him. From the moment I saw him that night I snuck Jeremy into Dominic's engagement party, I've had a bit of a thing for him."

"A thing?" Lil clapped her hands once in excitement before her.

Alethea shrugged one shoulder. "Okay, so I may have done repeated background checks on him just to see if I could find an unattractive photo of him. Nope. He was cute even as a kid. Except for that one time when he banged up his face a bit playing hockey. Nah, even then he looked adorably beaten up."

Shaking her head, Lil said, "Al, you scare me sometimes. Why not just ask him out?"

"I can't." Just the thought of it made her brain shudder.

"Really?" Lil asked with growing fascination. Alethea regretted revealing as much as she had. "You're not shy around men. You usually twist them up like emotional pretzels and spit them out."

"This guy is different. He's a war hero, for God's sake, with a Navy Cross. It's why Dominic hired him. Marc came home wounded, and made the news when he was turned down for a job at a department store. Unemployed war hero. The story went national. Dominic put him in charge of his security team. Trial by fire, so to speak. He's a self-made man with an impressive reputation in his field."

Lil's eyes rounded. "Oh, my God, I never thought I'd see the day. You finally found a man you respect."

"Don't build this up into more than it is. I like that he is who he is. No stories. No lies. No matter how deep you dig, you find more all-American, boy-next-door good guy. He put his brother and sister through college. Paid off his parents' home for them."

"And you wouldn't want to slip up and sleep with a man like that, would you?"

Alethea gave her an impatient look. "You, more than anyone else, should know why he's off limits to me."

Evidently, Lil had forgotten her earlier warning to stay away from him. "I dare you to call him."

"That may work on others, but it doesn't work on me. I get in enough trouble without your help. Can you imagine what everyone would say if I started dating Dominic's head of security?"

"If it stopped you from obsessing over every possible thing that could go wrong, and sneaking into hospitals just to prove you can, I think they'd love it. I should have Jake ask him if he's dating anyone."

"No. Lil, stop. I shouldn't have said anything. Don't tell Jake. Don't tell anyone what I said."

Looking mutinous for a moment, Lil then sighed in resignation. "My lips are sealed."

"I'm serious, Lil."

Throwing her hands up humorously, Lil said, "Why does everyone think I can't keep a secret?"

Alethea raised a hand and flagged the server to bring the bill. "Because we know you?" she asked, but there was no bite to her tone, only one good friend lovingly teasing another. "You know I'm kidding. Well, I'm mostly kidding. Can we talk seriously for a minute?"

Lil laid her fork down. "I can't get involved the way you asked me to. All I can do is ask Jake again if there are problems at work and suggest that he talk to you. That's as far as I'll go, Al."

"He won't tell you the truth."

In an instant, Lil was as serious as a heart attack. "We tell each other everything."

"Everyone has secrets."

"Not us," Lil said confidently.

Sitting back with a sigh, Alethea decided to try another approach. "What if he doesn't know how serious it is?"

Lil sat straighter. "Jake is one of the sharpest minds in the country. If there is a problem, he's going to see the big picture. If you have solid information, let's take it directly to him."

"What the hell is solid information? I pay people to keep their ears to the ground. I pay them well to update me on events even if they seem unimportant. It's because I get tidbits from inside, outside, underground, and overseas, and I see patterns where others might not. I'm not suggesting that I'm smarter than your genius boyfriend—"

"Fiancé."

"Fiancé, excuse me," Alethea said sarcastically.

"Wait, did you just say inside? As in, inside Corisi Enterprises? You have someone on your payroll there?" Lil's mouth dropped open in shock.

Said like that, it sounds bad. "I have since Abby left for China. Something you would have thanked me for if she'd gone missing."

"Oh, my God, Al." Lil stood, stuffed the various pieces of her phone into her purse, and swung it over her shoulder. "I can't listen to any more."

"Aren't you even curious about what I found?"

Checkmate.

Lil sat. "You found something?"

"Those glitches are not an accident. My person has traced two of them back through several decoys to one specific IP address."

"Then there isn't a question anymore. We have to take this to Jake."

"Not yet."

"What are you talking about? Jake needs to know this. As soon as they find the source, he and Dominic will annihilate whoever it is. Problem solved."

After the waitress returned with the paid bill, Alethea looked Lil straight in the eye and said, "We can't let that happen. Not until we know for sure he's guilty."

"You just said you knew who was doing it."

"No, I said it was coming through one IP address. We need more than that before we point a finger."

"Al, you always think we have to do this on our own, but Jake can help us. We don't have to be private sleuths anymore. You could be part of a team instead of working alone."

"Lil, it's Stephan's IP address."

Lil swayed in her seat. "No."

"Yes."

"Holy shit." Lil was quiet for a moment, considering the idea. Then she shook her head adamantly. "No. Stephan wouldn't do that. He loves Nicole."

"He's gone after Dominic before."

"That was before they got engaged." She shook her head again in shock and held a shaky hand up to her mouth. "You don't honestly believe he would do this, do you?"

"Money and power corrupt people. I don't know."

Lil held her purse tightly to her side, looking angry and miserable. "I don't know what to do with this, Al. I don't want to know this. I want to be happy. I love Nicole and I love Stephan. This would tear the family apart. Oh, my God, we can't tell Jake. He doesn't trust Stephan."

Although she hated seeing her friend upset, she knew she had to figure out if Stephan was behind these glitches—and that she needed inside information to do it. "This problem won't go away just because you refuse to deal with it. Do you really want to wait and see how it plays out, hoping for the best? What if Stephan is out to hurt your fiancé's company? Do you want to be the person who did nothing?"

"Give me a day, Al. Don't do anything else. Just let me think this through. For once, promise to do this my way. Promise me."

Lil put up her pinkie for a solemn vow.

Alethea didn't like it, but what could she do? She pinkie swore to wait for Lil's solution.

Marc was looking over video surveillance tapes from the new cameras he'd had installed systematically throughout Corisi Enterprises' office buildings. It had taken him almost a week to install them, since the work could only be done at night once everyone had gone home. He didn't tell the night security crew what he was doing, beyond saying that he was updating their system. The fewer who knew, the better. He'd used only his closest team to do it. If there was a mole, he was going to catch him.

Craig entered, a report in hand. "We've combed through the background checks of everyone who was hired in the last six months. Nothing."

"Then go back a year. Go back two. Keep looking."

"What are you hoping to find?"

"Nothing. I'm hoping you come back with nothing. But I have a feeling that might not be the case. I'm also demoting you."

"What? Without even a job review? Is this about the hospital incident?"

"No," Marc said impatiently. *That one was my fault. Alethea was right about the need for specially issued IDs. I should have thought of that.* "It's not an actual demotion. You're going undercover. Don't worry; your pay will stay the same. Your job is to be the most laid-back mailroom messenger Corisi Enterprises has ever seen. I'll talk to Ed in the mailroom. He may recognize you as part of my team, but I can trust him to keep it to himself. You'll deliver the mail, and rotate where you go. Find your way to wherever people are taking breaks. Look for someone who is driving a new car who shouldn't be able to afford to. Anything like that. One thing I know about moles is, they may be good at covering their tracks, but they can't resist spending their extra money. Smile. Flirt. Play nice. I don't care if you have to go out for drinks with every secretary we employ. I want the office gossip."

"Tough assignment." He gave a young, cocky smile. He stood taller, posed against the doorjamb, and practiced a Casanova smile.

"Focus, Craig. Don't date them, get close enough to find out if they know anything and then move on to the next. I'd do it myself if I wouldn't be recognized."

"I hope I don't break any hearts," Craig said with feigned concern.

Marc rolled his eyes skyward. "I'm sure they'll survive."

"That's cold, Marc. Really cold. What are we calling this covert operation? We need something catchy."

"Call it job insurance. You screw this up and I won't be able to save you from the wrath from above. Get in, get the information we need, and get out. No one can know what we're doing."

With a nod and a smile, Craig said, "Gotcha," and walked out of the room. A moment later, the earpiece on Marc's desk lit up. He picked it up and pressed a button that allowed the sender to access protected private radio communication with him.

Craig said, "The shark is entering the water. I repeat: The shark is entering the water."

"Are you the shark?" Marc asked in resigned humor.

Speaking just above a whisper, Craig asked, "Is this a test to see if I blow my own cover?"

Closing his eyes and striving for patience, Marc said, "Whatever you want to call yourself, have a report on my desk at the end of each day." He put the earpiece down. He'd chosen Craig because the man's quirky personality would allow him to move through the building without raising suspicion. His elite

RUTH CARDELLO

team was too seasoned, too hardened to be able to play the role of a mailroom messenger. Craig was the only viable option.

Returning to his desk, Marc turned his focus to the real wild card in the game. One that Craig would never be able to fool. He might call himself a shark, but Alethea would make a quick snack of an innocent like Craig.

His own ego was still smarting from his first encounter with her.

Alethea. As beautiful as she was cunning. Both Dominic and Jake had warned him about her, but their warning had come one day too late. His heart beat double time as he remembered their first meeting. With her long, wild auburn hair, deep emerald eyes, and athletically tight body, she had easily been the most striking and beautiful woman at Jake's engagement party.

He should have known from the way her attention had riveted on him that she had had an ulterior motive. The smile had come to her lips too easily. The flirting looks had been too blatant. Still, he'd been unable to resist the lure.

He'd deserved every critical word she'd written about him in her report to Dominic. That night he had, indeed, been weak and easily distracted. He'd wanted her with an intensity he'd never felt before. Like an ocean siren, she'd called, and he'd followed—leaving his duties unattended, something he'd never done in all the time he'd worked for Dominic.

Dominic's reaction had come in the form of a simple warning. "Stay away from Alethea. She's trouble."

Jake had given him similar instructions: steer clear of the wreckage that would follow any personal entanglement with Alethea. He'd done as they'd asked because, although he'd spent many nights remembering the one hot kiss he'd shared with her, his loyalty was to the men who had given him a chance when the rest of the world had turned their backs on him.

No woman, not even one who made sex with other women less tempting, would be the reason he disappointed them again.

Now Jake was asking him to watch Alethea—closely. Not something he minded doing, but something that held a risk of forgetting why nothing was possible between them. His personal feelings had to come second to his duty.

He needed to find out if she was involved in the recent coding errors. To do that, he would have to breach the defenses of a woman who had once demolished his with one sultry look.

How do you outsmart a woman who prides herself on outsmarting everyone else?

You play by her rules.

Which means there are none.

He remembered the look in her eyes when she'd seen him at the hospital. No matter how their first encounter had ended, the attraction was still mutual.

I can use that.

I may even enjoy doing so.

Calling her dominated his thoughts all day, but he forced himself to wait. To win, he'd have to choose his strategy and timing carefully. Luckily, he'd had almost a year to study his target.

And he had. He'd kept her on his radar, even when some would have said it wasn't necessary. Although she'd attended fewer and fewer of the social events he'd worked, when she had, he hadn't been able to look away from her. At first he'd tried to tell himself it was part of his job, but there was no denying the pleasure he found in watching her. Alethea entered a room with purpose. When she wanted to be the center of attention, her wild red mane flew loose—like the cape of a matador flaming the passions of men even as it lured them to their doom.

Doom might be a bit strong. Most of them left their encounter with her looking bemused. Her racy choice of outfits, lingering sidelong glances, and even her light flirtatious laugh was a means of distracting her target while she gained access to whatever information she sought.

She was a woman who was always in control.

A woman men fawned over, instead of challenged.

Someone who liked to win.

A devilish smile spread across his face. He knew exactly how to throw her and keep her off balance.

It rang once. Twice.

"Hello?" Alethea asked slowly, most likely because he'd blocked his ID.

Payback time.

CHAPTER *Five*

LYING IN BED, Alethea rolled onto her back when she heard her cell phone ring and groaned. She'd trained most of her international contacts to call her at a reasonable hour, but there were still a few who forgot now and then. She reached for her phone, placing it instantly on speaker and flopping backward against her firm pillows. Like the rest of her apartment, the bed was functional without being overly comfortable. Too much comfort made a person soft, vulnerable.

Something Alethea refused to ever be again.

"Hello, Alethea." A deep male voice echoed through her dark bedroom as if its owner were there with her.

Alethea sat up, instantly alert. There was only one man whose voice alone could have her body humming with anticipation. "Marc," she said, striving for calm, glad he couldn't see the way her cheeks warmed and her nipples strained against her cotton T-shirt, a side effect of the numerous nights she'd used his image as inspiration while she'd pleasured herself. Her voice was huskier than she aimed for when she asked sarcastically, "What did I do to merit a phone call?"

"I've been thinking about you all week."

The same way I've been thinking about you? she wondered, but wisely kept the thought to herself.

She relaxed back into her pillows and closed her eyes. She and Captain America had nothing in common. Even if her body was sure that wouldn't matter. "And you finally decided to thank me for my help at the hospital?" Okay, it was a jab, but she couldn't resist.

He answered smoothly, "Let's not talk about work. In fact, there is only one word I want to hear you say and that's—yes."

Don't ask. He's playing on your curiosity. "To what?"

His sexy chuckle resonated through her, sending warm tingles into her stomach and lower. "To everything."

"That's not going to happen."

"Scared?" he asked huskily.

Only of hurting myself in my haste to disrobe. See, that's why I can't say yes, because when something feels as good as being with you does, it never ends well. "No, just smart enough to know you wouldn't call unless you wanted something from me. What you're suggesting could get messy and complicated. You don't do either. What do you really want?"

"Oh, Alethea. So much smarter than the rest of us. If you can see right through me and my motives, then there is no risk in meeting me." He chuckled again. "Unless, you don't think you could control yourself."

"That's not a risk."

"Prove me wrong. Meet me for a drink."

Her rational side began listing all the reasons why that would be a bad idea. He worked for Dominic. Now, more than ever before, she needed to keep her head clear, if she was going to figure out what was going on. On the other hand, he might have inside information that could clear Stephan.

I told Lil I wouldn't do anything until we spoke again.

However, she did dare me to call Marc.

So, technically, I won't be breaking my promise.

"Okay, one drink."

"Excellent. Now say it."

"Say what?"

"Yes."

What game was he playing? "No."

His voice deepened, and hot desire shot through Alethea as he said, "You are a delicious challenge, Alethea. Keep fighting to control every situation. It'll make your eventual submission that much sweeter."

Alethea's heart thudded loudly in her chest as her body once again was at odds with what she was thinking. *Submission? Who does this guy think he's talking to?* With some irony, Alethea admitted to herself, *only a woman who just drenched her panties at the thought of him trying to make her submit.*

Cool. Play it cool. Don't let him see that he's getting to you.

"I thought you wanted to meet for a drink."

"We both know what you really want from me. Why try to deny it?"

"Wow, there probably isn't room for me and your ego in your bed, so I'm going to pass on that offer."

His low chuckle was about the sexiest thing she'd ever heard. It was playful, yet held a promise of determination. "I love the way you hide behind sarcasm when you're scared. It may turn off some, but I think it's hot. You can insult me all you want, Alethea. It won't change how the night ends. I know what you need."

A cold shower? What the hell is wrong with me? She angrily tucked her comforter tightly around her. "I don't need anything. I can have who I want, when I want, how I want."

"And that's why you're not satisfied. You don't want someone you can control. You dream of being taken, roughly, again and again. You want to be the one who begs for release. I know what you crave, and I can give you that fantasy and more. But you have to submit to me fully. That's what I like. That's what *I* need."

Alethea panicked and hung up.

Before she agreed.

Her phone vibrated and she checked her messages. He'd sent her a short text. "I thought you were braver than that."

She could almost hear him laughing, and an angry heat spread up her cheeks. *Bastard.* She threw her phone down next to her on the bed.

What an arrogant ass. Who does he think he is—God's gift to the vagina?

She mimicked his voice as she repeated his words, "No man has ever fully satisfied you."

Ridiculous.

And right.

Of course, she'd had her share of orgasms and sexual partners, but none so remarkable that they'd remained crisp in her memories. She'd kept the number to one hand by remaining in contact with one of the more talented of her partners, but even he was little more than a convenience. A girl could only invest in so many batteries before sex had to involve the real deal.

Maybe that's the problem. She tried to remember the last time she'd had sex and realized it'd been more than a year. *It's been too long. That's all this is. I'm a healthy woman in my prime.*

Marc is nothing special.

I should have met him for a drink just to scratch an itch and end this ridiculous fascination I have with him.

Why couldn't he ask her out, buy her a drink, and let her sneak out in the middle of the night while he slept, like every other man she knew? Why go all macho and all "You will submit to me"?

By saying that, he proved how very little he does know me.

I'll never submit to a man.

Okay, now and then in a passing fantasy, but that's fantasy. In reality I would never give anyone else control over me.

She remembered a therapist she'd spoken to back in high school, when her mother had thought she needed to talk out her feelings. The woman had warned her that she would never be happy if she lived the rest of her life on high alert.

Easy advice to give if you've never lost everything because of a threat you didn't know was there.

Had your father die and know it was your fault.

I won't relax as long as I have something to lose.

Someone to protect.

Relaxing, much like deep sleep, can wait until I'm dead.

42

Marc set his phone on the table, started undressing for bed, and smiled. He hung his suit in the closet and donned a pair of flannel lounge pants. Alethea wasn't going to meet him that night, but he hadn't expected her to. She was rattled, though, and that had been his goal.

He placed his wallet and watch on his nightstand beside photos of his family, and shook his head in amusement. His mother would have boxed him on the ear if she'd ever heard him speak to a woman the way he'd spoken to Alethea, and both of his sisters would have done the same. He'd been raised in a household of strong, opinionated females. His father was a retired Marine, just as his father had been before him, a fact that gave people the wrong impression of how he'd grown up. Born to older parents, he'd missed the deployments and had grown up in a solid two-parent home with a father who doted on his wife and spoiled his daughters. Stone men were fiercely protective of their family and country, but in the home, they were laid-back and more prone to humor than harsh words. His father often said there were times and places that required the worst of what was in a man; the home was not one of them.

They weren't a wealthy family, but they worked hard and raised their children to respect authority, education, and the value of a loaded Colt .45. He'd grown up with more than a little admiration for intelligent, independent women.

But there was something about Alethea that made him want to pound his chest and drag her off to the nearest cave—an urge that was only stronger now that he sensed a part of her wanted him to do just that.

Shit.

Focus.

I need to get into her head, not her pants.

His loyalty to Dominic was not going to be undermined by a paranoid redhead, no matter how gorgeous she was or how many cold showers it took.

43

He took his laptop to bed with him and searched the Internet for anything that would explain what motivated her. He'd read her personal history via a detailed background check, and it didn't add up. She'd been a model student until middle school, and then something had happened. Something serious enough to change the course of her life. The list of private schools that had thrown her out was impressive, speaking volumes about the financial clout her family must have had. The report stated that her father had died of a heart attack. Had she been there when it happened? It didn't say. There was remarkably little information about the incident.

Thanks to the social media explosion, his search revealed photos of Alethea and Lil at public events over the years. Proms. Parties with friends. Even someone as careful as Alethea couldn't keep all of her photos off the Internet. People had posted and tagged her. Lil had made an entire montage of the two of them during their senior year and put it on an old blog that both had likely forgotten about.

He smiled at a photo of the two of them standing in front of a school, side by side in their late teens, looking gloriously guilty. There were more recent photos of Alethea looking down at a newborn Colby in her arms with love in her eyes.

She obviously loved Lil and her child. How far would she go to protect them? Was Jake right? Were the software glitches Alethea's warning that there were holes in the Corisi server firewall?

Although he admired her loyalty to Lil, he knew what it meant.

He couldn't trust her.

And he had to stop her.

Across town, Alethea was doing her own research while giving her libido a pep talk. She hadn't slept, but that was nothing new. Her bed was covered with files she'd pulled. *Stop thinking about what tonight could have been like and focus on what's important.*

The early morning sun was just beginning to brighten the windows of her apartment. She'd slept for only a couple of hours, and then, not peacefully.

Why would Stephan still be targeting Dominic?

What could he want?

His family will have Isola Santos back when he marries Nicole.

His company is doing better because of his association with Corisi Enterprises.

Is it jealousy?

He had the opportunity to take Dominic down without being caught. But instead, he confessed and risked everything for Nicole.

To do what? To lull them into trusting him?

What could he possibly be planning that would be bigger than financially ruining Dominic?

She opened and closed one of the folders on her lap. It was a proposal for a business opportunity in Denmark. They wanted her to test the security for a new bank chain. It was an amazing opportunity for her and one that she normally would have jumped on.

How easy it would be to simply hand over what she knew about the Corisi computer glitches to Jake and walk away. No one was going to thank her for her involvement. *I barely know Stephan. It's not my responsibility to clear his name.*

My gut tells me it's not him, but what if it is? What if I sit on this information for too long because I don't want to believe that he's capable of it—because I don't want the fallout to hurt Lil?

What if that's what he's counting on? That no one would suspect him now?

I need to dig deeper.

I need to know if he's after Dominic.

And if he's not, I need to know who is.

CHAPTER *Six*

LIL INVITED HER two guests to sit and set four teacups on a serving tray. She didn't ask the staff to serve them. In fact, she'd given the staff the morning off. She didn't want anyone to overhear what she'd planned.

Marie Duhamel, Dominic's personal assistant and second mother, took the cup she was offered and placed it carefully before her. She looked at the fourth cup and raised an eyebrow. Lil pretended not to notice.

Don't be late, Alethea. Don't call me with an excuse not to come. This has to work.

Nicole picked up her cup and looked around the room. "Lil, you sounded nervous when you asked me to come over this morning. Did something happen? Is Abby okay? I saw her yesterday and she looked fine."

"It's not Abby."

Marie leaned across the table and put a supportive hand over Lil's. "Whatever it is, we're here for you. You can tell us anything."

Can I? Is this the right choice? Alethea and I have been here before—saddled with information that could save or just as likely alienate the ones we love. I almost lost Jake the first time because I lied. These people are my family. And we all want the same thing. We all want Stephan to be innocent. No one is going to be happy with the news—not Alethea, not Marie, and definitely not Nicole. But we can prove Stephan isn't involved— together. I'll make them see that.

After taking a fortifying breath, Lil said, "I invited Alethea to join us."

Marie's face tightened and she withdrew her hand. With forced politeness she said, "Well, what a nice surprise."

Nicole looked on sympathetically. "It can't be easy for you, Lil. I know how much you love her, but some personalities don't mix well with others and, unfortunately, Alethea has one of those personalities."

"You're being kind," Marie said to Nicole. "Very kind."

Squaring her shoulders in determination, Lil defended her friend. "Alethea has been a good friend to me for a long time. I know she can take things too far. She's impulsive, she's snarky, and she's suspicious of even the moon the moment she can't see it. But she's like a sister to me, so please don't speak poorly of her in front of me."

Marie's expression softened a bit. "No one is saying you can't be friends with her." Lil held her eyes and Marie added, "And we should probably all try to make more of an effort to be nice to her. You shouldn't have to feel like you need to defend her to us."

Nicole laid her cup down and smiled. "I can't believe she snuck into the hospital through the kitchen. That girl has balls. I'll give her that."

"I'm hoping you'll both give her more than that."

Marie cocked her head to one side. "What do you mean?"

Lil bit her lip nervously, then said, "She told me something and I don't know what to do with it. Marie, you're a problem solver. I need your advice. And, Nicole, you may know something that could clear all of this up before it goes any further. I trust both of you completely. I hope you'll understand why I brought us together."

Nicole went white. "You're making me nervous."

Alethea stood in the doorway, unannounced as usual. "No one told me this was a party."

Lil crossed the room to join her friend and took her by the arm. "Al, this is better than your way. I can't play detective with you this time. I have too much to lose. Tell them what you know. Let's work together to figure this out."

She tried to drag Alethea toward the other two women, but Alethea didn't budge. She looked from Marie to Nicole and back. "Throw me to the lions, why don't you? You think they want to hear what I know?"

With warming cheeks, Lil conceded her point. *This is going to work. It has to.* "Want? No. Need to hear it? Yes. I love you, Al, but I love them, too. Trust them. Trust me."

Alethea reluctantly walked up to the table where the two women were seated. Neither stood. She looked at Lil one last time before saying, "I have information linking recent computer glitches at Corisi Enterprises to Stephan's IP address."

Marie suddenly stood and aggressively threw her napkin on the table. "What kind of nonsense is this?" A moment earlier, Marie had appeared to be a mild-mannered older woman. Everything from her choice of a conservative jacketed linen dress to her delicate jewelry broadcast New York sophistication. Her civilized veneer thinned at the hint of a threat to one of her boys.

Lil intervened quickly. "It's not nonsense. If Al says she has information, it's true."

Alethea interjected, "It doesn't mean that—" but didn't have time to finish her sentence before Nicole cut her off.

"No," Nicole said loudly. She stood and covered her mouth with a hand that shook. Tears filled her eyes. "Stephan would never do anything to hurt me or my family. We're getting married. How could you think that he would be involved in anything like that?"

Alethea raised a placating hand, but her tone wasn't as kind as Lil knew was necessary to calm a woman who still worried that Dominic would never fully accept the man she loved. "Let's try to focus on the facts and not get emotional about this."

Her voice rising, Nicole said, "Not emotional? Not emotional? You little bitch. You stand there and tell me that my fiancé is trying to sabotage my brother's company and I'm not supposed to be offended by it?"

"I didn't say—" Alethea started impatiently.

No, this is going all wrong. They weren't listening to Alethea, and she was getting defensive. That didn't bode well for a good outcome. Lil cut in, "Nicole—"

"What evidence do you have?" Marie asked in a cold voice.

Flipping her long curls defiantly over one shoulder, Alethea answered sharply, "Does it matter? Either you believe me or you don't."

Clasping her hands before her until they were white, Nicole announced, "I don't. I don't believe any of this. And I don't have time to waste on someone who loves to stir up trouble." Before she left, she turned to Lil and asked angrily, "Do you believe Stephan's involved in whatever she's accusing him of?"

I'm not good under pressure. I wish Abby were here. She'd know what to say to Nicole to reassure her. "No, I don't. I don't want to believe any of this, but Nicole, you're the one who is closest to him. People make mistakes. He spent years hating Dominic. Is he over that? If anyone would know, it's you."

Backing away, with a voice that cracked with emotion, Nicole said, "I do know and I can't believe that you'd even ask that." She turned and walked out of the room.

"I didn't mean it the way it sounded..." Lil said sadly, knowing that chasing after Nicole would only make it worse. *Marie is still here. She'll know how to fix this.*

Alethea and Marie were standing nose to nose, two strong women who would never come to blows but who certainly knew how to tear each other apart verbally. *I can't let that happen.*

Lil groaned when she saw the fire in Alethea's eyes. She didn't respond well to confrontation. Some people avoided conflict; Alethea ramped up in the face of it. Angry with her? She'd be angrier. It was part of the fear Lil had always sensed in her friend. Alethea needed to be in control, and the moment she felt she wasn't she came out fighting.

In a cutting tone, Alethea said, "No one said Stephan is guilty. I don't know who would have access to his accounts or why he'd give it to anyone, but the path leads back to him."

"Of course it does. No, you didn't accuse Stephan, you just said enough to plant a seed of doubt." Marie bristled. "How miserable are you that you can't stand to see anyone happy?"

No. No. No. "Marie, stop. Alethea didn't organize this meeting, I did."

Marie continued to challenge Alethea. "These glitches, do they even exist? I've heard nothing about them, and the boys tell me everything. You know what I think? I think you're afraid you're losing Lil and you're willing to destroy anyone to stop that from happening."

Head high, Alethea said, "Do you honestly think I care what you think of me? I don't need to prove anything to you. Lil knows the truth."

Do I? Lil searched Alethea's face urgently. "I know you believe there is a problem, Al, but I'm not sure what to think this time. I know things have changed between us. That can't be easy for you. Lately I've seen a side of you, though, that I don't understand. You were cruel with Jeisa. I've never seen you like that before. I'm not saying you're making this up, but could you be wrong?"

Alethea's expression hardened. "So, you don't believe me either?"

"I didn't say that, Al, but do you see how this could ruin everything? Can't you let it go?" Lil looked helplessly at Marie and then back at Alethea.

"You know I need to uncover the truth."

Lil slumped a bit. "Even if this destroys our friendship?"

"Even then." Alethea growled, and walked out of the room, out the front door, and to her car.

In the quiet after she left, Marie said, "That is one interesting friend you have."

Lil hugged her arms around her waist and shook her head. "Don't, Marie. You don't understand her."

Gathering up her purse, Marie said, "That is one point I certainly can't dispute. However, I'd like to think I know you. You're happy, Lil. Don't let her ruin that for you."

After Marie left, Lil headed to the back of the house to relieve the nanny. Colby ran over and buried her face in her mother's leg. "Mama. Mama. Up."

Lil reached down and picked up her young daughter. "Were you good for Karen?"

Colby laughed and stretched her answer into a comically long word. "Gooood?" Then she shook her head solemnly. "No."

Lil hugged her closer and laughed out loud. "Me, neither. I think I really messed up."

Taking her mother's face between her little hands, Colby said, "Two minutes, time out."

If only it were that easy for adults.

CHAPTER *Seven*

ALETHEA DOWNED HER third shot of what the bartender had promised would knock her on her ass: Three Wise Men. Johnny, Jack, and Jim—a combination that shocked initially, then brought a blissful burn. She stacked the small empty glass on top of two others and waved the bartender over. She fully intended to drink until she either stopped hating herself or stopped feeling anything, whichever came first.

She should have changed out of her tight-fitting sleeveless tank dress. There were two men at the bar watching her closely. She assessed them for threat and dismissed both. One was large and soft. The other didn't look like he'd ever seen the wrong side of a fist. If either followed her out the door, she hoped she didn't end up in jail for the pain she would inflict on them.

One smiled at her when he caught her looking across at him. She shook her head and looked away. *Sorry, I can't find a man attractive if I know I can kick his ass.*

"Seems you've changed your mind about our drink," a deep familiar voice said suggestively in her ear.

Alethea didn't even look up. She just downed her fourth shot. "Don't fuck with me tonight, Marc. I've had a bad day."

"Apparently," he said dryly.

"How did you know I was here?"

"Would you believe gut feeling? Or should I confess to light stalking?"

Almost smiling, Alethea waved over the bartender for another shot. "Don't make me laugh. I hate everyone right now."

"Want to tell me about it?"

"No." She downed her fifth shot.

He took her purse and rifled through it, pulling out her keys and sticking them in the front pocket of his charcoal suit pants.

"What are you doing?" she demanded, with the first hint of a slur in her voice.

"You're not driving anywhere tonight."

"How I get home is none of your concern."

"Maybe not, but I'm not going anywhere." He took a seat next to her. The bartender brought another shot by, but Marc waved him away. "So tell me about this bad day."

Alethea closed her eyes, then leaned onto her elbows on the bar in front of her. "I'm celebrating my freedom from the responsibility of trying to make people see reality."

"You're not celebrating. You're wallowing."

Alethea tried unsuccessfully to stack her remaining empty shot glasses into a pyramid but missed. "You don't know anything about what's going on. Did Marie send you? She thinks I'm jealous of Lil's new life. I'm not. I don't want a husband and kids. I'd die of boredom in her perfect little life. But that doesn't mean I'm wrong."

"About what?" he asked quietly.

She looked up into his intense blue eyes and instantly regretted doing so. Even though they were slightly blurred, they looked just as beautiful. Maybe even more so because they were so close. Too close. Like those luscious lips of his that were pressed in a thoughtful line. It would be so easy to escape into them as she had into alcohol. "About life. If you have something you love, you have to protect it or someone will rip it from you." She snapped her fingers in the air. "Look away and you lose, just like that."

"What are you trying to stop Lil from losing?"

"Everything," she said angrily, and knocked the pyramid over, not caring about the glare the bartender gave her as some crashed to the floor. "But they don't see that. They think I'm looking for trouble where there is none. I'm done caring what they think of me. I should just let it all fall apart—then they'd miss me." She leaned closer to him until their lips almost touched. "Even you would miss me. Admit it."

Marc coughed. "This isn't a conversation we should have in a public bar. Come on, I'll drive you home."

He helped her up and she leaned against him. "If you think sleeping with me will get me to tell you everything, you're song... so wrong." She corrected herself as she stumbled over her words.

"We will be together, Alethea, but not tonight," he assured her with a cocky smile, walking her out of the bar, his arm around her waist to steady her.

Heaven. Too bad I probably won't remember this. He put her in the passenger seat of his car and buckled her in. While he did so, he was close, too close. She said, "I want to hate you, but you smell so good."

"Oh, my little warrior, you're drunk."

"Not enough. I can still feel my feet. I was hoping for absolute oblivion."

"Alcohol is never the solution."

Alethea shrugged. "Judge me all you want. I know I'm not perfect. I've made mistakes. Who hasn't?" As she spoke she sank farther into the seat and closed her eyes. "You think I want to be like this? I don't. I want to believe in the illusion of safety. But I can't. Ever try to write a letter to Santa after you're told he doesn't exist? My life is like that. Just like that."

His voice was unexpectedly gentle. "I was with you until the Santa reference."

Alethea's eyes opened slowly and she looked across the car at him. It might have been the alcohol. *Okay, it's definitely the alcohol.* But Marc sounded like he cared. The pain and fear she could normally conceal from the world spilled forth. "I lost my father because I was too trusting, too naïve to protect him." She looked out the window at the blur of traffic, felt instantly queasy, and turned back to him.

He glanced at her, studying her in a way that made her regret speaking so honestly. "Your father died of a heart attack at home, didn't he?"

What does it matter if I tell him? No one believes anything I say anyway. "That's what they told me, but there was this guy. And the papers. Then we moved across the country so fast. I knew what happened even before I *knew* what happened. You know what I mean?"

"I'd like to say I understand what you're saying, but you're not making much sense. Let's get you home. You can tell me tomorrow."

Tomorrow. She closed her eyes again. *Does it have to come? Can't we stay here? Just you and me. No problems to solve. No one telling me how they would love me if... if... if I weren't me. Just the sweet comfort of your body against mine, and just enough numbness to not care why it's wrong.*

She imagined the two of them falling into her bed, ripping off each other's clothing as they did. Despite how her head was spinning, she smiled.

"We're here," Marc said, and Alethea realized she must have passed out. *See, that's why I should drink more—I'm a lightweight.* The term amused her and she laughed out loud.

Marc gave her a puzzled look, which only made her laugh more.

While he half walked, half carried her through the garage beneath her building, she gave in to temptation and slid a hand beneath his suit. His stomach was rock hard, just as she'd imagined it. "Nice," she said.

She felt his sharp intake of breath before he took her hand in his and held it away from him. "You're not making this easy," he groaned.

She smiled up at him cheekily. "Because you want me. I know you do. I see the way you look at me." As they entered the elevator, he leaned her against the railing and stepped back. She swung an arm around for emphasis. "You were off limits because I didn't want to upset anyone, rock the cart, upset the boat... whatever. But now it doesn't matter. They're all angry with me anyway."

She stumbled and dropped her key when the elevator stopped at her floor. He picked up the key, then swung her up in his arms. She laid her head on his shoulder and breathed him in. Like her, he didn't wear artificial scents. His smell was delightfully, simply him. She knew she should tell him to go, but for just a moment she let herself savor being held. Not since she was a child had someone made her feel protected, and in his arms, she finally felt safe.

He opened the door with one hand, carried her through to her living room, eased her back onto her feet, and stepped away from her. Alethea fought the desire to follow him, climb back into those strong arms, and recapture the brief feeling of peace.

But she didn't. She stood there, swaying slightly, wondering why he looked unhappy when she'd offered him a night of pleasure.

He walked around her apartment, studying the bare walls and sparse décor. "Why don't you have better security?" he demanded.

What is he angry about? "I offered to let you spend the night and you're worried about what kind of alarm I do or don't have?"

He walked over and scowled down at her. "I imagined you'd have fifty bolts on your door and a high-tech security system."

She waved at the door and its basic lock and bolt. "I protect what's important. My computer is practically set to self-destruct if tampered with."

"You don't care if anything happens to you, do you?"

Those blue eyes looked right through her bravado and into her soul. Huskily, she admitted, "I haven't since that day."

His face tightened with anger. "Come on, let's get you to bed."

The idea had held appeal earlier, but now the room spun and Alethea's mouth suddenly dried. "I don't think it's a good idea anymore..."

A faint smile curled one side of his luscious, delicious lips. "I'd love to join you, but not like this."

"Excuse me," she said in a rush, stumbled for the bathroom, dropped to her knees, and threw up into the toilet. She felt his hands in her hair, holding it back from her face as she retched again. *Yep, I know how to turn a man on.* When she sat back on her heels, shaking and dizzy, he handed her a cool, wet towel for her face. "Just go, Marc."

He squatted down next to her, pushing some of her hair back behind her ears and said, "You need water, aspirin, and to sleep this off. Are you going to throw up again?"

Vomit again? No. Die of embarrassment—well, that was still a definite possibility.

"No." She stood up quickly. Her legs were like jelly beneath her now and the room tilted. "Probably not," she said with less certainty.

Marc swung her up in his arms. She closed her eyes and, despite her churning stomach, let herself enjoy the moment. There it was—that feeling of being cared for again. Even if it wasn't real, even if he would have done the same for anyone in her condition—it still felt unbearably good. He carried her to her bedroom and set her gently on the edge of her bed, then hunted through her bureau and returned with the ridiculous flowered cotton nightgown with the high neckline that her mother had sent as a present and which she hadn't had the heart to throw away. That was all their relationship was now: holiday and birthday gifts that revealed how little they knew each other. *I've worn gym shorts and T-shirts my whole adult life, but since I never see her, I guess she wouldn't know that.*

"Stand up, turn around, and strip," Marc said roughly.

She stood, narrowed her eyes, and wagged a finger at him. "Shouldn't *you* turn around?"

He shook his head and said, "I have to make sure you don't fall on your face."

Just how drunk does he think I am? In an act of defiance, she faced him and reached for the zipper of her dress. *I'm not ashamed of how I look.* Her fingers fumbled with the zipper and it snagged a few inches down.

He watched her with a combination of desire and amusement. "Let me help you."

She smacked his hand away. "I can do it myself." She grabbed the hem of her dress and pulled it up, forgetting how snug the material was. She gave it an angry yank upward and found her arms wedged tightly over her head while the cool air teased her exposed breasts and midriff.

With a growl he said, "Why are you so stubborn? There is no shame in needing help now and then."

She tried to pull away from him and almost fell forward, still trapped in the dress that was half up over her head. "I don't need you. I don't need anyone."

With one strong move, he hauled her back against him, held her struggling body with an arm around her waist, and pulled the dress over her head and off. In a flash, he replaced it with the nightgown and turned her to face him. "Everyone needs someone." He pulled back the covers, eased her beneath them, and said, "Don't go to sleep yet. I'll be right back with some water."

During his short absence, a deep sadness settled over her, as the alcohol brought out the truth she usually withheld even from herself. *You're right. I don't want to be alone. I want to be the friend Lil can invite to all of those family events she now throws. I do care what they think of me.*

I just don't know if I can be the person they want me to be.

She sat up when he returned and obediently took the pills he held out. Then she flopped back into her bed. The sweet oblivion she'd sought earlier arrived and she sank into a deep sleep.

Marc pulled a chair closer to her bed and settled himself into it. He wasn't going anywhere.

In sleep, she looked peaceful and delicate. It was difficult to reconcile her sweet features with the persona she projected to the world. He'd always assumed that her over-the-top behavior was driven by an addiction to adrenaline rushes and the need to be right.

That wasn't the woman who lay before him.

This woman had endured some trauma she couldn't face. In his years in the Marines he'd seen frontline action. He'd seen how the horrors of war affected people differently. Some became numb to it. Some left tormented by nightmares. War shaped a person, and never all for the good. No matter how they dealt with what they'd seen, with what they'd done—a part of them was forever changed.

Alethea's pain called out to his own, reminding him of his darker side that he kept boxed up and hidden.

He knew exactly what Alethea had been looking for at the bottom of those shot glasses, because he'd sought the same his first few months after leaving the Veterans Hospital. Drinking hadn't solved his problems; in fact, it was the reason he hadn't gotten that famed department store job. His bloodshot eyes had belied how he'd spent the night before his interview.

Which made the second chance Dominic Corisi gave him, after he saw Marc on the news, so undeserved. Dominic's computer empire was quickly growing, and he knew he needed security, but he was also one who didn't trust many people. Marc still shook his head when he remembered how Dominic had put him in charge.

Of course, Marc had needed the job, but he'd been brutally honest with the cocky businessman about his experience. "I don't know shit about corporate security."

Dominic had calmly informed him that he didn't care what was on his résumé. "The business side of security can be learned," he'd said. "But the kind of loyalty you showed your platoon when you went back to get more of them, even though you'd been shot—that's either in a man or it's not."

RUTH CARDELLO

There wasn't a day that went by that Marc wasn't grateful for the faith Dominic had shown him, and his loyalty had never wavered. He'd found his confidence again and enjoyed a lifestyle most envied. Money bred money. Although he wasn't in the same financial league as his boss, he was wealthy beyond what he'd ever expected. He would have said that nothing was more important than his job.

Until now.

With a sigh, Marc looked back at Alethea. He should have squeezed out every bit of information he could while she was vulnerable. It would have been easy enough to manipulate her and she likely wouldn't have even remembered it the next day.

But he couldn't.

Not even for Dominic.

Beneath her tough talk and confident smile, Alethea was hurting, and he couldn't ignore that any more than he could have left his men behind on the battlefield. In the past, they may have been adversaries, but they were more alike than different when it came to what he considered most important.

He wanted her.

Needed her.

Would find a way to have her.

He'd dated many women—even come close to loving a couple of them before things fell apart for one reason or another. But none had ever gotten under his skin the way Alethea had. None sent his blood pounding at the mere thought of touching her.

But it was more than that.

He respected her.

Wanted to hold her to him and comfort her.

Or shake some sense into her.

The temptation to crawl into bed beside her, hold her in his arms, and kiss away the pain he'd seen in her eyes was strong, but, however much he wanted to protect her, it was his job to outsmart her. He hoped to God she had nothing to do with the trouble at Corisi Enterprises.

60

Tomorrow. He'd figure out what to do tomorrow. For now, all he could do was watch over her.

A few hours later, she stirred in her sleep and moaned. Her eyes flew open and she asked into the darkness, "Marc?"

He fought and won against the urge to go to her. Instead he answered quietly, "Yes?"

"What are you still doing here?" she asked, sounding surprised and confused.

"Making sure you're okay."

She laid her head back on her pillow and closed her eyes, falling back asleep even as she spoke, "I told you I don't need you."

I know, he thought. *But you're wrong.*

CHAPTER *Eight*

HIS LIPS CLOSED over hers and Alethea moaned with pleasure, opening her mouth for him, inviting his invasion. He claimed her mouth with an abandon that spoke of his intense need for her. A need that also rocked her.

His hot lips moved across her cheek as he whispered, "You're mine, Alethea." One of his hands slid beneath the short hem of her nightgown and settled on one of her buttocks, squeezing it possessively. He rolled onto his back, taking her with him so she lay on top of him. With a strong, bold move, he whisked her nightgown over her head, settling her back against him, bare chest to bare chest. "That's better," he said huskily, then slid a finger beneath the hem of her silk underwear. "But why are you still wearing these?"

Alethea rubbed the soaked crotch of her panties back and forth against his arousal. "Because you're slow tonight?"

"I'll show you slow," he growled, and lifted her so she was straddling him. Then he started a hot, torturously slow worshipping of her breasts. He traced them first with the back of his hand, then circled her excited nipples with his calloused thumbs. He flicked their hardened tips until she was gasping from the pleasure of it. Then he pulled her forward and took one of her small breasts into his mouth, suckling gently. She felt the intensity of that caress shoot through her stomach as she rubbed herself helplessly against him.

He rolled onto his side and brought her with him. Taking both of her hands in one of his, he held them above her head and plundered her mouth while his tip teased her wet lower lips by sliding back and forth against them. With one strong move, he shifted so he was above her and spread her legs wide.

62

"You're mine," he said roughly. "Say it."

When she refused, he inserted just the tip of his shaft inside her, rolling his hips in a teasing move that had her thrashing wildly beneath him. "Mine to take as often and any way I want. Submit to me, Alethea. You know you want to."

She shook her head in denial, until he plunged so deeply inside her she cried out, a sound that he muffled with his mouth on hers. Then he withdrew and began the tortuous tease of rubbing himself against her swollen clit and folds. His tongue claimed hers. Her hands were held immobile above her while his free hand explored and claimed her.

She was defenseless to stop his possession of her, and so wet and ready for him that she couldn't deny how much she wanted to give in to him.

He plunged his shaft deep within her again, taking advantage of how her mouth opened wider when she gasped by claiming it even more deeply. Her senses were full of him and she was losing the battle with herself. He withdrew from her and began to lick his way down her chest, between her breasts, past her navel until his mouth hovered over her sex.

"You can't win with me, Alethea. I'm in control here. Not you. Say it."

She'd long since stopped caring what she was saying. She gripped the sheets on either side of her, her head thrashing back and forth as she cried out, "Take me, Marc. Take me."

The sound of her own cries woke her and she sat up with a jolt. "Marc?" The room spun. She squinted against the harsh morning sun, then dropped back into her bed, groaning in response to what felt like a sledgehammer crashing against her forehead.

It was a dream. Just another freaking dream.

Opening one eye cautiously, Alethea noted the chair that was still pulled up beside her bed.

And a nightmare.
I don't drink.
What was I thinking?

I wasn't.

As a collage of memories from the night before began to surface, Alethea closed her eyes again. *I threw myself at him and he ducked.*

She vaguely remembered him holding her hair back as she hunched over the toilet. *Lovely.* She didn't remember exactly how she'd gotten into her nightgown, but she did have a vivid memory of Marc watching over her while she slept.

Hopefully I don't talk in my sleep. She half smiled. *Maybe I do and that's why he ran.* She groaned again when she realized someone had installed carpeting in her mouth while she'd slept.

Pushing herself out of bed, Alethea trudged to the bathroom. The hot shower wasn't washing away the hurt she'd felt when Lil had questioned her motives, nor did it lessen her mortification about turning the hottest man she'd ever met into her nursemaid for the night.

Some days just suck. She looked at the calendar on the wall. *I can't even blame it on Monday. It's Tuesday.*

Beneath the spray of the shower, Alethea weighed her options for the day. *I can stay angry with Lil for not trusting me, angry with Marc for seeing me at my worst, and angry with myself for not handling either situation well, or I can do something about at least one of the reasons I hate myself today.*

You don't help someone because you know they'll thank you for it. You help them because they need you. Because you couldn't live with yourself if you didn't help them.

Something doesn't add up.

Why would someone go to the trouble of uploading glitches that could be fixed easily? Why make it look like Stephan is involved? Or is he? No, it doesn't make sense for it to be him. He'd hit Dominic with a more deadly corporate blow. Could both be a smoke screen to cover a more sinister plan? If so, what?

She opened her phone and scrolled down to a number she knew she shouldn't call. *Jeremy.* They weren't a team anymore. Maybe they never had been. *He was a good friend to me, but I didn't appreciate how good, until I screwed it up. I should have respected his relationship with Jeisa. I should have been happy for him, instead of worrying about what it meant for me and my career. Maybe even my ego.*

I killed that friendship because in my rush to get what I wanted, I didn't see how I was hurting those around me. I don't mean to hurt them. Does it matter, though, if the result is the same?

If I don't do something, I'm going to lose Lil—the only family I've allowed myself to have. She thought of her mother, who had remarried a couple years after the "accident," and how she'd never been able to forgive her for being able to accept the lies and move on. Like Lil, her mother didn't want to see anything that might threaten her happiness.

And I couldn't let her have that fantasy—even if the truth wouldn't undo our loss. I needed her to believe me.

I wouldn't back down.

Not even when it destroyed my relationship with my mother. Why couldn't I let her be happy? Am I the vindictive person Marie thinks I am? Am I wrong to keep digging when I know no one wants me to? Am I destined to repeat this pattern until I've driven everyone I care about away from me?

No, this is different.

I can't walk away until I know how serious this is.

It's not about coding errors. I know it. What am I missing?

Is Stephan involved in this or not?

There is only one person who knows for sure.

She padded out of the shower, applied a shield of makeup, and shook her hair out in rebellious free curls. Normally she dressed to blend in. She preferred to work under the radar, but the red dress she chose was her war paint.

An image of Marc surfaced, but she shook it off. This has nothing to do with how my ego took a beating last night. I don't know what I'm going to face today, and I'm not leaving any advantage behind.

It has nothing to do with the nearly impossible chance that our paths may cross today.

She slipped on her Louboutin stilettos, strode out the door and down to the garage. She peeled out as she drove off, not caring about the drivers she angered as she cut them off.

She was going to find Stephan, and no one—no one—was going to stop her.

"I found him." Craig sauntered into Marc's office, interrupting an otherwise tedious couple of hours of reviewing notes.

"Who?"

"Our mole. At least I think so. He fits the bill. He's in programming. He was living with his parents up until a few months ago. All of a sudden he's dressing sharp, driving a Bentley Continental, and throwing money around like he won the lottery. The secretaries call him Coding Casanova. They aren't interested in him, but they love to gossip about him."

Marc stood and stretched. "That sounds like exactly what we're looking for. What's his name?"

"Jim Whitman."

A quick search on his computer told Marc all needed to know. "He's relatively new. He was hired last June. June. That would have been when Dominic went to China to sign his big contract."

Also when the first serious hacking occurred.

He dismissed Craig and dialed Jeremy's cell number. "Jeremy, it's Marc. I need you to hack into something for me."

"Hey, hey, hey," Jeremy said with a laugh. "First, we never call it hacking. Second, we never talk about it on a phone where anyone could listen in. And third, I have a legitimate business now. I'm done with that lifestyle."

"Someone's on the wrong side of your firewall and I think I found him. I need proof to give Jake. Tell me what this guy is up to."

"Are you sure? It should have been airtight. Hang on, I can get remote access." There was a rustling noise, then a clatter of Jeremy's cell phone falling and being picked back up. "Who is it?" he growled.

"Jim Whitman," Marc said.

"I don't know him, but I will in about two minutes. Just using my password generator." A few seconds later Jeremy said, "And I'm in."

"What did you find?"

"Give me a minute. Getting in is easy. Wading through the crap in most people's email is the pain. Wait. He has an encrypted folder on *his desktop*. That's so cute. It's like putting a tiny safe in your backyard and thinking it'll protect your jewelry. It screams, 'Open me.'"

"So, open it."

"Done."

Marc paced as Jeremy typed.

"The good news is this is no Einstein. We're talking about basic coding and simplistic encryption. Eesh, he doesn't even have sophisticated taste in porn. You should see what this guy spends his lunch looking at."

"Is there anything in that folder that suggests someone is paying him?"

"No."

"Keep looking. Can you see if he's accessed anyone's mail or a department he's not supposed to?"

"I can try. Most would know to cover their tracks. Oh, look, he didn't. This little weasel has been all over the server."

"We've been experiencing coding glitches. Could he be uploading them... or whatever you do to get them in a program?"

"You don't know much about computers, do you?"

"No, but I'm a dead shot from a thousand yards with a sniper rifle."

"Point taken. Okay, so this guy is definitely gathering information for someone. I don't think he's the reason for the computer problem, but I'd say he knows who is. Give me a minute. I miss doing this."

After a series of guttural noises, some revealing his displeasure with what he found, Jeremy said, "Do you want the good news, the bad news, or the who-didn't-see-this-one-coming?"

"Just spit it out."

"I know what Jim was up to, and he's not a threat to your software. In fact, he's tracking whoever is."

"And the bad news?"

"He traced some code errors back to Stephan Andrade's IP address."

"Shit."

"Seriously, that's fucked up. I thought that guy was over whatever happened between him and Dominic."

"I thought so, too." *This just keeps getting worse.* "Was there anything else?"

"Yes, Jim sent out an email right after he found a connection to Stephan."

"Who? Who did he contact?" He knew the answer, but he hoped he was wrong.

"Alethea," Jeremy said, sounding more than a little put out. "I can't believe she replaced me with an idiot who doesn't even know to encrypt or erase his email. He thought deleting it was enough."

Alethea. What am I going to do with you? "Thanks, Jeremy. Can you do one more thing for me before you go?"

"Sure."

"I need a little something to help ensure Jim stays gone after we kick him out. Don't stop digging until you find something we can hold over him."

"My pleasure," Jeremy said, and started furiously typing again. As he searched, he said, "I'll also retrace his tracks and see if I can find anything he missed. Just a quick piece of advice: If Alethea thinks Lil and Abby are in danger because of this, she won't stop until she takes down Stephan, along with anyone who stands between her and that objective—even if it gets her killed."

Marc said with conviction, "That's not going to happen."

"Good luck, man," Jeremy said. "I have a feeling you're going to need it."

Marc hung up the phone and dialed Jake Walton's number. "Jake, we need to meet this morning, but I have to pick up a package first."

"You found something?"

"Oh, yes."

"Good, where do you want to meet?"

"I'll come to you."

After hanging up, Marc charged out of his office and down to his car. He called Alethea, but it went through to her voice mail. Trusting his gut, he headed toward Stephan Andrade's main office.

He ordered his team to set up a surveillance perimeter around the building. If she made it there before him, he wanted to know. He parked in front of the building and glanced into the main foyer, even though he had no expectation of seeing her there. It wasn't her style.

He stopped mid step when he spotted a drop-dead gorgeous woman in ridiculously high heels, a hot red dress, and telltale auburn locks, standing at the reception desk of Stephan's office.

Although he'd never been one to believe in destiny, he felt that he was meant to find her.

Stop her.

Save her.

CHAPTER *Nine*

THE PROBLEM WITH knocking is that you give people the chance to slam the door in your face.

"Do you have an appointment?" the older secretary at the main desk asked her.

Squaring her shoulders, Alethea said, "No, but I need to speak with Stephan Andrade."

The secretary looked her over and said, "You know he's engaged, right? That outfit would be completely wasted on him."

Alethea let out a calming breath. *She doesn't matter. This conversation doesn't matter. Don't give her a reason to refuse you.* "Can you just call to see if he's available?"

"Hon, he's not available. Men like him never are. If you'd like to leave your name with me, I'll forward it to his secretary. That's the best I can do."

Unprofessional. Rude. And there is no way she's a natural blonde. Again, all unimportant. "He must have a list of who you allow to go straight up. I know him personally."

The woman looked down at her desk, then back up without saying anything.

"My name is Alethea Niarchos. Check the list."

The woman scanned a paper on a clipboard, then some side notes. She looked up and her face went a bit red. "Hang on a moment," she said, before bending to speak softly into a microphone.

Two security men approached from across the hall. Alethea rolled her eyes. "You've got to be kidding me. Seriously? I'm on *that* list? Fine, I'll just call him myself to tell him I'm here."

She dug her phone out of her purse but, before she could input anything, the phone was snatched out of her hands from behind. Alethea spun, prepared to show her assailant why she excelled at kickboxing, then froze when she saw who had taken her phone.

"I'll handle this," Marc said smoothly to the approaching security men and to the stunned secretary. He gave them his card. His name alone was now big in his business.

The secretary let out an audible sigh of pleasure as she looked him over.

He dropped Alethea's phone into his pants pocket and took Alethea by the arm, guiding her rather forcibly toward the office building's front door.

"What do you think you're doing?" Alethea raged.

"Saving you from yourself," Marc said calmly, and stepped out of the building with her, still holding her arm.

She planted her feet—not easy to do, considering her heels—and refused to budge. "Take your hands off me or I'll do it for you."

He stopped and smiled down at her. "You could try."

She cocked one knee in preparation of doing just that, then stopped. With her heart beating wildly in her chest, she admitted to herself that it was good to see him again. Right. Wrong. It didn't matter. He'd come for her and that felt pretty damn good. Her eyes homed in on his lips, those wonderfully stern and kissable lips.

He pulled her flush against him and growled down into her ear, "The only choice you get is how you're getting in my car. Are you coming peacefully and willingly, or would you like to see exactly which pressure point causes temporary paralysis?"

If possible, his threat made him even more attractive. She squirmed against him, more out of the need to rub against him, than to get away, but he didn't know that. He held her tighter, and the feel of his body hardening sent a shot of fire straight through her. She should be angry with him. He was standing between her and what she had to do, and she felt confused as to why she wasn't fighting him.

She shifted her tush against his erection and reveled in his quick intake of air. *Oh, yeah— that.*

His breath was hot on her neck as he said, "I'll take you up on that offer, just not now."

His confidence served as a splash of sanity. She raised a foot to plant one of her heels into the toe of his shoe, but he twisted her body just enough to keep her off balance and take away the leverage she needed. She changed her approach and softened her stance in his grip. Widening her eyes and turning her head to look into his, she said, "I have information about what is going on at Corisi Enterprises."

"Great. You can tell me when your adorable ass is in the passenger seat of my car—and it will be there in less than two minutes, one way or another."

She almost smiled at his reference to her derriere, but instead put her chin out defiantly. "Your Neanderthal tactics don't impress me."

He growled in her ear and said, "Liar. Aren't you imagining what we'd be doing if we weren't in a public place? If I could rip that dress off you and end the pretense that we're both not hot for each other?" He moved a hand up to the back of her neck and said, "I'll carry you to the car if I have to. I don't even mind if you struggle. You're rubbing all the right places. But you know that, don't you?"

"Okay, okay," she said, her voice husky from a passion she was fighting to deny. "I'll get in your car. Now get your hands off me."

He released her a bit but retained a grip on one of her arms. Opening the door, he guided her into the passenger seat. "Bolt and I'll put you in the trunk next time."

"As if you'd do that," she scoffed, glaring at him, but she didn't move from where he'd put her. He was the only man she knew who might succeed at doing it.

He checked her seat belt, then secured his own and pulled into traffic.

"I could have you arrested for abduction."

"You're too smart to involve the law when you know you'd lose. Imagine what I could counter your claims with."

Angrily folding her arms across her chest, Alethea said, "I'm not a criminal. In fact, you stopped me from doing something that could very well have helped the people you work for. I can't tell you the details, but it's big."

He turned a tight corner and, with his eyes still on the road, said, "I know why you were there. I had Whitman escorted out of the Corisi building this morning, and he won't be back."

"Why would that have anything to do with me?" she asked innocently, hoping her voice didn't betray how disappointed she was to have lost her informant. Now, if Stephan wasn't behind the glitches, she'd lost her chance to find out who was.

When Marc raised a mocking eyebrow, Alethea snapped, "If you know everything, then you know why I have to see Stephan. He's the only one who knows if he's guilty or not."

Shaking his head, Marc asked softly, "And what did you think—that he would just tell you?"

Alethea looked out the window. "I'd have known the truth as soon as I accused him. It would have been in his eyes." Marc didn't say anything. "No pithy put-downs? I'm surprised you're not telling me why that was a ridiculous plan."

"Not ridiculous. Dangerous and possibly explosive. You would have gotten your information, but at what cost?"

"The truth is worth any price."

"Is it? It's worth your life?"

"When it comes to protecting the ones I love, yes."

She expected him to argue with her, but he didn't.

"I understand why you planted Whitman. The sister of your best friend had run off with a rogue billionaire and you thought the scenario was too good to be true. You wanted to protect Abby."

With a shaky, slowly released breath, Alethea said, "Yes."

"But things have changed. Dominic and Jake are not a danger to the women you love. You could work with them instead of against them." He reached out and put a hand on her tense thigh. "But you won't let yourself trust them."

She looked down at his hand on her leg and said, "I don't trust anyone."

"Except Lil."

Alethea turned her face away.

Very softly, Marc said, "When you're under fire, and I'm talking about the real deal, men are dying around you, and all your survival instincts are screaming for you to run—that's when you have to trust your unit. You have to believe that you are stronger together than you are individually. That kind of faith doesn't come easily. It starts with trusting one of them and builds."

"This isn't a war, Marc," Alethea said dismissively.

"Yes, it is, Alethea. It's your war. And you've been fighting it alone for too long."

What the hell did I tell him when I was drunk? "You don't know me. You don't know what I've been through."

He looked at her quickly before returning his eyes to the road. "I know something hurt you—and scared you. You deal with that fear by trying to control every situation. But control is also an illusion. This level of hypervigilance you're living at isn't healthy. If you continue down the road you're on, you'll lose everything—do you see that? Or you'll get yourself killed."

Tears sprung to her eyes, blurring the buildings they passed. "I'm not the one that matters."

He took one of her hands in his and held it on his leg. "Yes, you are. I'm not telling you to stop fighting for what you care about—I'm telling you that you're not alone. I care about the same people you do. Protecting them is just as important to me."

She met his eyes, her breath caught in her throat. Her eyes were focused on his profile as he parked the car. "Trust me," he said, unbuckling his seat belt and getting out of the car.

He opened her door and held out his hand. She stepped out and froze when she saw where they were. The Corisi Enterprises building loomed above them.

"What are we doing here?" she asked.

"Meeting with Jake."

Alethea stepped back and shook her head. Memories of her recent meeting with Marie and Nicole still held too much sting. "Maybe you're right—I shouldn't have gone to see Stephan. But I shouldn't be here either. Jake will never believe anything I say. He'll tell Lil that I came here and she won't forgive me for this."

He put a hand on her lower back and looked into her eyes. "I'll be standing right next to you the whole time." He dipped his head and whispered against her lips, "You can do this. Or walk if you're too scared. Your choice."

He didn't move. He just held her eyes and waited.

Alethea wasn't easily intimidated, but she was shaking in her five-hundred-dollar shoes. She'd grown used to risking her life, but it had been a long time since she'd opened herself to being hurt the way she'd feel if this was all just a ruse to get her into Jake's office.

Marc stood there, looking down at her with those piercing blue eyes.

She ran through a mental checklist of all the ways his plan could fail, but she couldn't bring herself to turn and walk way. If there was the slimmest chance he was right, this could very well be the crossroad everyone faced at least once in their lives. If you take one road, you find your happy ending. If you take the other, you spend the rest of your life wishing you'd been braver.

"Okay," she said, as they began their walk to the elevator together.

When they stepped inside, Marc pulled her into his arms and hugged her. She breathed in his scent and closed her eyes. It was a moment that ended too quickly. He set her back just before they reached their floor. His hand was firmly placed on her lower back again, giving her no opportunity to change her mind.

They stepped through Jake's outer office and Marc asked the assistant to announce their arrival. Alethea tensed instinctively while they followed her to Jake's door.

Marc leaned down and said, "It'll be fine."

She nodded and stood taller. She didn't fear Jake, but she was afraid to say or do something during their meeting that would end her friendship with Lil forever. Lil loved him and his approval mattered, even if Alethea had tried to pretend it didn't.

Jake stood when they entered. He looked disappointed at her arrival. "I was hoping it wasn't you."

Marc guided Alethea to a seat in front of Jake's desk and said, "She's not the source of the problem, but you won't like what she has to tell you either. Hear her out." He took the seat beside Alethea.

Jake sat back down and leaned forward on his desk.

Alethea thought back to how she'd given the news to Lil and the women. They hadn't believed her. Why would Jake be different? *Trust.* "I've traced the problems at your company back to a specific IP address. That doesn't mean that I know who is responsible for the code errors, but I do know how they are accessing your server."

"You're wise to not assume things are always as they appear. IP addresses can be compromised. I won't even ask yet how you know what's going on inside our server. I'm guessing that knowing would only serve to infuriate and distract me. Has that leak been dealt with, Marc?"

"Yes, sir, it has been."

"Good," Jake said, "we'll talk more about that later. For now, which IP did you trace it back to?"

"Stephan Andrade."

Jake sat back and rubbed a hand over his eyes. "Fuck."

Marc said, "It doesn't make sense for it to be him, though. He could have taken Dominic down with much less trouble. What would he gain from doing it now that he wouldn't have gained before?"

Sitting forward again, Jake rapped his desk with his knuckles as he spoke. "His thirst for revenge might have been too hard to put aside. He changed his tune fast. Maybe too fast."

Alethea said, "I could dig deeper, but I wish I had someone like Jeremy in on this."

Jake's eyebrows shot up.

With a slight flush of anger, Alethea said, "Not so I can see him again." She looked over at Marc and said, "We were never a couple. We were friends. Not even good friends. I used him. Yes, I know, I'm an awful person. But that doesn't mean he's not our best option when it comes to something like this. If someone is setting Stephan up, Jeremy could find the proof my sources couldn't."

"Already done. He's on it." Marc didn't look bothered by her statement. "And I'm not worried about your past."

Jake coughed. "Okay, let's focus on the problem at hand and not whatever you two are up to that I don't want to know about. It won't take Jeremy long to figure this out, but I'll call him and see what he needs. I was hoping not to bother Dominic with any of this. He's not going to be happy."

Oh, what the hell. "Could you mention something to Marie, also?" Alethea added.

Jake and Marc looked at her in confusion.

Alethea shrugged defensively. "She thinks I'm a liar."

Jake stood abruptly. "Marie knows? How did she find out?" Alethea didn't respond. Jake crossed to stand in front of his desk and said, "You told Lil."

Alethea stood and nodded. "Nicole, too."

Marc moved protectively closer to her side, sending a shiver of pleasure down her spine. She couldn't look up at him because she didn't want him to see how much his support meant to her.

Jake, on the other hand, was not as sure of her choices. "Is there anyone you didn't tell? I'm surprised you didn't go to Stephan yourself."

It was easier to face Jake's aggression than whatever was building between Marc and her. Easier, and infinitely less scary. She didn't need anyone to defend her. She always had, and always would, handle her own problems. Chin high, Alethea said, "I almost did, but I came here instead. Was that a mistake?"

Running his hand through his hair, Jake sighed. "No. I'm not your enemy, Alethea. You're practically my fiancée's second sister. I know how much you've done for her over the years. But you've also hurt her. Your involvement in this is done. Are we clear on that?"

Alethea didn't like to lie so she said nothing.

Jake was too intelligent to miss the meaning of her silence. He also knew that arguing with her would be a waste of time. Instead, he directed his next command to Marc. "I don't care what it takes, but keep her out of this. I'll be occupied with damage control here and at home. I don't want any more surprises, understood?"

"Yes, sir," Marc said, and then looked at Alethea. "What if I took her downstairs?"

A sudden look of amusement flashed across Jake's face. "Normally I would consider that a bit extreme, but in this situation I think it's a viable option."

I don't get the joke. What's downstairs that has them looking so pleased with themselves?

Marc forcefully guided her out of the office. "Come on." They walked past the main elevator to what appeared to be one reserved for maintenance only.

She stepped inside with him and turned toward the closing door. "What's downstairs?"

He pressed a blue button on the very bottom of the panel. "Something even you don't know about."

Although her curiosity was piqued, her stomach was churning—a time-tested indicator of trouble. "I'm sure it's fascinating down there." *In the jail cell or dungeon you want to lock me in.* "But I'll take a rain check."

"You heard Jake—it's my job to keep you occupied until Jeremy solves this. I know just how we could pass the time until then." He hit the stop button and pulled her into his arms. His mouth was hot and demanding on hers. All fight melted out of her, and she wound her arms around his neck. His tongue teased her with a quick flick, then thrust into her mouth, claiming it as his.

Desire doesn't care if it's unwelcome.

It doesn't wait for a situation that makes sense.

It whips in, crushes all rational argument for why it shouldn't be there, and sweeps a person away.

Alethea opened herself to him, moaning with pleasure when he pushed her up against the wall and ran his hands over her as if he had every right to. She was clutching him just as eagerly. She slid her hands beneath the back of his suit jacket and dug her fingers into the rippling muscles of his back, rubbing against him, wantonly seeking to deepen their connection.

As their tongues teased and explored each other in an intimate dance, Alethea imagined other places she would welcome his wet invasion. Would he thrust that tongue between her lower folds with as much relentless skill? No hesitation, just plundering and demanding a response that she was helpless to stop herself from delivering. To feel those teasing flicks on her clit, that hot breath on her thighs, those strong hands of his spreading her wider for his pleasure.

Oh, God, take me. Here. Now.

She was drenched and ready for him. He broke off their kiss and caressed her neck hungrily. She threw her head back and gasped when one of his hands slid boldly up her inner thigh and pushed aside the soaked satin of her thong panties. His middle finger thrust deeply inside her wetness and began to roll inside her, while his thumb found her eager clit and flicked it lightly.

In a hot circular fashion, his thick finger filled her and sought what others had often missed, the one spot that sent her over the edge. Sensing his triumph, he used his thumb to circle her nub while he kneaded without mercy at her most sensitive inner spot.

His other hand came up and pulled aside the strap of her dress and her bra, revealing her left breast to his hungry mouth. All she could do as he suckled her, nipped her, and plunged a second finger into her, was close her eyes and bite her lip to stop from calling out.

"Come for me," he said hotly against her neck. "Now."

She pushed her hands on his chest as her head thrashed from side to side. She didn't want to give him this power over her. She wanted to resist the pull of the orgasm that threatened to wash over her. "No," she whispered hotly.

"Yes," he said, taking her chin in one hand and forcing her to looking into his eyes. His thumb moved faster on her nub and his fingers pulled out and thrust deeper, harder than before, a combination of pleasure and pain that was impossible to resist. When the heat began to spread through her, robbing her of her ability to breathe, her eyes began to close from the intensity of it, but he shook her chin lightly in reprimand. "Share it with me."

Her whole body shook, and she clenched his fingers deeply inside her as she came with a cry. For a moment, just a moment, she was his. The feeling was terrifyingly good.

But it didn't last.

Almost instantly she felt vulnerable and exposed. She used her hands, hands that a moment ago had been clinging to the front of his shirt, to push him back from her. His pleased expression angered her and brought a defensive coolness to her voice, even as her body hummed with desire for his continued touch. "If we're on the bottom floor, why isn't the door opening?"

"Patience, Alethea. We're not there yet," he said softly, watching her expression closely. "Prepare to be amazed."

Seriously? She cocked an eyebrow at him. "Pretty confident about your abilities, aren't you?"

He backed her up against the wall of the elevator again. With one hand on the wall beside her head, he closed a hand over the breast she'd forgotten was uncovered and leaned down to growl in her ear. "I was going to wait until we were somewhere more comfortable for our first time, but if you push me to prove myself now—I'm ready." He took one of her hands in his and brought it down to rest it on his straining bulge. "More than ready."

Looking up into those intense blue eyes, Alethea panicked and pulled her hand free. Jake had told Marc to keep her occupied. *That's all this is.* Allowing herself to feel anything would only lead to hurt. *A man like him probably looks that way at anything female. Since the beginning of time, women have confused lust with emotion. He doesn't care about me. He sees me as a potential, convenient fuck. Don't forget that.* "Then it's a shame that I'm done. Sorry to get mine and run, but I'm really not interested in going any further with you."

A line creased his forehead, then disappeared, and he smiled. "Let me see if I can change your mind." He inserted what looked like a pen into a small hole beneath the elevator panel. A section of the metal panel slid aside, revealing a control pad. He typed in a code. A small camera popped out above the elevator buttons. Marc positioned his eye in front of it until a green light blinked and the elevator began to descend again. "I used a gaze-password authentication system instead of the mainstream retinal scan. It required individual calibration and an estimation algorithm from the computer nerds upstairs, but the result is a password that cannot be used by an imposter thanks to logged variations in gaze parameters."

Alethea sagged against the wall of the elevator as his foreplay entered an entirely new dimension, one that she was unprepared to fend off. "Does the algorithm include any biometric features?"

"Of course," he said cockily. "The Waltons are working on a genetic password system, but for now we had to settle for the technology available."

"What are you safeguarding?" she asked just above a whisper, unable to hide her curiosity.

A fact that he openly enjoyed. "Something Dominic didn't think he was into, but he changed his mind quickly enough once he saw the place. Intrigued?"

Utterly, and on more than one level. When the elevator finally stopped, it opened onto a hallway that looked like any other, except that it lacked windows. They both stepped out and the door closed behind them.

"Is this some kind of safe room?" It made sense. Many wealthy people had them in their homes and in their workplaces. *It's a dangerous world.*

"Something like that," he said, and guided her firmly down the hallway to a door. "Designing these is a passion of mine now. A secret and surprisingly lucrative one." Marc reached for the door, but stopped when Alethea tensed and pulled back. He looked down at her in concern. "What's the matter?"

Her head swam with images of what might lay behind the door. She'd read enough women's fiction to come up with seriously kinky options when she paired the words *secret* and *passion* together with a location. "I'm not into... I don't like..."

"Are you claustrophobic?" he asked, assessing the size of the underground hallway before meeting her eyes again. "No, that can't be it, but I've never seen you worried. What do you think is on the other side of the door?"

Her cheeks flushed bright red.

He cocked his head to one side, then burst into a deep laugh. "I like where your mind is going." He shook his head, a huge grin on his face. "Unfortunately, the reality is much tamer than what is flying through that pretty little head of yours." He pulled her to him, resting her hips against his arousal. "I'm sure we can think of something equally exciting, unless you're really into that sort of stuff."

"I'm not. I just said I'm not," Alethea huffed, placing her hands on his shoulders to push him back, but her own body betrayed her when his lips grazed her ear. Her hands fisted the material of his jacket and she shuddered against him. She was used to being in charge with a man, not whimpering for more each time they touched. Even though he wanted her, he didn't stumble over himself trying to please her, and that was even more of a turn-on.

"It'd be a shame if we never made it past this hallway since there is so much to see inside."

He leaned down and kissed her lips, even though they pursed with irritation. "Come on, let me show you what I do in my spare time."

He opened the outer door, typed in another security code, and swung open a thick metal door that looked like it was constructed to keep out a nuclear war. He closed it behind them and typed in another code. They stepped into a tinted glass octagonal room with multiple doors. Alethea forgot her concern as her curiosity soared.

More than just a hot body.

More than a hero.

He secretly believed in covert preparation.

She let out a dreamy sigh. When he looked down at her quickly, she gave herself a mental shake. She followed him through the glass doorway and exclaimed, "Holy shit."

Marc puffed with pride and closed the door behind him. The domed area they entered was lined by building façades, giving the illusion of being outside even though they were underground. The cement paths were lined with grass, and the ceiling was an LCD screen showing clouds and sun. A waterfall, and what looked like a lazy river, comprised one entire wall.

"I based the indoor garden on Japanese technology but with a few modifications. The lighting changes throughout the day and simulates the benefits of sunlight. I also flash ultraviolet light at night to increase vitamin D in some of the plants. No bees here, so for now I have installed a pollen duster, but I'm still working on improving that system. This pod is self-contained and a bit like an underground terrarium. It can, but doesn't need to, connect to the five other pods that branch off from the room where we entered. Technically, someone could live down here for decades."

Eyes wide, Alethea walked ahead of him and studied the mix of technology and nature. "You did all this?"

He smiled, took her by the arm, and led her through the center toward the façade of a house that belonged in the suburbs, with its porch and picket fence. "I drew up the plans, but Dominic's geek squad made it a reality. Welcome to my home for the zombie apocalypse."

Alethea looked at him doubtfully. "Seriously?"

"Or asteroid collision, chemical or nuclear war, alien invasion... whatever."

She searched his face. "I can't tell if you're joking or not."

He opened the door to the house. "Good." He led her through the living room to another door, that in a normal home, would have led to the basement. Behind the door was a thick metal hatch designed to keep water out. "I'm particularly proud of the next room."

Alethea waved an arm to reference her surroundings. "It's better than this?"

"Oh, yes."

He swung the hatch open and held out his hand to her. She took it, following him down another corridor. "We're no longer under the Corisi building. Dominic owns several storage facilities behind it that line the dock. I wasn't sure if what you're about to see was feasible, but I couldn't resist attempting it."

They stopped at another thick metal door, this time with nothing more than a large hand lever to open it. "Close your eyes," he ordered softly.

She shook her head stubbornly. "That's not my style."

He pulled her into his arms. "Then you'll never know what's back there. I don't care. I have more than enough to entertain myself with right here." He pushed her hair aside and began to kiss her neck, loving how her breath became labored and how she sagged a little against him. He lost himself in the pleasure of her taste, her scent, the curve of her breast beneath his hand.

She pulled back, breathing heavily. "You can't take me all this way and not show me what is back there."

He murmured against her lips, "Take you? I like the way that sounds. How about right here, right now?" He slid a hand up the hem of her dress and cupped her sex. *God, she was still wet and ready for him.* This time he rubbed her through her satin panties. It was tempting to take her now on the floor or against the wall—or both—but he wanted more than she'd given him the first time.

She squirmed against him, reaching behind his neck to pull his mouth fully down to hers. "Open the door for me," she commanded softly.

His breath caught in his throat and his blood surged downward. "No." She wasn't in control here and it was important that she understood that. He eased her skirt back in place and stepped back from her. "I want you like I've never wanted another woman, but I won't settle for what you've given others. Give me what you hold back. Close your eyes for me. Trust me."

A silent war raged between them. Neither giving in, neither backing down.

Eventually curiosity won over caution. She folded her arms in front of her and closed her eyes with a dramatic sigh. "Fine."

He took her by the arm and opened the door behind them. When he saw her open one eye slightly, he covered both with his hand and urged her farther into the room, not stopping until they were beside his bed in a transparent tunnel beneath the Manhattan River.

"Open your eyes," he said, as he removed his hand.

Her beautiful red lips rounded in awe. "What is this place?"

"My bedroom."

She spun as she assessed both the truth of his claim and the creative architecture of the structure. "You sleep here?" Forgetting him for a moment, she walked the length of the room, touching the clear walls and looking into the water above.

"Not usually. The concept was nothing new. There are hotels that have similar rooms, but they don't have this." He lifted a remote control, clicked, and the glass wall now showed an image of vivid blue water filled with tropical fish. Another click, and the bedroom looked out on a majestic mountaintop. "Plus, that's not glass. It's a prototype polymer a friend of mine owns the patent for. It's bulletproof and able to withstand shock waves, with or without the buffer of the water above. Even if exposed, it should provide as much protection as the rest of the facility."

"Against zombies," Alethea said dryly.

"Against anything," he said, wrapping his arms around her waist and pulling her back against him. "It couldn't take a direct torpedo hit, but since no one knows it's here, that's unlikely. Secrecy is a key component."

"Then why show me?"

Alethea held her breath and braced herself for the answer. *Because I'm never getting out of here alive? Because, with my track record, no one would believe me anyway?*

He turned her in his arms. "Because I've never seen anyone fight harder for those they care about than you do. You've been a royal pain in my ass since Dominic met Abby, but that doesn't mean I can't see what motivates you."

Completely taken by surprise, Alethea said defensively, "You think you know me, but you don't."

He tipped her head back and ran a thumb gently up her jaw. "You try to look so tough. So jaded. Too bad I know you're scared."

She stiffened in his arms. "Scared? I put my life at risk on a weekly basis. I'm not afraid of you."

He gripped her chin to stop her from looking away. "Now who's lying?"

She whipped her chin free of his grasp. "Let me go."

He held her even as she pushed against him. "Do you think you're the only one who has ever been hurt, Alethea? The only one who has lost? Aren't you tired of hiding? Of pushing everyone away?"

It's what I do, she thought, fighting a swelling panic that she was beginning to believe only he could trigger within her. "What do you want from me?" she snapped.

He rested his chin against her forehead and sighed. "I want you. What you're proud of and what you consider too ugly to show anyone else. I want it all."

She shuddered against him, her knees weakening at his words even while she reminded herself why they were really there. She was an assignment. Granted, one with perks, but this was not a date. A part of her admired his determination. And she couldn't even fault him for using their sexual attraction against her. Manipulation Techniques 101. Basic, but proven effective many times. Although she stopped short of intercourse, apparently Marc didn't have the same policy. "Well, you can't have it all. I appreciate the tour and the... erm... elevator ride." She mustered through what was surely a blush. "However, it's time for me to go."

"You can't leave," he said calmly, but he released her, allowing her to step away from him.

"Don't make this awkward, Marc. You're a nice enough guy, just not my type..."

To her surprise he didn't look the least bit bothered by her announcement. "Seriously, neither of us can leave. I set the lockdown for twenty-four hours. As hard as it was to get in here, it's even more impossible to get out. It's meant to stop people from panicking and opening the door too early."

Alethea charged out the hatch door of his bedroom, out of the house, and to the door they'd originally entered. She pulled on the doorknob, pressed a few buttons, then spun on him angrily. "What the hell are we going to do in here for twenty-four hours?"

From a few feet behind her, he said dryly, "We could go back to the initial plan."

She advanced on him. "Open the door, right now."

"No can do," he said smugly.

She stopped just before him, her chest heaving angrily. "You're way too smart to not have a fail-safe plan. What if I had a heart attack? You'd need a way out. You could get out of here if you wanted to."

A large grin spread across his face. "Can't get anything by you. You're right. I could open the door, but I'm not going to. I promised Jake I'd keep you contained for a while. Sex would have been nice, so if you change your mind I'm still open to the idea. But either way, you're not leaving until I let you out."

"I haven't met a system yet I couldn't beat," Alethea said defiantly.

"Test it. You won't break out, but it'll be entertaining watching you try."

She cursed under her breath.

He reached across, threaded a hand through her hair, and pulled her to him, claiming her lips with his for a long deep kiss that left them both breathing heavily. "Would now be the wrong time to tell you how hot you look when you're angry?" She raised a hand to slap him, but he caught her hand easily and brought it to his lips to kiss, growling, "I love it when you act like you don't want it, too. It makes me want to prove to you just how easily I could have you moaning and begging me for more. Is that how you like it? A little rough?"

"I like a man who listens when I say no."

He took her chin roughly in his hand and held her face so she couldn't look away. "I have never forced a woman and I never will. All you have to do to get me to stop is tell me that you don't want this."

She stood rigidly in his arms and lied. "I don't want this. Now can I go?"

He set her back from him. "No, but you're free to try."

He walked away, leaving her beside the waterfall, cursing him, but also mulling over his words.

She headed straight for the exit and studied his security system. No matter how strong something looked, everything had a weakness.

Chapter *Ten*

"I HOPE TO hell this is important," Dominic said, as he stepped into Jake's office. He'd promised Abby he'd spend more time at home, at least for the initial month after the birth. He didn't like disappointing her, but Jake had been adamant that his presence was required.

Jake stood and whistled when he saw Dominic. "You look like shit."

Dominic made a face. "I'm doing the night feedings while Abby heals. Sounded easy enough, but Judy could eat all night. She falls asleep in my arms, but as soon as I put her back in the crib she starts to cry, so I've been sleeping in the chair in her nursery and it's hell on my back."

"Abby's not breast-feeding Judy? Even the CDC advocates for it."

"I'm not talking to you about this."

"Did you read the report I sent you? There is enough statistical evidence to safely say that it's linked to high IQs. Some have implied it's linked to healthy metabolisms. Not all of the benefits are known yet, but there is no man-made formula that rivals it."

"Do you know what has also been linked to living a longer and healthier life?"

Jake leaned against the corner of his desk and shook his head. "No."

"Telling me whatever the hell you thought you couldn't say over the phone, because I'm pretty sure whether or not we're breastfeeding Judy was not it."

Raising his hands in defeat, Jake said, "You shouldn't have asked me to read up on the subject if you didn't want me to have an opinion about it."

Dominic made a gurgling sound in his throat, then sat heavily in one of the chairs. "I'm too tired to hit you, but I will remember this conversation for later."

"Marie won't help out? Your mother would likely love to take a few shifts."

Dominic groaned. "Abby and I talked about it. The first few months are important bonding time. Judy needs to know that when she needs something we'll be there for her."

Jake shook his head. "You've already lost control of the situation, haven't you?"

Dominic closed his eyes for a moment and laughed tiredly. When he opened his eyes, he joked, "God, yes. With all the trouble we've gotten into over the years, did you think it would be diapers and midnight feedings that would do me in?"

Jake took the seat across from his friend and said, "You love it, don't you?"

With a huge smile, Dominic nodded. "I'm happier than I ever thought I could be—definitely more than I deserve to be." He studied Jake's expression and some of his good mood faded. "But you didn't ask me to come in today to hear about this, either."

"You're right. We have a problem, and the deeper I dig the worse it looks."

Sitting upright, all fatigue left Dominic. "At Corisi Enterprises?"

Jake stood and walked over to his desk, picked up a folder, and threw it down on the table in front of Dominic. "It started before Judy was born. At first it was a series of simple coding errors. I looked into each of them and they seemed unrelated, but they bothered me. The glitches were too systematic. So I looked into tampering. Our server should be airtight. I didn't have anything concrete, just a feeling, so I put Marc on it."

"Good, what did he find?"

Jake poured Dominic a Scotch. "You need to know that we don't have all of the information yet. Jeremy's working on it from California. I gave him full remote access. He should have some answers soon."

Dominic stood and flexed his shoulders. "What are you not telling me?"

"Alethea planted someone in our IT department last year. We found and removed him, but what he discovered is the real problem."

"Worse than an internal leak of God-knows-what information?"

Jake nodded. "There was no leak. Seems Alethea planted him when you first met Abby. She was under the impression she needed someone on the inside in case you didn't return from China with Abby. Alethea's mole told her about the coding errors, so she had him investigate where they were coming from."

Dominic didn't say anything; he just stared at his friend with a stony expression of displeasure.

"Her informant traced several of the issues back to one external IP address."

"I thought Jeremy had secured our server."

"He did, but this person built themselves an access point that we didn't even think to look for. Or at least that's how it looks right now. We don't know exactly how it happened yet."

"What do you know?"

"I know that I hope we're wrong about who's involved in this."

Dominic closed the distance between them and growled, "Who? Who the hell are you talking about?"

"Stephan. The trail leads back to your sister's fiancé."

A heat of fury rose up Dominic's neck and face. He turned to leave, but Jake blocked his path. "I know that look, Dom. Don't do anything you will regret. We don't know if it's him for sure yet."

"Oh, it's him. Give me one reason why I should let that little bastard live."

Jake didn't move out of Dominic's way. He kept his voice reasonable and said, "Because your sister loves him and you could lose her over this. We'll uncover the truth—possibly by today. The informant Alethea used wasn't in Jeremy's league. His conclusions may have been flawed or deliberately produced by whoever is doing this. Acting without all the facts could cause larger problems."

Dominic stepped forward aggressively and Jake stepped back, hoping his friend would heed his warning. Just before stepping out of the office, Dominic snarled, "You've cleaned up the Alethea situation?"

"The leak has been dealt with effectively. He's no longer an issue."

"And Alethea?"

"Marc has her contained downstairs."

"Downstairs?" Dominic pointed at the floor with emphasis and almost smiled. "I wonder if she can get out."

Jake shrugged. "Hard to say. Marc is good." As Dom headed toward the door, Jake asked, "Where are you going?"

"Home. You have twenty-four hours to figure this out, then I'll deal with it my way."

Across town, Lil held her niece and sat with Abby in the living room of her newly renovated, midtown Manhattan mansion. Once an exclusive private club, it was now filled with baby swings and strollers. Colby played at their feet with wooden slices of fake food lined with Velcro, that allowed her to stack them into sandwiches.

Abby noted the tight lines on her sister's face and worried for her. This should be the happiest time of her life. She was living with Jake and he'd adopted her daughter. The only remaining piece of the puzzle was the formality of their wedding.

It was amazing how much had changed in a year. She'd never felt closer to her sister. "What's wrong, Lil? Is Colby keeping you up nights again? I thought she was done teething."

With a sad smile, Lil said, "No. Yes. I mean, yes, she's keeping me up, but no, that's not the problem."

"You know you can tell me anything."

"Can I, Abby? I'm not sure. I need advice, but I'm not sure you could help me with this one."

Fear gripped Abby's heart. They'd come so far. What could Lil be involved in that she'd be afraid to share? Everything was going too well not to fear that something could bring it to a sudden, crashing end. "I love you, Lil. Without knowing what this is about, I can't promise to know what to say, but if you need me, I'm here. I'll always be here for you. No matter what happens."

"It's Alethea." Lil raised her hand to stop Abby from jumping in. "I know what you think of her, but this is more about me than her."

Mouth pressed tight, Abby nodded and pretended to eat the wooden hamburger Colby handed her.

Lil couldn't meet her sister's eyes when she said, "I know she takes things too far, but she does it because she cares. She only broke into the hospital because she cares about you."

"Some people send flowers," Abby said sarcastically, then stopped herself. "Sorry. Go on."

"She found an issue at Corisi Enterprises and wanted me to help her figure it out."

"Tell me you didn't get involved in one of her wild schemes. You promised you wouldn't."

"I didn't."

"Why is she still sniffing around our business? Isn't there enough trouble out there in the world to occupy her?" When Lil jumped to her friend's defense, Abby said, "I know. I know. She does it because she cares. Or so you always tell me. What did she find?"

Lil told her. She told her everything, from the coding errors to Stephan's possible involvement. Abby remained quiet, the flush of anger on her cheeks the only indication of how she was feeling. "She wanted me to help her find out if it's true, but I told her that I wasn't going to do it her way this time." She adjusted Judy's bib. "So, I took her to see Marie and Nicole, and we told them everything."

"How did that go?" Abby asked in an uncharacteristically unkind manner.

"Worse than I imagined. Nicole was furious."

"Do you blame her?"

"No. But Al wasn't saying that Stephan is guilty, she was saying that all the trails led back to him."

"Semantics, wouldn't you say?"

"Not to Al. She doesn't want him to be guilty any more than we do." Lil met her sister's eyes and confessed the part that bothered her the most. "Marie accused Alethea of making the whole thing up because she's jealous of how close I've gotten to you and everyone else."

"I probably would have thought the same."

Lil wiped a tear. "See, that's the problem. You want to think the worst of her. You only see what she does wrong. You never give her credit for always being there for me. And when I've needed her, she's always been there."

Abby picked up Colby and hugged her, a tear rolling down her cheek. Her young niece laughed up at her, clapping. She'd missed too much of her first few months of life. "I would have been there for you. I wanted to be part of your life so desperately. The harder I tried to hold on, the more I lost you."

"That wasn't Al's fault." Lil said, tears of her own entering her eyes. "And you have me now. Isn't it time to forgive her for our problems? I've been putting off my wedding waiting for the two of you to work things out, but I need to know. Am I waiting for the impossible?"

Colby squirmed to get down and walk around the room. Abby released her to the floor. Sometimes the tighter you hold someone to you, the more you lose them. She'd learned that lesson the hard way. Still, Alethea hadn't made raising Lil any easier. In fact, it had often felt like a tug-of-war between them: Abby, pulling for Lil to stay safe and make good choices, and Alethea, pulling her in wild directions full of morally vague high-risk situations. *Old news, I guess.* "I don't know. You just said she upset Nicole. How can I overlook that?"

"She didn't. I did. I messed up. I thought Nicole would want to help clear Stephan's name."

"Oh, Lil."

"I know. I made it worse. I've called Nicole about a hundred times, but she's not answering my calls. Al isn't either. She asked me if I believed her and I said I wasn't sure that I did."

"What do you want me to say, Lil?"

"I'm asking you to help me, Abby. Help me figure out what to do. I never meant to hurt anyone."

The little devil on Abby's shoulder whispered that this chance wouldn't come twice. She could tell Lil that some friendships are not fixable. All she had to do was tell Lil it was time for her to let Alethea go, for the sake of the family, and there was a good chance this time she would.

Life without Alethea—the idea had appeal.

But Abby looked down at her niece and thought about what Lil had said. *Alethea didn't make the problems between Lil and me. She didn't cause the rift. And no matter how I feel about her, she's been a good friend to Lil.*

I may not like her, but Lil loves her.

"Always better together, Lil. I believe that. Let's get them all in the same room and we'll hash this out."

"That didn't work so well the first time."

"I'll talk to Marie and Nicole. Families fight, Lil, but then they make up. If Alethea really does want to be part of this family, she'll show up."

"I don't know if she'll come. It got ugly last time. How do I convince her this time will be different?"

"Tell her I'm on her side."

Lil's eyebrows went up. "Are you serious?"

Abby walked over and put her arm around her sister. "You're right. It's important for me to put the past in the past. You love her, so I'll try to. This time I'll really try."

Even with Judy in her arms, she hugged Abby. "That's all I can ask for, I guess."

I can pray for a bit more than that. "Stephan has to be innocent."

"Don't worry, Alethea won't stop till she finds the truth."

Somehow that doesn't make me feel better.

CHAPTER *Eleven*

AFTER THOROUGHLY TESTING every aspect of the security system and attempting every mode of communication with the outside world, Alethea sat down on the bench in the grassed area beside the waterfall.

"Give up?"

"Go to hell."

"Come on, let me enjoy this moment. You thought escape would be easy. Your comprehensive testing was impressive, but why not just admit that you're stumped? Did you try the vents?"

"Yes."

"Genius the way I looped them back through the air purifier, wasn't it? They lead exactly nowhere." He sat next to her on the bench.

"I noticed."

"Each pod has its own air system in case one fails. Working with an unlimited budget helps."

"Do your victory dance. You beat me. This time."

He put an arm around the back of the bench and played with one of her curls, even though she shifted away from him when he did. "Does it have to be a competition between us? I earned this gloat, but I'd rather relax and enjoy this time together." He pushed the hair off the back of her neck, exposing its curve and blowing gently on it. He took a remote out of his pocket and, with a click, the ceiling of the bunker became a twinkling night sky.

Alethea fought a smile, then looked at him, shaking her head with humor. "Seriously?"

He gave her a shameless grin and wiggled his eyebrows.

98

"A fake night sky will not get me to forget that you've locked me in against my will."

Marc shrugged and stood up. "You can focus on the details, but I intend to enjoy this unexpected day off." He took off his shirt and laid it on the bench beside her, then stepped out of his shoes.

Alethea hated to admit it, but unlike most people, Marc looked even better with his clothes off than on. His chest was perfectly cut and lightly dusted with hair. She wanted to reach out and touch his firm abs. "I told you I'm not interested."

He turned away from her, dropped his pants to the floor, and dove into the deep water in front of the waterfall. The image of his perfectly toned ass momentarily stole her breath. Wiping the water from his face when he surfaced, he smiled at her. "There you go, making it all about sex again. You've never gone skinny-dipping just for the pleasure of it?"

Alethea folded her arms across her chest. "No."

There was very little that she did simply for the pleasure of it. She didn't relax her guard long enough to.

He swam to the edge in front of her and rested his arms on it. "You're quite a puzzle, you know that? I used to think you were a badass. Next you'll tell me you're a virgin, and I'll drown from the shock."

"Of course I'm not a virgin. I've had plenty of sex—alone and with others. I just don't want to have it with you."

A lusty smile spread across his face. "That's not the impression you gave me in the elevator."

His comment soured her mood. "That was a mistake." She said more quietly, "One I don't want to talk about."

"Then come swim," he suggested. "I promise to keep my hands to myself."

"You expect me to believe that?"

"Yes," he said seriously.

When she didn't move, he said, "People can't disappoint you if you don't trust them, can they? Beneath all that bravado, you're not very brave at all, are you, my little warrior?"

Not brave? Ha. She stood up and stripped naked, slowly, enjoying the fact that his jaw dropped open and his eyes widened with pleasure. She stood proudly before him and smiled, then dove in and surfaced beside him, close enough to hear his breathing change and see his eyes dilate with excitement. "I told you—I'm not afraid of you," she said, and shook her hair, loving how it drew his attention to her bare shoulders and lower.

He took a deep breath and said, "Yes, you are." He leaned forward as if he would kiss her, but didn't. "But you shouldn't be, because I'm on your side."

Thankfully, he swam off to do laps, leaving Alethea aroused and angry at the same time—a condition she was beginning to associate with being around Marc. She started swimming too, if only to give herself something to do besides gawk at a man she wasn't sure whether she wanted to kiss or strangle.

Having her so close and not being able to touch her was torture, sweet torture. *Thank God I didn't promise not to look.* Watching her beautifully toned arms slice through the water, and the glimpse of her breasts just beneath the water, had him painfully aroused. He gave up trying to pretend, swam to the edge, and propped himself up with an arm on either side to savor the view.

If mermaids look anything like her, no wonder sailors dive to their doom.

Her delightful bare ass arched above the waterline each time she reached the end of the fake river and dove to turn. As she swam by him, he saw what looked like a half smile on her face and chuckled. She knows exactly what she's doing to me and she's waiting for me to give in and chase her. That's what she's used to.

She tempts.

The man chases.

She gives only what she wants to.

Safe.

I could let her win, agree to her terms, and the reward would be a night between those sweet thighs. One night of sex would be no different than any hookup I've ever had.

And that's the problem.

I don't want just one night. I want to know what scares a woman the FBI considers more of a liability than an asset. Someone to hire when they need her, but not someone they want on their payroll.

Someone so good at what she does that, like NASCAR, people watch in fascination, waiting to see her crash, even as they cheer her on. Like Dominic, she made more enemies than she did friends.

He had to admit that he'd spent more than a few evenings imagining how good it would feel to humble her a bit. Her bold, take-no-prisoners and win-at-all-costs attitude elicited a strong emotion in many people.

And I'm only human.

The more time he spent with her, however, the more he saw that she didn't want to win—she needed to. She wasn't driven by fame; in fact, even in the midst of intense public scrutiny of those near her, she'd managed to stay under the radar. Keenly intelligent with the ability to read most people, she was a master manipulator.

But to what end?

Money didn't impress her.

She could have parlayed her connections into a position of power, but she hadn't.

Every once in a while, if he looked closely enough, he glimpsed, what he'd bet his life on, was fear. Not the I've-had-my-heart-broken surface shit, but the wake-up-terrified-and-sweaty kind of mental scar that comes from being brutally thrown into hell and then deposited back on earth. A scar you hide, even from those you love, because some things are too ugly to share.

He understood scars, internal as well as external.

Watching Alethea tirelessly swim back and forth before him gave him time to come to a decision. Sometimes you have to tear something down before you can build it up stronger.

She shot him another look as she swam by. Their eyes met and fire sprang between them.

You'll be mine, Alethea.

But not on your terms.

Marc smiled, turned, and hauled himself out of the pool. Not bothering to conceal how much he'd enjoyed watching her, he waved to her when he caught her checking out his erection. She turned her face away and coughed as she swallowed water unexpectedly. He laughed and picked up his clothing, tucking it under one arm.

Lesson one: Laughter heals.

He scooped up her clothing and rolled it into his. He'd only made it a few feet away from the pool, and was still chuckling, as he imagined what she'd say when she stopped drowning and realized what he'd done.

Suddenly she was before him, gloriously angry, dripping wet, and blocking his way. He didn't think he'd ever seen anything sexier than the defensive jujitsu stance she took. "Drop my clothes before I drop you."

He stopped, but, even though he wanted to do as she asked— if only to free up his hands to pull her to him—he didn't. Instead, he looked her over slowly and said, "I wonder if they make martial-arts porn. I never thought it could be sexy until just now."

A red flush started between her breasts and spread up her neck and across her face. "I'm deadly serious."

Despite her angry tone, her nipples were pursed in hard little nubs that were nearly impossible to look away from. Looking down didn't help. Lean, muscular legs led upward to an exquisitely trimmed line of pubic hair. He swallowed hard and shook his head. When his eyes met hers, he was fighting to keep his breathing normal. "As much as I'd love to wrestle with you,

I said I wouldn't touch you. But you're making that a hard promise to keep."

Her eyes dropped at the word *hard,* and his dick twitched and throbbed, growing more beneath her perusal. She referenced his eager erection and said, "Could you cover that up?"

He looked down, then back up with a smile. "Find it distracting? You should be on this side of it." The red on her cheeks deepened. He tossed her clothing to her. She slipped her dress over her head and stepped into her underwear. "We both know I want you—hiding it won't change that. And you can cover up as much as you want, but every last inch of you is burned into my memory now and will keep me up many nights." When her eyes dropped back to his penis, he laughed out loud again. "I love that dirty mind of yours, Alethea. I really do."

She stepped back angrily.

He turned to walk away, then stopped. He caught her eyes over his shoulder. "Try to keep your eyes off my incredible ass as I walk away." He turned from her, then looked back and caught her still watching him. "I knew you couldn't help yourself. Fine, look all you want. And just so you know, unlike you, I don't have a no-touching policy. Touch all you want."

She said something rude under her breath.

He laughed as he reentered his fake house.

Swimming in the heated pool had been excruciatingly wonderful, but for the sake of his sanity, he was going to take a shower.

An ice-cold one.

Two, if that's what it took.

Fully dressed again, Alethea paced the inside of Marc's bunker home. It was almost midnight. *I'm not sleeping here. I'm done. I have been more than understanding. But I refuse to stay here one more moment with that... that... streaker.*

103

No matter how gorgeous he is.

This is kidnapping. Illegal detainment.

There has to be some way to contact the outside world from here.

None of the phones worked, and the computer wasn't linked to anything. He'd taken his cell phone, along with hers, into the shower with him. She thought back to the scene at the pool and groaned. I should have smiled sweetly and taken his phone while he wasn't looking. Why the hell did I strip and dive in with him?

The truth was painful to admit to herself.

Because a part of me wants to finish what we started on the way down in the elevator. I want to test out that bed beneath the river. She thought back to how he'd stood naked and exposed, not to mention fully aroused, while talking to her. *I guess if you're that well endowed, why not wave it around? Who does that? He's ridiculous, and irritating, and... sexier than any man I've ever met.* His easy confidence was a relief from men with fragile egos who were easily intimidated when they realized what she did for a living.

My mother always said that men don't like smart women. I hate that so many have proven her right. If I bleached my hair blonde and limited my vocabulary to two-syllable words, I'd probably be married by now.

Not that I want to be married.

I don't need a man.

I admit it would be nice to have someone to come home to, but not if it requires pretending to be someone I'm not.

What's wrong with being a strong woman? With knowing what I want and not being afraid to go after it?

Like Marc.

What would he say if I told him I've changed my mind?

She flopped herself into one of the generously cushioned chairs. *A few hours in captivity and I've lost my mind.*

She shivered at the thought and rubbed her arms.

"Miss me?" he asked from right behind her. She nearly jumped out of her skin in surprise.

Her eyes grazed his bare chest and dropped lower of their own volition. He was wearing a low-slung pair of lounge pants. "You're in pajamas?" she asked, her throat so dry her words came out in a croak.

"Yes, disappointed?" He wiggled his eyebrows at her and laughed when she quickly denied it. He threw a pair of flannel lounge pants and a T-shirt at her. "This is all I have, but you're welcome to them if you'd like. The pants have a string tie."

Alethea bunched the clothing in one of her hands and sat up straight. "What's next, you offer to cook me a meal like we're friends?"

He moved to stand beside her chair. "If you're hungry, I have about five things I know how to make, but the food here is all canned or dried. Still, better than nothing."

She stood angrily and glared up at him. "Are you deliberately not getting my point, or are you dense? I don't want to be here with you and I'm not going to pretend I do. I don't want to swim with you, I don't want to eat with you, all I want is—"

He leaned down and covered her mouth with his. With a groan he pulled her closer and she forgot what she was saying. She opened her mouth to him, meeting his tongue eagerly with hers. They wrapped their arms around each other as their tongues danced and teased.

She slid her hands up his flat stomach and loved the feel of his muscled chest. His heart beat wildly beneath her touch. He rubbed himself against her stomach, his dick growing larger and harder as he did. She closed her eyes, but that only allowed her to vividly remember the intimate details of how he looked.

With two confident hands, he eased her dress up over her hips and held her against him as he slid her panties down, his mouth never leaving hers. He put a hand on her hips and lifted her until she straddled his waist and was kissing him from above, cupping his head between her hands.

The feel of him rubbing against her wet center as he carried her to his bedroom excited her further. He stopped near his bed and she clung to him with her legs and arms as he sheathed himself in a condom.

He tore his mouth free of hers and braced her shoulders against the wall. Raggedly he said in her ear, "I have to be inside you. Now." And with one strong upward thrust he was, and she cried out from the pleasure of it. He stopped, letting her adjust to his size.

His mouth was hot on her neck while one of his hands held her waist and the other parted her rear cheeks and caressed her intimately. She moaned and moved her hips urgently against his, wanting, needing to feel him move within her.

She arched backward and he impatiently pulled her dress down on either side, exposing her breasts. He nipped at her, grazed her with his teeth, and took her into his mouth while his tongue circled her sensitive nipple. All the while, he held her exactly as he wanted her and pounded into her, deeper with each thrust, until she was opening her legs wider and calling out his name in pleasure.

He paused and said, "You are so tight. So goddamn tight."

She writhed against him. Quivering with need. "Don't stop," she begged. "Don't stop."

"I've wanted to do this since the moment I first saw you," he whispered in her ear, rolling her hips back and forth, easing himself in and out of her as he did so. "It's even better than I imagined. You're amazing."

He thrust into her. Withdrew and thrust again. Each time bringing her closer and yet not completely to an orgasm. She clenched around him, dripping with excitement and almost mindless in need.

"You—" he started to say.

She covered his mouth with her hand and cried, "Just shut up and fuck me."

She felt him smile beneath her hand and he pushed her more firmly against the wall. All pretense of taking it slowly fell away and he was slamming into her with an abandon that she welcomed and matched, thrust for thrust.

She came first, crying out with a loss of control she'd never allowed herself before. She was sobbing with an almost overload of sensation, and her cries only excited him more. He pounded into her, faster and faster, harder and harder, unyielding in his demand for her submission. This was a primal taking, a claiming. Beyond either of their control.

Then the unbelievable happened: she felt herself soaring again. Heat flooded her stomach and she dug her nails into his back as she clenched for a second orgasm, feeling him bury his face in her neck and shudder as he joined her.

They stood there, with him still inside her and her legs around his waist, as they both caught their breath and slowly came back to their senses. He groaned and chuckled as he kissed her collarbone. "I hate it when I break a promise. I just couldn't figure out how to do it without my hands."

She met his eyes. "Is everything a joke to you? Put me down."

"Let your guard down, Alethea. It's okay to laugh. You don't have to protect yourself from me."

She couldn't take any more. She shifted until she broke their connection, then continued to squirm until he released her enough so that her feet were firmly back on the floor. "Don't. Don't pretend this is anything but what it is. This isn't a date. You're being paid to keep me out of the way and that" — she waved her hand in the air beside her—"that was just the result of two people being thrown together in a stressful situation."

He studied her face, then broke out in his cocky smile. "Your job must be more exciting than mine, because this is not the norm for me."

She shoved him back a step. "You're not funny."

He closed the distance between them and was suddenly serious. "Well, now you've hurt my feelings. Looks like I'll have to do my best to impress you with my other qualities."

The evidence of the quality he was referring to nudged her sex, hard and ready, as he swept down and plundered her mouth with another deep kiss. A part of her clung to the knowledge that none of this was real, but the rest of her felt it was too good to pass up. These memories would have to sustain her, because she would never put herself in this situation again.

He stopped, raised his head with a funny expression on his face, and asked, "What are you thinking about?"

She tried to pull his mouth back down to hers and said, "It doesn't matter."

"Tell me," he demanded.

"No."

Alethea wasn't sure what reaction she expected to her refusal, but she didn't expect him to pick her up, swing her over his shoulder, and carry her to his bedroom. He tossed her down on his bed.

Oh, no, he didn't.

Oh, yes, he did.

This isn't one of my fantasies. This is real.

Still naked, she was on her knees and scrambling past him, but he caught her, flipped her onto her back and, before she knew what he was doing, he'd secured both of her hands above her head with handcuffs.

Lying beside her, he said, "I know what you're thinking—what man has handcuffs under his bed, right? They were a gag gift from a buddy of mine. I figured I should keep them here in case I had to ride out the apocalypse. In case things got boring." He smiled down at her as if he couldn't see the fury in her eyes. "Not that you're boring. Trust me, you're the opposite of boring, but you need to learn to trust people."

Pulling against the cuffs angrily, Alethea snarled, "And you think this will do that? All it's going to do is be my defense for why I strangled you the second I was set free. 'Your honor, look at the bruises on my wrists. He had it coming.'"

Marc ran a hand up one of her arms to just below where the metal met her wrist. "You won't have a single mark on you if you don't fight it."

She tried unsuccessfully to whip her arm away from his touch but was impeded by the restraint. "You might as well tell me not to breathe. I'm going to free myself and when I do, you will regret this."

"I see the problem."

"Thank God. You're coming to your senses. Get the keys now and maybe, just maybe, I'll forget this ever happened."

Propped up on one elbow, Marc looked down at her as if she were a puzzle he was solving. "You can't turn it off, can you? Everything is a fight to you."

"Do these handcuffs come with earplugs? Because there are laws against torturing people with your psychobabble."

Instead of rising to her taunt, he laughed. "I'm beginning to get you. Really get you. You're scared right now, aren't you? That's why you're on the attack."

I'm not afraid of anything, but I'll go along with this if it has the potential to provide a window of opportunity. "You don't think that locking someone in a bunker, then tying her to a bed, is cause for concern?"

"I would never hurt you, Alethea. Do you believe that?"

She looked away. "Then let me go."

He turned her face back to his and those beautiful blue eyes seemed to see her soul. "Just this once, let yourself be in a situation where you're not in control."

She shook her head.

He leaned down and whispered in her ear. "What's the worst thing that could happen? You find you enjoy it?"

She glared at him.

When she didn't say anything, he said, "If you really want me to take off the cuffs, I will. All you have to do is say it." He ran a lazy finger over her collarbone and down the side of one breast. "Or you can trust me to take care of you. That's what the cuffs are about. Trust. Yes, they leave you vulnerable, but everything that matters in life leaves you vulnerable. And sometimes you win by not fighting."

His words washed over her, filling her with a warmth she couldn't deny.

All I have to do is tell him to remove the cuffs and this is over.

No man controls me, not even for the sake of sexual experimentation.

I don't do restraints.

So why am I not demanding my freedom?

He didn't gloat as she would have expected a man to. Instead, he quietly waited for her decision.

An unexpected tear came to her eye and in a thick voice she said, "If you hurt me, I'll kill you. Literally. Slowly. In the most painful way I can think of."

Real shock showed on his face and he touched her cheek with a gentle hand. "Hey, it's okay to be scared. Trusting anyone is always scary."

He leaned down, took one of her breasts between his teeth, and pulled ever so gently on her nipple, sending a rush of heat straight through her. There was no denying how his touch affected her. She gasped with pleasure when he ran a hand down her stomach and cupped her sex possessively.

Tempting her.

Teasing her.

Waiting for her to say the words she didn't want to say: "I hate you right now."

He raised his head. "I can't tell if that means, 'Yes, keep going,' or 'No, get the hell off me, you pervert.'"

She rubbed her pelvis against him and moaned. To hell with being in control. Just this once, she wanted to be taken.

Her eyes flew open and met his.

I do trust him.

He trailed his kisses down her side, over her quivering stomach, and continued moving until his face was above her lower, throbbing lips. He put her legs over his shoulders and arched her upward so her sex was spread open and ready for his mouth. His breath was hot on her, but still he waited. "Tell me what you want, Alethea."

She arched further on the bed, bringing his mouth in light contact with her mound. "You know what I want."

He rubbed his chin lightly on the outside of her. "That's the fun of being on this side of the handcuffs—I don't have to give it to you until you give me what I want. Tell me how you like it, Alethea."

Her legs clenched around his neck and she hated the truth, but she admitted it to him anyway. "It doesn't matter. I don't really enjoy it. Not like other women do."

He met her eyes and a line creased his forehead. "Not this time. Tell me, do like this?" He delved his tongue deeply inside her, and the heat of it seared through her. With one hand, he parted her so he had unobstructed access to her most sensitive spot. He blew lightly on it, then flicked his tongue back and forth across her excited nub.

She tried to relax, but she couldn't. Her mind raced to justify why. *I don't have a problem with trust. Would you leave a five-dollar bill on a public counter and expect it to be there later when you return? That's not paranoia, that's being realistic.*

"Or do you like this better?" He took her nub between his teeth and gently tugged, sending wild sensations through her. She gripped the chains of her handcuffs and arched with pleasure, but couldn't turn off her inner voice long enough to fully enjoy it. *Maybe I should fake an orgasm so he'll move on to something else.*

"Or maybe you prefer this?" He plunged two fingers inside her and worked them rhythmically while suckling on her and using the stubble on his chin to roughly caress the surrounding area.

Oh, that's nice.

That's really nice.

She closed her eyes and pushed herself against his mouth. He rewarded the move by alternating his lapping with his fingers and chin. Each time he withdrew to switch, she felt the separation profoundly. Each time his mouth returned, the fire beneath his touch grew more intense, until it was almost painful and she cried out.

"That's it," he said against her inner thigh, as his fingers pumped in and out of her dripping sex, and the heat of his breath caressed her exposed clit. "Come for me, Alethea."

She was powerless to resist his command. Her body was already tightening around his fingers. She thrashed back and forth, clinging to the cuffs as the most intense orgasm she'd ever experienced rocked her body.

He kissed her thigh and said, "I'd say you enjoy that just fine."

He lowered her onto the bed and rolled away for a moment. When he rolled back, he was sheathed in a condom. He settled himself above her, keeping his weight off her. He slid a leg between hers. She opened them wide and cried out with need when he slipped only his tip inside her. She wanted him deep within her. Wanted to be filled with him.

He licked the curve of her neck hungrily and thrust into her roughly. He pulled out, teased her with his tip, and thrust roughly inside her again. This time when he withdrew she was grasping for him with her legs. His strong fingers bit into the soft flesh of her ass as he lifted her off the bed and changed his position, then pounded into her. Pleasure and pain mixed and heightened each other.

As their rhythm increased, she felt herself near orgasm again and gave herself over to it. She trusted Marc to take her where she wanted to go and bring her back to earth safely.

They came in unison and collapsed together back onto the soft bed. She felt him release her hands from the handcuffs and marveled that she didn't feel relieved at the freedom from them. He took her mouth hungrily in his and she opened herself to him. In that moment there was no fear. No walls. They were one.

When the kiss ended, she opened her mouth to say something, but he gently laid a finger over it to silence her and said, "Just enjoy this for a moment longer."

She spoke despite his finger. "How do you know I wasn't going to say something nice?"

He dropped his hand, smiled across at her lazily, and reached down to pull a blanket over both of them. Then he lay back and tucked her against his side. "Okay, I'm ready. Say it."

Alethea laid her head on his chest. "I don't hate you."

He chuckled against her hair. "I know you don't."

In the quiet seclusion of their bunker, in this place outside of time, Alethea felt closer to him than anyone else, and felt compelled to explain herself. "You were right. I was afraid." She waited for him to make a joke out of her admission, but he didn't. He rubbed her back with one of his strong hands, and that comforting move encouraged her to open up more to him. "I barely sleep. I wake up terrified. I go to bed terrified. I never feel safe. Not in friendships or relationships. I'm always waiting for an ugly truth to be revealed."

"Those are some deep scars, Alethea. What happened to you?"

She shook her head and closed her eyes. There had been a time, long ago, when she'd tried to get people to believe her, but she'd learned the hard way to keep some things to herself. "Nothing."

He took her chin in his hand and raised her face. She reluctantly met his intense blue eyes. "You can trust me with more than your body, Alethea. I don't care who has let you down in the past. I'm not them."

What if he doesn't believe me? What if, like everyone else, he dismisses it as something I came up with for attention? With a shaky breath, Alethea said, "My father was murdered."

Rubbing a thumb almost absently across her jaw, Marc said, "The police records said he had a heart attack at work."

"They were doctored. And how do you know that?" *Duh, because it's his job to have anyone associated with the Corisis*

113

investigated. And I'm part of that job. "Did you enjoy sifting through my personal life?"

"Absolutely," he said lightly, then became serious again. "So, you think the police lied?"

"Yes. The day he died, a man came to our home and said my father had left important papers on his desk. I let him go into his office. I didn't know my father was involved in anything dangerous. My father was dead by that night."

"No chance it was a coincidence?"

"That's what my therapist said. Mother hired her to convince me that those two events were completely unrelated, but I have always gotten this nauseous, anxious feeling when something is not quite right. Like when we never saw his body. They said the morgue had to do an autopsy and then accidentally had him cremated before his funeral. A slipup my mother didn't protest. Why? Because she must have known we couldn't see him without discovering the truth."

"What truth?"

"I don't know. She would never admit it and I've only collected crumbs of proof. Not enough to prove anything. Someone had my father killed. Someone powerful enough to be able to cover it up and have fake police reports written."

"Do you think he was involved in something illegal?"

He believes me.

"I've spent most of my life trying to find that out."

"Have you told anyone about this?"

"Not since middle school. Even Lil doesn't know. I involved her in some of my attempts to dig up proof but never told her why. I let her believe they were just crazy stunts I did for attention. I love Lil, but she's not exactly a vault when it comes to keeping a secret."

Letting out a deep breath, Marc held her closer. "You can trust me with your secret, Alethea."

She looked up into his eyes. "I believe you, Marc. I don't know why, but I do."

114

"We all have secrets," he said softly. He ran a hand gently through her hair, then said, "I understand fear, Alethea. I know what it's like to not be able to sleep at night because your mind won't turn off and exhaustion is preferable to the images you'll see in your dreams. I'm not a hero. I'm just a man who thought enlisting would pay for the education my parents couldn't afford to give me. A man who ended up in the wrong place at a bad time."

"You went back for five men who had been shot. That's heroic in my book."

"I barely remember that part of the day." He looked up at the ceiling as the memories took him far away from her. "We were doing a routine patrol in what was supposed to be a friendly village. A roadside bomb went off that took out the lead Humvee. Sniper fire split our unit in two sections. I knew I was a dead man. No one was getting out alive. Men were dropping beside me. I don't remember doing the acts they say I did. I remember being scared. I wanted to run for cover, but I couldn't leave everyone. I knew those men. I knew their families. I knew they wouldn't leave. I vaguely remember the Apache helicopters arriving and then nothing else. I woke up in a hospital and they called me a hero, but they're wrong. Those men died anyway. I didn't actually save anyone. I should have died with them." He took her hand and laid it on the scar he had on one side of his abdomen. "They sent me home to heal, but you don't heal. You never heal. And you never forget." He tucked her head beneath his chin and said, "All I can do is get out of bed every day, go on, and try not to hate myself."

"You did the best you could in what was a horrific situation. It's not your fault they died."

"And if your father was going to be murdered for what he knew, there was nothing you could have done, even if you had known." He hugged her closer to him. "But knowing that doesn't make sleeping easier, does it?"

"No, it's doesn't," she said sadly into his chest.

He reached over for a remote and dimmed the lighting in the room. "You're the first woman I've told about that day. The women I've dated couldn't handle it. They want the hero. They don't want to know the truth."

Deep in her chest her heart soared, even as she warned it not to. Real panic set in soon afterward. She would have bolted if there were a way out of the bunker, but, since that was impossible, she retreated into her mind and pretended to fall asleep.

Marc watched her and wondered if he was right to push her. He knew she wasn't sleeping. "What is going on in that beautiful head of yours?" he asked in her ear, and felt her tense against him.

She met his eyes angrily. "Do we have to do this?"

He played with one of her long tendrils. "You're not going to threaten to kill me again, are you?"

She pushed ineffectively at the arm he still had wrapped around her waist. "Stop."

"What?"

She waved a hand around them. "This. The after-sex pillow-talk flirt. Why bother? If I wasn't locked in here with you, I'd be long gone."

He sat up and pulled her to him until she was pressed against his chest, looking down at him. "What is this about?"

She opened her mouth to deny it, but closed it again with a click. She just glared at him, anger warring with another emotion in those beautiful green eyes. "We end the moment that door opens. Why pretend that's not what's going to happen?" When she shifted away from him, he pulled her back.

"You want the truth? I like you. You're borderline paranoid and abrasive as all hell, but I don't care. I can't get enough of you. I love to watch you work a room. You can talk your way around most people with an ease that should be logged in the *Guinness Book of World Records*. And the way you find flaws in security plans—it's like magic. A real gift. I've never been with a woman who excited me on so many levels. This isn't just about sex. I'm not going anywhere. Not tonight. Not after we leave here." Settling himself back down on the bed, he wrapped both arms around her again. "What would happen if you let yourself believe in us?"

She tensed against him and said, "Us?"

"Yes, us. Go to sleep, Alethea."

He expected an argument but didn't get one. It took her almost an hour, but her breath finally deepened, and she turned and buried her face in his chest. He hugged her closer, his heart beating wildly in his chest.

Not with desire as it had earlier, but with something he'd never felt before.

He wanted to be her haven—her hero.

Chapter *Twelve*

ALETHEA WOKE UP alone and padded into the main part of the house. Sunlight streamed through the window, but since it was simulated, she wasn't sure what it meant, time-wise. She found her dress hanging beside a change of clothing in the bathroom. Linen pants and a simple silk blouse. Yesterday she'd dressed for a battle. Today she chose the tamer option. She showered and readied herself the best she could.

Returning to the living room, she hugged her arms around her and took a moment to savor the memories of the night before. Her cheeks warmed at the memory of how she'd woken in his arms, how they'd made love tenderly, wordlessly, and then fallen back to sleep wrapped around each other. A deep, refreshing sleep she'd thought impossible to achieve in adulthood.

As she stood smiling, she acknowledged that she felt at peace with what they'd done. She was filled with a calm that had little to do with the orgasms she'd had and everything to do with how it had felt to sleep in Marc's arms. To hear the steady beat of his heart in her ear, and for the first time in nearly a decade, feel safe.

Safety is an illusion, she reminded herself harshly.

Just like allowing herself to believe that Marc is here because he wants to be. This is his job, and last night was no doubt an entertaining way for him to pass what would otherwise have been a tedious amount of time locked away from the world.

He'd said all the right things to her.

But that's what men do. They say whatever they think a woman wants to hear.

118

She spotted him on his phone, walking up and down the path near the lazy river. Who was he talking to? Dominic? Had Jeremy cleared or convicted Stephan?

Either way, their time in the bunker was likely over.

I should be happy.

I can get back to my life now.

She thought of her empty apartment and her schedule that, although full of work-related appointments, lacked a social component. No need to rush home, since no one is waiting for me. Not even a cat.

Oh, my God, I'm losing my mind. Is this what happens when everyone around you gets engaged or married? You start to think you need that for yourself? I don't. I've done perfectly fine on my own.

Marc spotted her in the window and started toward her. Sauntered, really. Practically whistling. He was perfectly groomed in one of his charcoal suits. His short brown hair was perfectly styled and he had the look of a man who had spent the night doing exactly what they'd done.

When he sprinted in the door, smiling, she asked harshly, "Did you get the go-ahead to let me out of here?"

His smile didn't waver. "Morning, sunshine. I wanted to be there when you woke up, but you were sleeping so peacefully, I decided to get some work done instead. I see you found the clothes I left you."

"Did you have them delivered or were they here already?"

"I like to call it being optimistically prepared." He winked. "And it worked out well last night."

Her cheeks warmed a bit at his reference to the handcuffs. *Distance. I need to distance myself if I'm going to be able to regain my balance here.* "So what is the plan for today?"

He studied her expression for a moment, then said, "Jake wants to see both of us."

"Did Jeremy find out anything?"

"He didn't say, but he told me to bring you up to see him as soon as you were ready."

She'd never been one to avoid confrontation. Better to go up and get it over with. Without hesitation, Alethea said, "I'm ready."

Marc tossed her cell phone to her.

Alethea caught it easily and held it up between them. "You trust me with this now?"

He closed the distance between them with two large strides and took her face in his hands. "Yes," he said, and claimed her mouth hungrily.

It took everything in her to not throw her arms around his neck and give in to the waves of desire that rocked her. She kept her hands clenched at her sides, but moaned with pleasure when his tongue swept over hers in an intimate greeting.

When he stepped back, Alethea stood immobile for a moment, unable to disguise her longing for what she was determined to refuse. She shook her head to clear it and said, "Let's get out of here then."

Now, before I forget this isn't real.

Before I throw myself in your arms and beg you to take me back to your underwater bed.

She checked her phone log simply to give herself something to look at. Lil had called. Repeatedly through the night. Alethea had never ignored her, but the sting of their last encounter was still fresh. If her time off the grid had made Lil regret not trusting her, perhaps it was not a bad thing.

She looked up to see Marc watching her closely. He said, "Our time here is over, but we're not. Far from it." He turned and walked out the door of his underground house, leaving her with little choice but to follow behind him. Each door they passed through required a passcode of some sort. The level of security was as impressive on the way out as it had been on the way in.

Inside the elevator, Alethea stood beside Marc and stole a glance at him. He was firmly back in work mode. Gone was the man who frolicked, hilarious in his state of undress, and teased her. Just like her, he had a face he showed the world, and it was firmly back in place.

What had he meant they were far from over? Did he imagine because she'd slept with him once—okay, three times—that he had some sort of weekend pass to her? If so, he was in for a harsh letdown.

They went all the way to the top floor where very few were allowed. Jake's secretary announced them through her intercom and instructed them to go straight to Jake's office.

Jake stood when they entered and crossed to greet them. He didn't waste time on pleasantries. He waved them to take a seat. Neither of them did. There was an energy in the air that wouldn't allow even a pretense of relaxation. "Jeremy should be here in a couple hours. I'm flying him in. He spent the night retracing Whitman's findings and he's come to the same conclusion. All paths lead back to Stephan."

Marc swore. "Does Dominic know?"

Jake ran a hand through his hair in frustration. "I haven't told him the latest bad news, but I spoke to him yesterday. I was hoping we'd find something to clear Stephan. Nothing. I don't get it. Dominic is not going to sit back and wait for us to solve this. I've asked my parents to help Jeremy with this."

With the Waltons' involvement, Alethea didn't doubt that the culprit would be found. However, Jake was right that Dominic was the time bomb in this scenario. Could they uncover the truth before Dominic went after Stephan and the entire situation flew out of control?

"You're that sure he's innocent?" Marc asked.

"I'm that sure we need him to be," Jake answered. "You don't want to see what Dominic is capable of if Stephan is using his sister as a cover. He won't care if he goes to jail over it."

At least Jake wasn't in denial when it came to the nature of his best friend. Nor was Marc, judging by how he seemed to silently agree.

"What do you need me to do?" Marc asked.

Unable to stop herself, Alethea cut into their conversation. "If we work backward from the assumption that Stephan isn't guilty, then we have to conclude that whoever is setting him up is better than Jeremy."

Jake stopped pacing to look at Alethea. "I've never met anyone better than him."

"Yes, you have. Sliver."

The mention of the man whom they had thwarted less than a year ago brought a frown to Marc's face. "I thought he'd been dealt with. Isn't he underground somewhere, licking his wounds and reduced to repairing DVRs or something?"

Alethea started pacing the room. Her mind raced with possibilities. "What if we weren't as successful as we thought and this is all connected? What if Sliver is taking another swipe at Dominic, this time using Stephan? We don't know the man Stephan gave Dominic's Chinese server access codes to. What if it was Sliver? Someone like that wouldn't have rubbed shoulders with Stephan without planting some sort of backdoor entry into his system. And he would be smart enough to use Stephan's history against him."

Jake rubbed his chin. "It sounds a bit far-fetched. Not impossible, but improbable. Stephan knew his hacker. He worked for him."

Alethea's eyebrows shot up. "Exactly. The ones who can hurt you the most are the ones you've let closest."

Although Marc didn't look happy with her comment, he nodded in agreement. "Stephan is either a villain or an unsuspecting player in someone else's game. Sliver's real name was Stanley, wasn't it? Jake, have you ever crossed paths with someone by that name?"

"No, not that I know of."

Tossing up a hand in frustration, Alethea said, "If Sliver was methodically coming after Dominic, and smart enough to use a decoy perpetrator, I'm pretty sure Stanley could be an alias."

Jake and Marc exchanged a look. Jake said, "Alethea, your theory is based on too much conjecture and not enough fact.

That's a lot of effort to put into what is currently presenting as little more than coding errors. Easy enough to find and fix. Hardly worth the trouble your conspiracy theory requires. Do you have any evidence linking Stephan and Sliver?"

Alethea shook her head and conceded, "No."

Marc stepped closer to Alethea and asked, "Then what makes you think you're right?"

He wasn't being sarcastic; he was interested, so Alethea answered honestly. "It's a hunch I have. Just a gut feeling."

Marc looked down at her and nodded slowly. "If you're right, this security breach goes beyond what Jeremy can patch. I'll increase my men around Dominic and his family, but the players in this game may already be planted deeply."

He believes me.

What if...

No, don't read more into this than there is.

Jake went to stand beside his large office window and said, "Dominic gave me twenty-four hours to handle this. You have much less than that. He's meeting me here in"—he glanced at his watch—"seven hours. Bring me something before then."

Without another word, Alethea and Marc headed out of the office together. "Come on, I know where we need to start."

Alethea fell into step beside him. "Where?"

"We need to talk to Stephan."

Oh really? As they headed down in the elevator to the parking garage, Alethea asked, "What happened to that idea being explosive and there being other, better ways, to deal with this?"

"This is different."

"Really? How?" *Because now it's your idea?*

"We'll be talking to him together."

Together.

A word that was every bit as terrifying as it was meant to be reassuring.

As the elevator stopped and opened out onto the parking garage, Marc held his arm in front of the door and motioned for her to step out. "Ask him what you had planned to. Let's see what his answers reveal."

Somewhat bemused, Alethea stepped into the garage. Marc fell into step beside her. "And what are you going to do?" she asked as they reached his car.

He opened the passenger door for her. "Make sure he doesn't kill you."

See what sex gains you? No threatened truck ride for me today.

Alethea shook her head. *Now is not the time for quirky inner dialogue. Focus.* She slid into the passenger seat and watched Marc quickly cross in front of the car, open the door, and join her. They were out of the bunker and still together.

Well, sort of together.

Once again, an outside force postponed what she knew was coming: the awkward promise to call that neither of them would follow through with. Last night hadn't changed the fact that they had no business being together.

Her phone rang. It was Abby.

Abby?

Had Lil tried to call her all night because something had happened to her? *Oh, God, my best friend is dead and I was too busy screwing Mr. "I'm Back in My Suit So I'm All Business" to answer my phone.*

No, wait. If Lil was dead, Jake would know.

Breathe.

She swiped her phone to answer. Marc looked at her for confirmation that they could pull out. Alethea waved for him to go and mouthed, "It's probably nothing."

"Abby," Alethea said in a tone she hoped sounded welcoming.

"Alethea, I wasn't sure you'd answer a call from me."

I live my life on the edge. "Why wouldn't I?"

"Lil said you're not answering hers."

Alethea looked across at Marc and said, "I lost my phone for part of yesterday, but I have it now."

"I've been there. There's nothing worse than losing your phone."

As they left the garage, the bright daylight blinded Alethea momentarily. *If you only knew where I'm headed.* "Yeah, nothing."

They were awkwardly, uncomfortably silent for a few minutes, and then Abby said, "I'm calling to invite you to my house for tea tomorrow afternoon."

"Tea?" Alethea choked on the word in surprise.

"Yes. Listen, I'm just going to be blunt here. Lil told me about the fight the two of you had and even about your latest— let's call it—*concerns* with someone we both know would never do what you think he did."

With an impatient sigh, Alethea was instantly defensive. "I never said he did it. In fact—"

Marc laid a hand on hers. She met his eyes. With a shake of his head and a slicing motion of his hand near his neck, he told her to keep her next words to herself.

Maybe he's right. Involving Abby could blow their chance to confront Stephan alone. Gritting her teeth, Alethea said, "I don't see how tea with you would help this particular situation, Abby."

"It won't be just me, Alethea. I've invited Marie, Nicole, and Lil. Let's talk this out and put it behind us."

Oh, hell no.

"Wow, tempting," Alethea said slowly. "Still, I have to decline. My schedule right now is... hectic."

"This is important, Alethea. You're the one who always says that your friendship with Lil is a priority to you. Show her you mean it. Come for tea tomorrow. I promised her I would be in your corner, and I will be. But you have to want to make this work, too. I can't fix this for you. And unless we all find a way to get along, I can't see things getting better. I, for one, am ready to forgive and start fresh."

Alethea held up the phone and, with her hands wrapped around it, made a motion like she was strangling it. *Saint Abby is ready to start fresh? And what? Forgive me—for which crimes exactly?*

"So, will you come tomorrow around two?"

"Sounds wonderful," Alethea said. And highly unlikely to ever happen since by then, there was a chance that Dominic and Abby would be frantically trying to bury a body. "See you then."

When she hung up, Alethea directed some heated expletives at the dark screen. "Who the hell does she think she is? 'Come for tea.' 'Let's fix this.' I don't need her approval or her help. I'm not even sure I need Lil anymore."

Marc pulled the car over to the sidewalk. "Then walk away. Get out, call a taxi, and fly off to some international job. Why meet with Stephan and remain involved if you have no investment in the outcome of the situation?"

Alethea spun in her seat and snarled, "I should. They never thank me. They treat me like I've wronged them in some way when all I've ever tried to do was be a good friend to Lil."

"And keep her safe." Marc said softly.

"Exactly," Alethea said.

"And to be safe, she shouldn't trust anyone you don't. She shouldn't let others close enough to hurt her."

"You're twisting this around." She reached to unbuckle her seat belt, but he blocked the move by grabbing her hand. "The last thing I need is for you starting to judge me."

"Hey," he said, "I'm on your side."

"Really?" she growled. "It doesn't sound that way."

"You love Lil. For whatever reason, she has become your family. You're close to losing her over this and it scares you. If you want to be alone, really alone, then go. I won't try to stop you. But it's a choice you're making, not something Abby is doing to you. If you can walk away and watch this family implode from a distance, then Abby is right—you don't deserve to be part of it."

Alethea glared at him. "You're probably the only person in the world who could make staying involved and risking my life sound like the right thing to do."

"Because it is. They need you."

"And if I'm wrong? If this all blows up in my face and we discover that Stephan is a sociopath who wasn't smart enough to take Dominic down when he had his best opportunity?"

"Then you pick yourself up, dust yourself off, and go have some fucking tea, because your friend Lil is going to need you even more when her sister loses control of the husband she thinks she has tamed."

"I really do hate you," Alethea said, but a corner of her mouth curled in a suggestion of a smile.

He pulled back into traffic. "I don't mind that," he said. "It makes me imagine all the ways I could win you over again, slowly—all night, if that's what it takes." He shifted in his seat and smiled at her. "Don't distract me. We have to stay focused." He put his hand on her thigh and gave it a sensual caress. "At least until tonight."

Tonight? One last booty call for the road? She put her hand on his to stop its progress. "I'm going with you to talk to Stephan and then I'm going home, alone. As in, not with you. Last night was great, but it's over. Now get your hand off me before I break it."

With a quick move that took her by surprise, he turned his hand and laced his fingers with hers. "I love it when you talk tough, but save it for tonight. We really do have to focus."

She looked down at their linked hands in confusion. It was over, wasn't it? He didn't mean what he said about not going anywhere, did he? "What are we doing?"

He raised her hand to his lips and kissed it. "Who the hell knows, but it feels good, doesn't it?"

She had to agree he was right.

Well, agree silently, in her head.

She wasn't ready to give him that.

Not yet.

CHAPTER *Thirteen*

WALKING INTO STEPHAN'S office building was an entirely different experience for Alethea with Marc at her side. He called up to Stephan and was waved on by the security at the entrance. Alethea didn't bother to hide her irritation as they rode up in the elevator. "Of course he has time for you."

With a flash of a smile, Marc said, "Temper, temper. When all this is done, we'll see about getting you off the naughty list." A teasing light danced in his eyes.

She was about to tell him where he could shove his offer, but the elevator door opened and then all that mattered was confronting Stephan. Without looking at Marc, Alethea said, "Let me do the talking."

Marc put a hand on her lower back and spoke softly into her ear. "I had every intention of doing just that."

She looked up at him quickly in surprise. "Really?"

A hint of a smile pulled at one side of his otherwise firmly set mouth. "Absolutely. There is no one better than you when it comes to pushing someone's buttons, and the angrier he gets the more likely he is to have an honest response."

We'll have to talk about your backhanded compliments later. Alethea frowned. "Not funny."

"Because it's true," Marc answered, his expression purposefully blank, but she saw the hint of humor in the line that appeared near one of his eyes as he fought back what she would have bet her life was a smile.

They didn't need to announce their arrival to the secretary since Stephan was standing at his office door. "Come on in." His eyebrows shot up when he recognized Alethea. "I have about fifteen minutes before my next meeting. What brings you two here?"

Marc stepped forward and shook Stephan's hand. "Thank you for seeing us with so little notice."

"Anytime, Marc. You know that." He looked at Alethea with a less friendly expression. "You're keeping interesting company lately, though."

Alethea held out her hand to Stephan and didn't lower it even when he didn't immediately move to shake it. "I almost came to see you yesterday, but things didn't work out."

Stephan met her eyes, acknowledging that he was aware of what had happened, and shook her hand for no other reason than that she refused to lower it. Their touch was brief. He turned and led them into his office, telling his secretary to hold his calls.

He sat at his large glass desk, leaned forward on his elbows, and motioned for them to sit in the pristine white chairs before it. "Well, you're here now. To what do I owe this pleasure?"

Alethea sat first, waited for Marc to take the seat beside her, and then said, "I was wondering if you and Nicole have set a date for your wedding."

Stephan steepled his fingers. "Why the interest? Are you looking to work it?" He looked at Marc. "No offense, but I have my own people."

"None taken," Marc said and sat back. Simply watching.

"You and Nicole seemed so in love the last time I saw you together, I figured you'd be married by now."

"Not that it's any of your business, but we decided to wait for the excitement to die down a bit. We're happy, no need to rush. Nicole wants to let Abby have her time with the baby and help plan Lil's wedding." He looked at his watch. "Listen, I have to be somewhere in ten minutes. Get to the point of your visit, because I highly doubt it is to ask where we're registered for gifts."

"Is it difficult seeing Dominic as happy as he has been? You hated him for a long time. I know you've said that's a thing of the past. But you can't truly be happy for that bastard. He beat you."

Stephan stood. "I don't like where this is going."

Alethea smoothed her linen pants and shot Marc a deliberately sly smile. "You don't have to pretend with us. We hate him, too. The way he flaunts his wealth. The way he uses his power to manipulate those around him. I don't know about you, but I'm sick of being forced to worship at the altar of the Mighty Dominic Corisi. I'd love to see him humbled a bit."

Glaring at them, Stephan said, "Marc, is this some sort of sick joke?"

Marc shook his head. "I'm afraid not."

Alethea pushed her agenda. "Think about it, Stephan. Right in this room we have three people who have different ways to access his defenses. He'd never see it coming. You could finish what you started, and we could make sure that he wouldn't be able to retaliate."

Stephan searched both of their faces. "You two are serious."

Alethea stood, preening herself deliberately. "We couldn't be more so." She walked closer to Stephan and leaned into his personal space suggestively. "Nicole is wonderful, but I'm sure the thrill of being with her has worn off. You've had time to think about how close you came to beating Dominic, haven't you? And you regret not following through. I don't blame you. He may love your family, but he'll never accept you. Not really. And watching him with your father, that can't be easy. He's exactly the son your father always wished you were, isn't he? Strong. Perfect. A winner. How does it feel always coming in second to him, even with your own family?"

Red spread up Stephan's neck. He walked away from Alethea and went nose to nose with Marc. "I'd expect this from her, but you? After everything Dominic has done for you? I hope for your sake that you're armed today and willing to shoot me right now, because neither of your lives will mean much after today. You don't mess with my family. I would kill you, but you're not worth the jail time." He pressed a button on his desk and said, "Anita, have security come to my office. I'd like to have some trash taken out."

Four men arrived. Two flanked Alethea and two Marc.

With a sigh of relief, Alethea looked across to Marc. "He didn't do it."

Marc nodded in agreement. "Thank God."

Stephan crossed the room to confront Alethea. "What the hell are you talking about?"

Marc positioned himself just off Alethea's side—close enough to intervene physically if necessary. "Someone has been accessing Dominic's server and planting coding errors using your IP address."

Alethea faced Stephan: chin high, eyes unrepentant. "We had to know if you were involved."

Stephan looked at his security men, then the duo in front of him. Then he waved the men to the door. "Give us a few minutes." Once they were alone again, he said, "How do I know you're not lying right now? I haven't heard about any problems at Corisi Enterprises."

Marc met his eyes. "What would I have to gain by hurting Dominic? He's made me a very rich man." Stephan nodded at Alethea. Marc shook his head. "Not even for her."

Alethea threw her hands up in the air. "Seriously, you can believe I am after Dominic but not Marc?"

A glimmer of the man she'd seen in the bunker surfaced as Marc postulated the reason. "People naturally trust me. It's my strong jaw."

Alethea rolled her eyes. She had to admit to herself, though, that watching him hold his own with Stephan was turning her on. Like her, he wasn't intimidated by wealth or power, and it made her impatient for a repeat of last night.

Stephan cut into her burgeoning erotic fantasy. "If there are problems with Dominic's server, why are you two here and not with him?"

Alethea scolded her raging libido. *Now is not the time to lose focus. Stop imagining Marc naked. This is important.* She directed her next comment to the man in the room she didn't want to pounce. "We think you're innocent."

"You?" Stephan repeated with growing anger. "But not Jake and Dominic? Or did they send you?"

Marc raised one hand hastily and said, "Let me take over, Alethea. No one knows we're here. Jake is trying to clear you. Dominic is..."

"Plotting my death, probably."

Another realist. Her opinion of him rose a bit. "You can't blame him, really, after what you did... or tried to do to him last year. And the cyber trail leads directly to your doorstep."

Stephan turned away and slapped his hand forcefully down on his desk in frustration. "I made a mistake last year. A horrible mistake, one that almost cost me Nicole and my family, but things were different then. I was different. I don't know how this is happening, but it's not me." When he turned around his face was twisted with torment. "Does Nicole know?"

"Yes," Alethea said quietly. The sadness in Stephan's eyes tore at her conscience.

"When? How long has she known?"

Alethea looked at Marc for help, but when none was given she admitted, "Two days. I told her two days ago."

Stephan moved back to the seat behind his desk and slumped into his chair. "That's why she's been weird." He searched Alethea's face with an expression akin to desperation. "What did she say when you told her?"

She'd always felt that whatever was gained by speaking the truth outweighed any hurt it caused, but she was having difficulty meeting Stephan's eyes. What if Nicole left him over this? *I shouldn't have involved Lil. I should have handled this myself.* Alethea searched for what to say that would alleviate some of Stephan's pain. "She said she didn't believe me. Accused me of making it all up to cause trouble."

"It must be eating her up to not ask me." He shook his head sadly. "She's been hurt so many times by those who were close to her. Even me. I swore I would never hurt her again. Who would do this? How could they do this? I have state-of-the-art firewalls. I've never had an issue."

Alethea walked to the front of his desk and said, "What can you tell us about the man you gave Dominic's access codes to last year?"

Stephan stood, suddenly alert again. "You think he's involved?"

Alethea nodded. "He worked for you, didn't he?"

"Yes, for a short time. He was one of the best coders I've ever met. When he left two years ago, he sent me a prepaid phone and gave me a phone number to call. He said he could plant a virus that would take Dominic's whole server down. Then he gave me the number of someone who would get me the information he needed to do it. At the time it sounded tempting, but something I would never actually do. I should have thrown the phone away. I was wrong not to. I was obsessed with beating Dominic. You were right about that, Alethea—I hated coming in second to him. I thought he deserved what I did. I was wrong. When I tried to call off the deal, he said he'd make me pay if I did. He could be behind this."

Marc asked, "What was the man's name?"

"Jack. Jack Mineoff."

Alethea threw up her hands. "An obvious alias."

Stephan shook his head in confusion. "We do full background checks on everyone who works here. That was his name."

Hand on one hip, Alethea said the name again, slowly. "Jack Mee-noff? Seriously? Jack Me Off? No one would do that to their child. This guy was screwing with you from the day you hired him. He has to be Sliver. That would give him the skills he'd need to create a false background."

Marc countered, "But what links him to Dominic? Why repeatedly go after him? What's the connection?"

Alethea turned to Stephan. "Did he ever mention Dominic?"

Stephan shook his head. "Not beyond offering to upload the virus to his server. He said it would make him famous." He held up a hand and said, "Give me five minutes." He walked out of the office.

Marc crossed to Alethea's side and put his hand on her lower back, caressing the tension he felt there. "Jack Mineoff. Good catch. And Stephan believes us. We're going to catch this guy, no matter how many aliases he creates."

Alethea nodded sadly.

"What's the matter?" Marc asked, sensing her mood declining.

She shook a bit beneath his hand. "People will always believe the worst about me, won't they? No matter what I do."

He turned her to face him. "I won't. I know what you risked to come here." He lifted her chin with a finger and said, "So strong on the outside. So easily hurt on the inside. If you let people see the real you, they'd love you."

As I do.

He didn't say the words, but they rocked him to his core. This woman fiercely fought for those she loved and secretly yearned to be accepted by those very people. It made him want to protect her from them or demand they see her as he did.

Across town, Abby was folding the napkins on her dining room table for the third time. She'd given her staff the happy news that they would have not only this afternoon free but also the next. She wasn't sure how either meeting was going to go, but she was sure neither would benefit from an audience.

Marie had arrived early to help with Judy so Abby could get dressed. Only Marie would come early to help prepare for her own visit. Abby couldn't imagine what she would have done without the woman she considered her mother-in-law. Her support made the absence of her own mother easier to bear.

"Judy is sleeping. She didn't want to. It's like she knows you're having company and doesn't want to miss anything. So much like her father."

"Dominic spoils her. All she has to do is whimper and he picks her up. I told him she needs to cry it out and he said he's not ready to do that yet. Maybe by the time she's in her teens?"

"He's going to turn her into a holy terror."

Abby smiled and sighed. "Not if I can help it. Can you believe that, of the two of us, I'm going to be the disciplinarian? She's going to walk all over him."

Marie smiled. "As little girls do with their daddies."

Abby nodded, taking a moment to savor the wonder of how her life had changed. "My father never could say no to me or Lil."

"My husband would likely have been the same with our son," Marie said wistfully, reminding Abby of the extent of her loss: both husband and child over the years.

"Marie, I'm so sorry. I didn't mean to..."

"Oh, hush. It's me who should be sorry. I don't know why I brought it up."

Abby put an arm around the older woman's shoulders. "Because you loved them and you still miss them."

Marie's eyes shone with emotion. "I do."

"Is that why things didn't work out with Romario?" Abby asked.

With a purposeful sniff, Marie said, "It was a ridiculous idea to entertain for even a moment. Dating? At my age? I don't need a man when I have family around me."

"You're not that old."

"Too old for what he wanted," Marie said, and then flushed.

Abby laughed. "Why, Marie. I do believe you've been holding out on me. What happened?"

"Nothing," Marie said firmly. "And it was for the best. My boys are here. This is where I belong."

Abby hugged Marie closer and said, "I was the same. All set to live one life and then Dominic came crashing into mine. Do you still talk to Romario?"

"I told him not to call me anymore."

"And?"

Marie blushed. "He calls anyway. He says he's not going anywhere. He knows what he wants..."

"And that's you..."

Marie made a *tsk-tsk* sound. "All that chest-thumping should be left to younger men and women youthful enough to appreciate it."

Abby moved away to double-check the plate settings. "You can tell me it's none of my business, but I think Romario genuinely cares for you. Why not give love a second chance?"

"I can't—" She stopped before she lied. "Abby, your generation probably doesn't understand, but I married the first man I slept with. I've only ever been with my husband. I don't know how to be the wild woman Romario wants. I haven't had sex in almost a decade, for God's sake."

There was a pregnant pause.

Marie closed her eyes for a moment. "Did I just say that out loud?"

Abby returned to her side to give her another hug. "You did, but that's okay, just don't let your fears cost you what could be the best chapter of your life. You've helped everyone else find love. Give Romario a chance."

Nicole walked into the room. "Give Romario a chance to what?" When Marie's cheeks reddened, Nicole's did, too. "Oh, I'm so sorry. I didn't realize you two were having a private conversation."

Marie straightened. "Abby and I were simply discussing nonsense to pass the time until you arrived."

Abby frowned at her but went to welcome Nicole. "I'm so glad you came. I hope you're hungry. I cooked lunch today. It's ready to be served, so please sit down and I'll be right back."

Nicole offered, "Would you like some help?

Abby shook her head. "Oh, no. It's very simple."

Abby returned in a flash with quiche and served the two women.

"Where is Judy?" Nicole asked.

"Sleeping," Abby said. "So we probably have only half an hour left of peace. Then she's up, she's hungry, she's wet... I don't understand how people say you should nap when they nap. By the time I clean up, go to the bathroom, pop some food in my own mouth, it seems like she's awake again and demanding another meal."

Marie cut into her quiche. "That stage lasts for such a short time. It puts ten years on you, but it goes by in the blink of an eye."

Abby said, "I thought I wanted more, but I'm waiting to see if we survive this one before we try again."

Nicole laughed. "I've never seen my brother looking so tired. I wonder how Stephan will handle fatherhood?"

Abby asked, "Speaking of Stephan, how is he?"

Nicole's face closed a bit. "He's fine. Why wouldn't he be?"

Abby put her napkin beside her plate. "Lil told me what happened. All of it. She's afraid she hurt you."

"She didn't," Marie said. "Alethea was up to her old antics again."

"I'm glad you brought her up," Abby said smoothly. "It's Alethea I want to discuss today."

Nicole put her hands on her lap, her face purposefully blank. "I have nothing to say about that woman."

Abby said, "I realize that she's hard to understand..."

Marie countered, "Are you actually defending her?"

With a deep breath, Abby plowed forward. "I'll admit to having my own problems with Alethea, but Lil is upset. I spent too many years without my sister to risk losing her again because I can't put the past behind me. Lil told me that she feels she can't get married while Alethea is at odds with us."

Marie shook her head sadly.

Nicole said, "I love Lil like a sister, you know that, but I'm not going to pretend—"

Abby cut her off. "I'm not suggesting we pretend anything. I'm suggesting that we figure out a way today to forgive Alethea. For Lil."

Marie said, "I'm sorry, I believe that life is too short to hold grudges, but I can't forget how she treated Jeremy. He adored her and she used him."

"That's true," Abby said. "But this isn't about Jeremy. He's happy now. He doesn't need her anymore." She looked at Nicole. "And all of us have made bad decisions at one time or another. I've made mistakes. You've both made mistakes. Families work through problems. We can work through this."

Silence.

"When I was teaching and my students had trouble getting along, I would have them list what they liked about the other person. It made them realize they were focusing on one or two things instead of the whole person."

Silence.

"Okay, I'll go first. Alethea is..." Abby's voice trailed off as the first words that came to her were not flattering. She started over. "What I like about Alethea is..."

The three woman looked at each other for a painfully, long time.

Most likely to simply break the silence, Nicole said, "She has good taste in shoes."

An awkward silence followed as none present could immediately come up with an additional compliment. Eventually, Abby groaned and laughed, covering her face with one hand. "Come on. We can do better than that. Alethea is loyal to Lil. No matter how much I worry every time she lures Lil into a new calamity, I know she would die for my sister."

Marie grudgingly admitted. "She's very intelligent."

Nicole said, "And she doesn't hold back what she thinks."

Abby nodded, her eyebrows raised in sarcasm. "No, she certainly doesn't do that." After taking a fortifying drink of water, Abby added, "Without her, we would have lost Dominic's business."

Nicole made a face as she admitted, "Dominic would have never forgiven Stephan if that had happened. So I suppose I'm grateful to her for uncovering the back door."

Abby said, "She tests all of our security systems. Granted, we ask her not to, but Lil says she does it because she cares. Maybe that's what we should try to do. See Alethea through Lil's eyes. Why does Lil love her?"

Marie said, "Lil told me how Alethea was there with her in the delivery room when Colby was born. When Lil has needed someone, Alethea has consistently been there, at least according to Lil."

Nicole said, "Lil told me that Alethea defended her throughout high school. She never felt alone."

Abby wiped away a tear that crested over one lid. "She was there for Lil when I couldn't reach her. Lil says she gave her unconditional support when I didn't."

Nicole got up and hugged Abby. "Oh, Abby, you did the best you could."

"Did I? How have I spent so many years resenting someone who did so much for my sister? How can I still resent her? All Lil wants is for me to stand next to her at her wedding and pretend to like her. Why can't I do that for my sister?"

Marie said, "Fear is an ugly thing, isn't it? You're afraid to lose your sister again."

Abby nodded. "I blamed Alethea for so many of the problems I had with Lil. She kept her out late. Even got her arrested once. But they were kids. They're women now. Lil doesn't want me to parent her anymore and I have to stop—somehow."

Nicole whispered, "Alethea doesn't stop. She has to dig and dig until she finds the truth. I'm happier than I've ever been. If this isn't real, I don't want to know."

Marie said, "You don't mean that, Nicole. And it is real. Stephan loves you. Anyone can see that. Jeremy says that

Alethea only sees the worst-case scenario and works backward from the idea of 'what if it were true.' She didn't accuse Stephan because he did anything. She accused him because she can't imagine a world where he wouldn't do something like that."

"I know you're right," Nicole said. "That's why I haven't said a thing to him. I know it's not true."

Abby said, "I've never really given Alethea a chance. Lil says she's not close to her own family. She considers us her family. What if she doesn't know how to trust people? We could show her. We could take the first step and really open up to her. Look at all we have. We're incredibly blessed. Maybe she would relax if we opened up to her first."

When neither of the other women said anything, Abby added, "For Lil."

Marie nodded. "You're right, Abby. I've never hidden my dislike of her. That's not fair to your sister or to Jake. If Lil is putting off the wedding until we sort this out, then it's time for us to put this all behind us."

Nicole let out a shaky breath. "I love Stephan. Alethea asking questions won't change that. I can forgive and forget if I know that doing so means that much to Lil."

Abby picked up her fork. "Okay, it's settled then. I'd like both of you back here tomorrow afternoon for tea. I've invited both Lil and Alethea. Let's show them that we can make this work."

Marie made the sign of the cross and appealed to the heavens. When Abby and Nicole looked at her, she said, "We're going to need all the help we can get."

CHAPTER *Fourteen*

OUTSIDE JAKE'S OFFICE, Marc offered Stephan a short reprieve. "I can go in first, update him on what we know, and then tell him you're here."

Stephan won Marc's respect by shaking his head and saying, "If this problem is a ripple effect of what I did last year, I'm not going to dance around whose fault it is. It rests firmly on my shoulders. I appreciate your support, but I don't need it. Jake will listen to reason. And Dominic..." Stephan sighed. "I'll figure out something."

Marc spoke briefly to the secretary and then Jake opened the door himself. "Stephan, come in."

When Alethea stepped forward to go inside, Marc held her arm and led her to the couch in the waiting area. Most men would have let go of her arm when she shot them the how-dare-you glare she sent him, but Marc only tightened his grip. She didn't belong in there, not yet. *If she's right, they'll come for her.*

Neither sat as they waited.

Between gritted teeth, Alethea said, "Get your hand off me."

"Can't do that. They need time to sort this out before they involve us."

"So, what do you expect me to do—wait here until they bestow an invitation on us?"

"Yes."

She said something rude under her breath.

Marc hid a smile. Patience was one quality his little warrior lacked. There were worse faults a person could have. Patience could be learned; loyalty couldn't. The more time he spent with

141

Alethea, the more he respected what drove her decisions. Even though she approached problems with a battle-axe when others would have used a more delicate tool, she was driven—almost obsessively so—to protect the ones she cared about.

A strong, loving woman whose worst enemy was herself. He didn't know how he was going to do it, but he wanted to help her find the kind of family she sought. Here with the Corisis, if possible; elsewhere, if necessary.

The secretary addressed them. "Mr. Walton will see you now."

Still holding her arm, Marc looked down at Alethea and said, "This time, let me do the talking."

Her lips pressed into a straight line of displeasure.

"Do you trust me?" he asked softly.

She glared at him and then looked down. "Yes."

"Then follow my lead here. This is a tricky situation. Jake knows what you think is going on. Stephan may. Don't ram your theory down their throat. Let them come to it naturally. I've already increased security. The situation is being dealt with."

"I can't just—"

Marc turned her to face him. "Yes, you can. The goal of a good security team is to protect without scaring the shit out of the people you work for. We'll watch, Alethea. If you're right and this is a small piece of something bigger, we'll find the proof and we'll stop the bastard responsible. But Jake deals with facts, and all we have right now is server breach."

Dressed in a dark suit and looking every bit like he belonged, Jeremy Kater walked into Jake's outer office. He stopped when he saw Alethea, then continued toward them.

He shook Marc's hand and then Alethea's. "Jake called and said Stephan is here. I should have guessed you'd be here, too." He nodded at Alethea.

Marc let go of Alethea's arm and placed his hand on her lower back. Did she have feelings for him? They'd been friends for a long time.

Oh, my God. I'm jealous. I'm never jealous.

That's because Alethea is the first woman who actually matters.

Alethea asked, "Did you bring Jeisa back with you?"

Jeremy's expression became guarded. "No, she stayed in California. She is in the middle of a big fundraiser."

Alethea nodded and gave a small smile. "You look happy, Jeremy. I know I haven't always appeared to be happy for you, but I am."

Relaxing a bit, Jeremy said, "Thank you. For the first time I feel like I'm where I'm supposed to be, doing what I was meant to do." He looked from her to Marc and back. "I hope you find the same, Al."

Marc was tempted to proclaim she had, but he held his silence. This was not the time or the place.

Alethea tensed beneath Marc's hand, but she didn't look back at him. She asked, "Did you find anything to help Stephan?"

Jeremy shook his head in frustration. "Not yet. You think he did it?"

Alethea stood straighter. "No, he's innocent. I know he is. The proof is there if you dig deep enough. If I were you, I'd ask myself how Sliver would set him up."

"Sliver?" Jeremy frowned. "Why would he go after Stephan? If Sliver wanted to hurt Dominic, wouldn't he choose someone closer to him?"

The secretary behind them said, "I'm sorry to interrupt you, but Mr. Walton is losing patience."

As the three of them headed toward the door, Jeremy's tone revealed he was beginning to see the merit of Alethea's idea. "Sliver would know how to cover his tracks, but why waste his time with easily fixable coding errors?" He stopped before opening the door. "You think the errors are a decoy, don't you? Something to keep us chasing our tails."

It was apparent that through years of working together Jeremy knew Alethea well, and it gave Marc a twinge of jealousy. But he knew Jeremy's chance, if he'd ever had one, was in the past. Still, there was a bite to Marc's tone when he said, "Enough. Let's go in."

Jake turned when they entered. "Jeremy. Good. We're all here. Stephan has offered to give you full access to his server. I want you to take my parents over there and find out who is doing this." He turned back to Stephan and said, "Everyone in this room wants to clear you. And we will. Hopefully before this explodes. I was hoping to have something concrete by now." He was referring to Dominic—another person who hadn't been blessed with the patience gene.

The door to Jake's office flew open and Dominic's voice boomed through the room. "Which one of you thought having this meeting without me was a good idea?"

Jake went to his side and said smoothly, "You gave me twenty-four hours, Dom. So technically, you did."

Dominic strode to the middle of the room and faced Stephan. The air was charged with the threat of imminent violence. "If I find out you're involved in this, that you've been using my sister to get to me, there won't be any place on earth you can hide from my wrath."

Normally sarcastic, Stephan wisely chose not to be for once. He met Dominic's angry gaze with the steadiness of an innocent man. "I love Nicole. I don't know how this is happening, but you have my full cooperation and access to whatever you need to figure it out."

Letting out a breath that sounded a bit like a hiss, Dominic didn't look away from Stephan as he asked, "Marc, you're a good judge of character. Do you believe him?"

Without hesitation, Marc said, "I do."

Dominic swung to look at Jeremy. "Jake must have you looking for proof. Have you found anything?"

"Not yet."

Looking around slowly, Dominic's attention settled on Alethea. "What do you think?"

Everyone stopped breathing...

"He didn't do it. Someone must have access to his IP address." Marc waited for her to say more, but she didn't.

Dominic punched his leg. "Shit. I wanted it to be you."

Stephan's eyebrows rose. "Sorry?"

Still angry, Dominic took his phone out of his pocket and opened his messages. He held his phone up so everyone could see a photo. "I received this from Stephan this morning."

It was a slightly blurry color photo of Judy sleeping in her crib.

Stephan said, "I didn't send that. I haven't been in your child's bedroom."

Marc moved closer. "Can I see it?" Dominic handed him the phone. "It was taken from her baby monitor. I know that feed."

A chill settled in the room. Jake asked, "Are we sure Abby didn't send it?"

Marc handed Jake the phone. "It's from Stephan's email."

Rising to his full height, Dominic roared, "How could someone access Judy's monitor? I thought we were using encrypted video."

Alethea interjected, "My guess is Abby didn't get that memo."

Dominic turned to Marc. "Marc, I want the security at my house doubled."

"Already done, Dom."

Shaking with a fury that had no outlet, Dominic growled, "What did you know that you failed to tell me?"

Jake accepted the blame easily. "I told him to keep it between us until we could confirm that we were dealing with more than a simple hacking."

Grabbing his phone back from Jake, Dominic snapped, "I'd say we're dealing with a hell of a lot more than that. I want the bastard who thinks it's funny to taunt me with my daughter. And I want him now. What do we know?"

Jake said, "All we have is a theory."

Looking down at the photo on his phone as if it caused him physical pain, Dominic snarled, "A theory?"

"Alethea's," Jake clarified.

Dominic spun back to address Alethea. Marc kept a hand on her lower back and felt her tense beneath his aggressive approach, but she kept her expression calm. She took a breath and said, "I think it's Sliver."

"We dealt with him. Jeremy, you said that we sent him so far underground he wasn't a threat worth pursuing."

Jeremy looked uncomfortable and admitted, "I may have underestimated his obsession with you. This isn't someone trying to make a name for himself. This is personal. Vendetta level."

Marc said, "Alethea believes that Sliver could be the same man Stephan gave your server codes to last year. He worked for Stephan in the past. That would have given him the opportunity to access his server as well."

"What are you basing that on?" Dominic asked forcefully.

Alethea raised her chin and said, "A gut feeling."

"So why the photo of my daughter?"

"A taunt and a warning. He wants you to know how close he is."

"I want this guy. I don't care what it takes. No one threatens my family and lives. Do we understand?"

Stephan stepped forward and said, "Dom, every resource I have is yours in whatever way you can use it."

Rage still simmering close the surface, Dominic said, "Hope you're not holding out for a thank you. You gave this bastard access to my family."

Stephan corrected him. "Our family."

Rubbing his eyes in frustration, Dominic took a deep calming breath. He looked across at Marc. "I don't want to scare Abby, but I want my home to be a Secret Service wet dream."

Marc nodded. "Consider it done." He stepped away to make a couple of calls to his men. When he returned, Jake had a large dry-erase board out and was making a web that had Dominic in the middle.

Jake said, "There has to be a piece we're missing." He put a line connecting Dominic to Stephan. He drew another line connecting Dominic to Jeremy and then to Sliver. An additional line connected Sliver to Stephan. "What is the pattern?"

Alethea asked, "Jeremy, when did you first notice Sliver online?"

"About two years ago, I guess."

She asked, "When did *Jack* leave your company, Stephan?"

"About that time."

"It has to be him," Marc added. "But why connect with Jeremy?"

Alethea studied the board. "I don't think he meant to. I believe that's the only mistake he made. Jeremy challenged his ego online. If this is the same guy, he thinks he's smarter than everyone else. We used that successfully against him last year. We can use it again."

Jeremy looked across at Marc and said, "Alethea excels at shit like this."

Marc watched Alethea study the web on the dry-erase board and couldn't agree more. Alethea continued, "You know this guy. His name isn't Stanley or Jack, but you know him. He's someone who feels wronged by you. Who has a reason to hate you, Dom?"

With marker poised, Jake said, "We're going to need a larger board."

Marc added, "It wouldn't be anything recent. This guy has a festering hate."

As Jake and Dominic brainstormed for people involved in deals where the other side might have felt cheated, the list did indeed overflow onto sheets of paper.

Alethea suggested, "What if we broke it down by year? Work backward from when he started working for Stephan."

Jeremy watched the growing list and whistled, "Dom, you're lucky you're still alive." He looked at Jake. "Is your list as long?"

Jake held up two fingers. "Two, maybe three shady deals."

Dominic's eyebrows rose. "Really? And here I thought you believed in doing everything above board."

Jake shrugged. "I'm only human."

Alethea pointed to the list. "Add those deals, too."

When they had an exhaustive list, Alethea paced the room and said, "Is there anyone on this list who would have the skills to pull this off? Maybe someone isolated from society by their awkward level of intelligence?"

"Hey, hey," Jeremy said, "not all geniuses lack social skills."

Jake opened his mouth to agree, then closed it with a snap. "She's right. That type of personality profile fits this scenario."

Eyes collectively went to Jeremy, who bristled a bit under the sudden scrutiny. "Don't look at me. I didn't know any of you before Alethea asked me to hack into your system."

Alethea instantly stiffened, apparently preparing for them to adapt her theory to include her.

Before things got more heated, Marc said, "The likelihood that it's someone in this room is slim, and doubting each other is just what this guy wants. That's why he used Stephan. We're not going to get anywhere if we don't trust each other." He picked up the stack of papers and said, "I suggest we start here. I'll track down what everyone on this list is doing now. Location. Financial standing. Everything."

Dominic rubbed his forehead roughly. "That's going to take you awhile."

"Yes, sir."

Dominic nodded in approval.

Jeremy started toward the door. "I'll go back with Stephan and see what I can find on his side."

Jake walked over to a briefcase and took out a laptop. "I'll pour over our records to see if we forgot anyone."

Dominic checked his watch. "I'm going home." Then he strode out of the office.

Alethea said, "I—"

"You should stay close to Abby and the baby," Marc said, not giving her a chance to finish her sentence. "Give Dominic tonight with them, but you have the perfect excuse to spend the day with them tomorrow."

"The tea? Are you kidding me? You want me to sit there having scones while the rest of you figure this out?" She looked ready to stomp her foot like a petulant child.

He wisely suppressed his amusement. There would be time later to kiss that pout off her lips. "That's where we need you. Close. Watching without alarming them."

Jake inserted, "I agree. They don't need to know about this yet. So far all we have is a theory based on coding errors and one photo. There is no need to scare them. We have all angles covered." He took in Alethea's obvious displeasure with the idea and said, "Why don't you help Marc with research tonight? I'm sure he could use your help."

Alethea shook her head in disgust and turned to leave.

Jake stopped Marc when Alethea was through the door. "Marc, you need to keep this contained until we can figure it out. Alethea is as potentially volatile as she is an asset. If it gets out that we're onto this guy, he could disappear before we can nab him. And I want him."

"Then I'd better catch up with her fast," Marc said, and strode to the door. "I'll do my best, but she's not going to fall for the bunker thing twice."

Seated beside Marc in his Lexus, Alethea closed her eyes for a moment to clear her head of the jumbled emotions surging through her. Stephan was where he needed to be. Dominic and Jake were aware of the gravity of the situation and would remain on high alert until whoever was doing this was caught. With Jeremy and Jake's famous computer-geek parents working on the IP address that led back to Stephan, it wouldn't be long before they could trace it back to the true origin, and with Marc working the other end they should be able to flush out even the best alias. Whoever was doing this was close and he was getting cocky.

Which meant he'd probably slip up.
And we'll catch him.
Tea with Abby and Lil? Bullshit.
I wish they'd say what they think.
They don't want me involved.
Does Marc seriously think I didn't hear the exchange between Jake and him as he left?
Marc's main job is to contain me, by whatever means necessary.

She thought back to the night before and a wave of nausea rose within her. *It's still all about keeping me occupied and out of the way. I knew it wasn't real, but there is a difference between knowing it and hearing it said aloud.*

With a slow, calming breath, Alethea opened her eyes and said coldly, "My car is still at Stephan's building. I'd appreciate it if you took me there."

Marc started the car and drove toward the exit of the garage. "I need your help with the research tonight."

Gripping the clasp of her seat belt, Alethea kept the ice in her tone. "We both know you don't. I heard what Jake said as we left."

Marc's jaw clenched, but he pulled out into the street traffic without hesitation. "That's a shame, but it doesn't change anything. You're coming home with me tonight."

"Really? So, we're back to manhandling to get me where you want me to be?"

The hot look he gave her sent a flash of responding desire through her. The business-first Marc was gone, replaced by the man she'd woken next to in the bunker, who was looking at her like he wanted to pull the car over and take her right there. *Job or no job, he wants me.*

A sexy smile stretched across his lips, and there was a glint in his eye that said he was enjoying their exchange. "Too late to pretend you don't want this as much as I do. You will spend the night at my place. I'll leave how you get there up to you."

Alethea looked out the passenger window to give herself some distance. "Last night was fun, but not necessary to repeat. It's been a long day. Drop me off at my place, and I'll pick up my car myself tomorrow."

He didn't answer, just kept driving. Since he was headed toward neither Stephan's office nor her apartment, she could only conclude that he was stubbornly driving to his place. She turned back toward him and snapped, "I don't want to spend the night with you. Not even the evening. I'm not sure I can stand five more minutes in this car before I snap and grab the wheel." When he looked at her quickly, she warned, "Don't think I won't do it. The risk of injury is worth it to get the hell away from you."

However Alethea expected Marc to respond, she didn't expect him to take one of her hands in his and chuckle as if she'd made a sweet joke. He raised her hand to his mouth and kissed it. "Now all I can picture is how you looked in that jujitsu stance when I took your clothes. You were so angry. I've never met a woman who could be that fierce while naked."

Alethea tried to pull her hand free. "I'm extremely serious."

He laid her hand on his thigh beneath his. "I know. That's what makes it so hot."

Alethea would have pulled away, but the heat from his thigh burned up her hand and through her. Memories of how that thigh had felt bare and rubbing against hers the night before sent a blush up her chest and warmed her cheeks. She wanted to be angry with him, but all she could picture was how he'd looked naked: confident and teasing. And how it had felt to wake in his arms, knowing that he was watching over her.

She wanted him as she'd never wanted anyone before.

And he knew it.

He also knew she would never hurt him.

No wonder he was laughing at her. She'd given him all the power.

She decided to try another method. Turning toward him, she deliberately looked down, then up at him from beneath her lashes, rubbing her hand ever so slightly up and down his thigh. "Take me to my place, Marc. Please."

He studied her expression briefly as he drove. "You're good. I wish I could say yes, but you know I can't."

"Because Jake told you to watch me."

He didn't look comfortable with answering, but he did. "Yes."

She whipped her hand off him and clenched them in her lap. "And none of you think I should be part of this, do you? People pay me big money to test their security systems. My skills are in high demand internationally."

With a slight frown, Marc said, "Next you'll say we hurt your feelings today."

She folded her arms over her chest and looked away.

"Seriously?" He chuckled again, patting her thigh. He spoke with the sweet tone one would use with a child when they find their actions adorable. "Oh, I didn't know you were so sensitive."

She looked out the window. "You're such an asshole."

He pulled up to valet parking in front of an uptown apartment building. "I can carry you upstairs. I doubt the valet will say anything—I already tip him outrageously well. I'll tell him that we love to role-play. It won't be the strangest thing he's seen if he's lived in New York for long. Or you can maintain your dignity and walk. Up to you. I'm easy."

A young valet opened her passenger door. She stepped out. Marc was beside her in a flash. She said, "I could get away if I wanted to."

He smiled. "Maybe."

As they walked side by side into his apartment building, she said, "I'll help you with your research tonight, but that's it. You sleep on the couch. We're not repeating last night."

His hand settled on her lower back as they entered the elevator. As soon as the door closed he pulled her to him, his mouth hot and demanding. Her hands splayed across his strong chest. Everything she'd said, both to him and herself, faded away in the face of their intense desire for each other.

Maintaining their kiss, he carried her to his door and, after typing in a code with one hand, opened the door, swept her inside, and then slammed the door behind him. He returned her to her feet and ripped at her clothing. She tore at his with every bit as much enthusiasm. Buttons flew. It was an animalistic need to mate. No gentle foreplay. Only a burning desire that demanded to be sated.

Normally Alethea was acutely aware of her surroundings, naturally scanning and assessing, but right now she felt nothing beyond Marc. Marc's lips on hers, on her neck, on her breasts. The feel of his pulsing shaft in her hands. His hands were everywhere, rough and demanding.

He lifted her so her legs wrapped around his waist and the room suddenly tilted. She put a hand out to steady herself and grabbed the banister. He perched her on the carpeted edge of a stair and sank to his knees, parting her legs roughly.

Alethea buried her hands in the plush rug and gasped as his tongue plunged deeply inside her. He slid a hand beneath her ass to position it as he wanted and lapped at her, suckled her, claimed her with his mouth.

She was gasping and close to orgasm when he stopped and repositioned himself above her. She hungrily took him deeply into her mouth, and he moaned. One of her hands gripped the back of one of his rock-hard thighs while her other cupped and caressed his balls. He surged and grew in her mouth. Feeling him shudder with pleasure, she welcomed him deeper, filling her with echoing pleasure.

When she thought he would come in her mouth, he withdrew, and she closed her eyes, knowing the pause in pleasure was temporary. She heard him open a wrapper and then he was kissing her neck again.

"Alethea," he said roughly, and she opened her eyes.

He plunged deeply inside her, and she cried out his name. He lifted her so her shoulders bore some of her weight and held her before him so he could pound with a leverage that had her crying and begging for more. It was unlike anything she'd ever experienced. Powerful. All consuming. Leaving both of them shaking from the intensity of their simultaneous orgasm.

He withdrew, lifted her gently in his arms, and carried her up the stairs to his loft bedroom. He disposed of the condom, then rolled onto the bed beside her, taking her into his arms and kissing her forehead.

His leisurely kiss rocked her to the core. It was tender and sweet and full of a promise she wasn't ready for. Still, it was as impossible to deny as breathing.

Between kisses, he said, "We can't fall asleep. I have a lot of research to do tonight. I really could use your help."

She buried her face in his chest. "I told myself this wouldn't happen."

He raised himself above her and pushed her hair out of her eyes tenderly. "I didn't promise myself that. You're all I thought about all day. I shouldn't let anything distract me right now. We have no idea how dangerous this situation is. But you're all I can think about. How do you think that makes me feel?"

She laid a hand on his cheek. "So this isn't about your job?"

He smiled down at her. "Hey, I'm dedicated, but not this dedicated. I know we don't make sense. Career wise, I have everything I've ever wanted. I'm at the age when I could settle down with a nice woman, have some kids, and maybe get a dog."

She glared up at him. "A nice woman, huh?" She went to roll away, but he held her beneath him. "Unlike me?"

He kissed her deeply, kissed her until she almost forgot what she was angry about. Almost. When he raised his head and saw she was still miffed, he said, "I used to think that being with that kind of woman would make me a better man. Instead I found myself dating one after another, not caring much about any of them. On the surface it was good, but when I look back they've blended into one sweet woman with a name I can't remember because they didn't matter."

Don't listen.

Don't believe him.

"But it's different with me?" she mocked. Believing would lead to wanting more from him, and he'd already said he didn't want to be with her.

He kissed her collarbone. He put a leg between hers and ran a hand over her wet center. "I want you more each time I have you." He dipped a finger between her lower lips. "I want you again. God, we have so much to do tonight and all I can think about is sinking into you again and again while you call out my name. That's how you're different."

She almost scathingly told him that he was talking about lust—plain and simple. And that was natural, but his finger found her G-spot, and that inner caress wiped her head clear of all coherent thought. She dug her hands into his hair and pulled his face down to hers, delving into his mouth with the same boldness he'd claimed her with earlier. His fingers found a rhythm of pulling out and sinking into her that renewed the wild need within her.

Her rebuttal would have to wait.

It was three in the morning. He and Alethea were still hunting for anything they could find on the names Dominic had given them. He was at his desk on his main computer on one side of the living room, and she was seated on the couch with his laptop. Marc didn't have a problem working on something through the night; in fact, that's how he'd designed most of his bunker.

Normally, however, a night of work didn't overlap with marathon sex sessions. He was having trouble focusing on the last page of names. Partly because they'd gone through so many without finding anything notable, but mostly because he knew

exactly what Alethea was wearing—or rather, not wearing—
beneath the long T-shirt he'd offered her.

He was close to putting the list aside and carrying her back to
his bed, which concerned him. His personal life and his work
had never been at odds. His loyalty to Dominic and the security
of his family and business had been his top priority for many
years.

*Someone sent him a photo of his baby, for God's sake. This
is serious.*

He typed in the next name on the list and forced himself to
look away from Alethea. Howard Voss. Net worth: $20 million.
Majored in psychology before founding a network of online
blogs. He'd accused Dominic of trashing him publicly, but it
hadn't hurt him too much because he'd turned around and sold
his network for millions. He'd gone on to create software that
bounced traffic from sites seamlessly and which had generated
him a substantial income. He'd also started two online
magazines. Nothing about Dominic since. No evidence that he'd
been hurt long term. In fact, he was doing better now, than he'd
been back when he'd made the accusation. No, Voss didn't have
the time or the motivation to go after Dominic. It was also
doubtful that he had the hacking skills. Marc made a few quick
notes beside his name and moved on to the next.

He looked across at Alethea and fought back the immediate
impulse to close the distance between them. Instead he asked,
"Are you finding anything?"

Alethea looked up with an ironic smile. "That you don't
cross Dominic. He was brutal when it came to business. I see
how he made his money. He was relentless."

"Daddy issues," Marc said. "He needed to prove he was
better. That kind of obsession blurs a man's morality."

"That's the first negative thing I've ever heard you say about
Dominic. I thought he was your idol."

Turning his seat toward her, Marc said, "I owe him. He gave
me a chance when I didn't deserve one. I don't know where I'd
be today if I'd never met him. But that doesn't mean I'm blind

to his faults. It also doesn't mean I don't regret some of what he's asked me to do over the years."

Alethea's eyes widened. "Such as?"

Marc smiled at her. "If I told you, I'd have to kill you." He stood up and stretched. "And I'm starting to like you."

He loved the way her eyebrows rose, causing one light line of irritation to crease her beautiful forehead. "Starting?"

Giddiness filled him and he plopped beside her on the couch, resting his arm along the back of it behind her. "It's a process." He pulled one of her curls playfully.

She swatted at him. "What, are we back in school now?"

He twirled a long red curl around one of his fingers. "Did the boys pull your hair?"

"When I was little, frequently. It drove me crazy."

"I bet you kicked their asses."

"I didn't, actually. I used to cry. But that doesn't work, does it?" She reached back and grabbed his hand, stilling it. "You have to make them stop."

He turned his hand in hers and linked their fingers. "I heard a rumor there is something adults use to resolve conflicts. I believe it's called communication."

Alethea shook her head. "Ha ha. You're hilarious."

"I'm also right. I know you don't want to go to the tea later today with Abby, but look at it as an opportunity."

"To give them all a chance to tell me what they think is wrong with me?"

"No, to let them see you. There is nothing wrong with you. You're fiercely loyal. Brilliant. Fearless." He ran a finger down one side of her exposed neck. "And funny. Lil is lucky to have a friend like you. Abby may be jealous of you. She may feel threatened by how close you are to her sister. When people are afraid, they lash out." He tapped her nose lightly in reprimand. "You, more than most."

"Why do you care if I get along with them or not?"

He tucked a finger under her chin and turned her face to his. "Because I care about you. If you want those women to accept you, you're going to have to play by their rules." He picked up one of her hands and kissed it. "Keep the claws sheathed. And don't tell them anything."

"I'm surprised you're not coming with me to make sure I don't."

He said, "You know how important it is to keep what we know to ourselves. If it gets out, we could lose our chance to catch this guy."

Alethea tightened her fingers around his hand and held it to her stomach. "I won't say anything."

He leaned down and kissed her neck. "I know. I trust you. Put all of this out of your head while you're there and try to find a common ground with these women."

"That's easy to say." Alethea looked at the ceiling and blinked away the tears that threatened to spill over. "I've been friends with Lil for more than ten years and I've never been welcome for holidays or family events. It never bothered me much, because Lil didn't have much of a family, but lately it hurts."

"And yet you've remained friends."

Alethea closed her eyes for a moment and when she opened them, Marc knew she was temporarily far away. "I can't imagine my life without her. We've been through so much together, and we've always been there for each other. She and Abby were fighting constantly, and my mother and I weren't close. We became each other's family, I guess. I love her."

Marc pulled her into his arms and hugged her to him. The feelings she'd expressed for her friend touched him deeply. It made him want more than to have her in his bed again. He wanted to hear her speak about him with that level of emotion—and more.

He wanted to be her family.

He stood up and took her by the hand. "Come on, let's go to bed."

She looked down at the paper on her lap and said, "I'm not finished with my section."

He tossed the paper on the coffee table. "I'm not either. I'll do it in the morning. Right now I want to hold you."

She stood and looked up at him, and he'd never seen anything more beautiful than the almost shy smile she gave him. "Okay."

He swept her up into his arms and carried her to his bed. He laid her down and pulled the shirt over her head, then shed his own clothing. This time wasn't about rushing or slaking a thirst. This was about holding her to him, bare skin to bare skin. Sex could wait. The list could wait. Nothing mattered except having her there with him.

He drifted off to sleep with her in his arms.

But awoke alone.

Alethea hesitated before ringing the doorbell at Abby's house. She adjusted the front of her carefully chosen silk blouse. Her hair was tied back conservatively. The style of her pants was classic and nondescript. Even her makeup was toned down. *Yes, I chose my most expensive pair of Manolo Blahniks, but a girl needs a bit of a confidence boost sometimes.*

Fearless?

Ha.

Give me a firefight any day over a room of women who want to talk.

She'd found respite in an hour of sleep within the haven of Marc's arms, but her churning stomach had woken her. She'd stared at the dark ceiling until she acknowledged that sleep would not return. She'd shifted and replaced herself with a pillow, pausing to appreciate the outline of Marc's muscular shoulders and back in the dimly lit room.

If she were looking for a relationship, which she wasn't, a man like Marc would hit almost every criteria on her perfect match list. He was intelligent without being socially insecure. Strong without being threatened by her own strength. And flawed. Thank God for his flaws. She certainly had a good share of her own.

A man like Marc could accept her as she was while still pushing her to be better—no different from the way he pushed himself. Unlike any man she'd been with in the past, the more time she spent with Marc, the more she respected him. He was honest, blunt, and he genuinely seemed to want her to be happy.

Alethea swallowed hard. She didn't want to fail here today. For Lil. For herself. And, remarkably enough, for Marc. She wanted more than anything to tell him she had navigated what was sure to be a minefield of temptation, held her tongue, and left this meeting with a workable truce. They may never be friends, but they could find a civil middle ground. One that allowed her to be close to Lil without the friction it presently caused.

Taking a deep breath, Alethea rang the bell and braced herself.

The door swung open and Lil pulled her through and into a tight hug. "You came, Al, I knew you would."

Tears welled and were successfully contained. Alethea hugged her friend back, then said, "I will always come when you call, Lil. Always."

Lil met her eyes and gushed, "When you weren't answering your phone I thought you were angry with me about springing Marie and Nicole on you. I honestly thought it would make it better, not worse. I feel awful about how that went down."

Calm. Peace. Control. Truce. "I was just as much at fault as anyone else. You know how I get when I lose my temper. But I wasn't ignoring your calls. I lost my phone for a bit and things got a bit crazy. Know that no matter how bad you feel, I am just as sorry."

Lil held her friend's hand and said, "And here I am again, asking you to give them another shot. I wouldn't blame you if you turned tail and ran, but Abby promised she'd be in your corner. She wants to work things out between the two of you."

Alethea nodded. "I want the same thing. I want to be standing next to Abby at your wedding. I know how much that means to you and I'll do anything to make sure you have that moment."

Lil bit her lip with worry before she said, "Just one thing. Don't bring up Stephan or your theories. Keep to safe topics. If they ask you, tell them that you were wrong and thought you'd found something but you haven't."

Oh, Lil. "I'm not a good liar."

"For me. Just this once. Let Dominic and Jake deal with their business issues—issues you wouldn't even know about if you weren't so paranoid. I know what you said you found, but you could be wrong, couldn't you? People make mistakes. Things look one way, but they turn out to be totally different when you look closer. Let this one go. Don't cloud today with possible apocalyptic scenarios. Let them see the side of you I love. Just be you today."

Lil sounded so much like Marc that Alethea fought back emotional tears again and hated herself for the weakness. *Just be me. I don't know who I am when you remove what I do.* Like Marc, Lil was asking for what felt like the impossible.

Don't expect things to get better if you do what you've always done.

I can do this.

I can be the friend Lil needs.

I can smile and keep my mouth shut.

"I won't let you down, Lil. Don't worry. I'll play nice."

Lil linked arms with Alethea and walked through the foyer with her.

Abby met them halfway. Her smile looked a bit forced, but she gave Alethea a kiss on the cheek. "Welcome. Everyone is already in the atrium."

"Everyone?" Alethea asked, her mouth suddenly dry.

Abby stopped and turned. Her expression changed, becoming more sympathetic and open. "Only Marie and Nicole. The house is empty. Dominic's mother is watching Judy and

Colby." She paused, then said, "I'm glad you came today, Alethea. Sincerely. I know we've had our issues, but I'm hoping we can find a way to start fresh today." She looked away and then back. "You've been a good friend to my sister and that is what I want to focus on. You love Lil and so do I. It's time for us to find a way to get along."

Say as little as possible.

With a tight throat, Alethea nodded. "I'd like that."

She followed Abby into the atrium. Marie and Nicole stood when she entered. A tense silence filled the room for a moment.

Marie crossed the room and gave Alethea a kiss on the cheek. "Alethea."

Alethea almost laughed as a clip from an old mafia movie flashed through her mind. Kiss of welcome or of death?

No jokes.

No sarcasm.

Be good.

I should hug the old bitty just to see what she'd do.

No, behave.

Maintaining what she hoped was a friendly smile, Alethea said, "Nice to see you again, Marie."

Nicole walked up to her, hands clasped tightly before her. "What you said about Stephan really hurt me."

Alethea took a calming breath. This was about a truce, not the truth. "I'm sorry. It wasn't my intention to hurt you." That much was true anyway.

White-faced, Nicole asked, "Do you still believe that Stephan is trying to sabotage my brother's company?"

I never said...

Doesn't matter.

"No, I don't."

Not letting up, Nicole pushed, "So, you were wrong."

Alethea glanced at Lil, who was practically wringing her own hands as she waited. *Lie. It doesn't matter what she thinks of me. Not being able to get along with her hurts Lil. Put aside your damn pride and just fucking lie.* Face tight, Alethea said, "Yes, I was."

With an audible breath, Nicole relaxed a bit and covered her mouth with one hand as she said, "Oh, my God, I knew you were, but I needed to hear it."

Abby stood beside Alethea and said, "Why don't we all sit down?"

They sat in a circle around an antique table while Abby served tea and passed a plate of scones.

Alethea took her cup obediently and placed it before her. Unlike the other women, she didn't reach for sweetener or lemon.

Marie asked, "Not a tea drinker?"

Instantly defensive, Alethea sat straighter, but bit back the first five responses that came to her. Finally she said, "Not really, but this is a nice treat."

Lifting the teapot from the tray, Marie said, "This particular blend is from Ceylon. They say it teases the palate with a hint of ginger and is best with a slice of orange. Milk does not complement it."

"Thank you," Alethea said, and reached for an orange slice. "I appreciate the tip."

Abby said, "I hope you're here long enough to see Judy when Rosella returns with her. She's getting so big so fast. Colby will be happy to see you, too."

Don't ask.

Don't get involved.

"So Rosella took them out?"

Abby nodded. "Yes, they needed the fresh air. She took the double stroller and is walking them both at Central Park."

"With security?" Alethea asked before she could stop herself.

Abby's face darkened a bit with irritation. "Of course with security. Look at this place, it's a virtual prison with all the men Dominic has patrolling it. It was bad before Judy was born, but thanks to your little hospital stunt, I can barely move without tripping over a bodyguard."

Lil said, "Abby, that's not really fair. Alethea saw a potential problem and she exposed it. We're lucky it was her and not a rabid fan or reporter."

Abby sighed. "Alethea, I know you did it to help, but you upset everyone the way you did it. From now on, please pick up the phone and tell me, or Dominic. I can give you Marc's phone number. He's Dominic's head of security. Call him with your concerns next time and I promise to be grateful for your help."

Bite your tongue.

She obviously has no clue what's going on.

But that's okay, because it's being handled.

Nicole said, "I don't know how you put up with this side of Dominic, Abby. It's too much. He tried to give me my own security detail and I turned it down."

Lil laughed. "He did the same for me when we first met. I had to threaten to call the police, remember, Abby?"

Abby smiled at the memory. "I do. You accused him of being worse than me."

"He was," Lil said. "Thank God Jake isn't like that. We have a regular home security system and that's it. I couldn't handle living like you do, Abby."

Marie interjected, "Dominic does it because he loves her. He lives a high-profile life. Even more so than Jake. That level of celebrity comes with a cost. He's just trying to keep his family safe."

Alethea said, "Lil, a bodyguard might be a good idea for you and Colby, too."

Lil shook her head. "No way. I'm careful about where I go and that's good enough for me. For special events, yes, I can see how we need it to deal with the press, but I don't want to live with a constant shadow."

The hair on the back of Alethea's neck went up at the knowledge of how unprotected her friend was. She wanted to demand that she do more for herself and her child. She wanted to spill the details of everything she knew. But she didn't.

All she knew so far was that Stephan's IP address was involved in the coding errors and someone had sent a photo of Judy through his email.

Neither was enough to convince anyone present they were facing a potentially lethal threat. They wouldn't believe her. Nothing would be gained, and Marc would never trust her again.

Abby put down her tea and said, "The reason I asked all of you here is because things have gotten rocky between us lately and I believe we've lost sight of what is important. We have a wedding to plan. Lil, stop putting off the date and pick one. We'll all be there."

A huge, hopeful smile spread across Lil's face. "There is nothing I want more than to have the people I love the most at my side that day." She looked back and forth between Abby and Alethea. "I love you both so much. I couldn't plan a wedding while you were at odds. But seeing you here together, I know we can work this out. I want to drag all of you wedding dress shopping, cake tasting, make you listen to a slew of possible bands."

Abby hugged Lil. "You deserve to have your big day without worrying whether we can get along or not. The past is the past. All that matters to me is whatever happens from this day on."

Lil reached across and took Alethea's hand in hers. "I couldn't have said it better than Abby did. A fresh start sounds good to me."

Nicole joked, "And the sooner the better. Stephan and I would love to be next."

Marie looked across at Alethea and said, "I've judged you harshly in the past, Alethea. I'm protective of my boys and I adopted Jeremy the moment I met him. Jeisa, too. I can't say I agree with how you treated either of them, but I can agree to let the past be the past. You impressed me today. I didn't know what to think when Abby suggested this meeting. But I can see that you genuinely want this to work out as much as we do. You've done a lot to help those I care most about, and I hope this is the start of a friendship between us."

The next two hours passed quickly as they chose days to get together, possible locations for Lil's wedding, and in general laughed over fun ideas they tossed around. Alethea didn't mention the challenges each proposed location faced when it came to security. She didn't share what all those days would mean to her work schedule and projects. No, she smiled, laughed, and did her best to avoid saying anything that could rock the boat.

She excused herself to go to the bathroom and Lil came with her, hugging her all the way. "Al, today worked out better than I dared dream it could. I'm getting married. I'm actually getting married, and you're going to be there."

She hugged her friend back, fighting the voice within her that screamed to be careful. *Abby was right. The past doesn't matter here. I bring it to every encounter I have. Is that why I can't be happy? I find ugly everywhere because I look for it?*

Just for today, I want to see the world the way Lil does.

She hugged Lil and gave in to an enthusiastic bounce. "You're getting married. You're really getting married."

They giggled together just as they had when they'd been much younger, and it felt good.

They returned from the bathroom, both smiling and laughing.

Abby's phone beeped and she checked it. She smiled and then frowned. Holding the phone so everyone could see the photo, she said, "Stephan just sent me a photo of the babies and Rosella at the park. That's weird. He's never sent me a text before. It doesn't look like they even know he's there."

She looked at Nicole, who shrugged and then at Alethea—who froze.

166

CHAPTER *Fifteen*

ACROSS TOWN, MARC placed his list of names on Dominic Corisi's desk. "With Alethea's help I went through every name you gave me. There is a brief summary next to each. We used every source we could to learn what these people have been up to and determine if they have the skills needed to pull this off. I wish I had good news for you."

Dominic looked over the list quickly and then handed it to Jake. "Jeremy, tell me you found something."

"I found a network of dummy IPs that lead backward from Stephan's. The good news is that Stephan's not doing this. The bad news is, whoever is doing this—he's good. Real good. I hate to say it, but I think Alethea is right on the money with this one. Someone put a whole lot of effort into this... over a few years. If we stop looking at the coding errors as the problem and think of them as a taunt, we're dealing with one sick bastard."

Jake said, "But one that Stephan may have met. If he worked for him, there has to be a photo of him. Or surveillance video. Something."

Jeremy said, "There is no record of Stanley or the other alias at Andrade Global. They store their surveillance videos digitally, and those files have been wiped clean. I guess we could have Stephan work with a criminal sketch artist, but other than that, we're at a dead end.

Marc looked at Dominic. "Can I use your computer?"

Jeremy's eyebrows rose. "No offense, Marc, but if there was something to find here, I would have found it."

Jake agreed. "I've gone through every possible online database we have. Nothing. It's like this guy never existed. If we're even hunting for the right guy. There is nothing that says the man who worked for Stephan and the guy who is doing this are the same person."

Undeterred, Marc walked behind Dominic's desk and took his seat. He stopped and looked at Dominic. "Password?"

Dominic told Marc and then shrugged. "I don't know why I use one when apparently everyone can access everything regardless."

Marc accessed the Internet and followed his hunch.

"What are you hoping to find?" Jeremy asked.

Marc answered, "Just give me a minute."

Dominic looked around the room angrily. "Where the hell is Stephan?"

Jeremy pointed his thumb at the window in a vague reference of location. "He's working with Jake's parents to secure his server. It'll take time to find and close every access point."

Dominic growled, "I don't like this. I don't like this at all. Who would go this far just to fuck with me? What could they get out of it?"

Marc spun Dominic's monitor around and asked, "Dominic, do you recognize anyone in this photo?"

Dominic walked over, flanked by Jake, and bent to look at the photo of a man looking irritated by the birthday cake on his cubicle desk. "Who is it?"

Marc straightened. "That's Jack the first year he worked for Andrade Global."

Jeremy nodded in admiration. "Social media. You're a genius, Marc."

Shaking his head, Marc said, "Not a genius, just savvy to the fact that everyone posts everything online and I figured the coding department at Andrade Global wouldn't be anything different. You can wipe databases clean, but try getting someone to take down an embarrassing photo of you. This one even had him tagged. I bet it meant nothing to him at the time and he forgot all about it."

Jake said, "Dom, we know him."

Dominic looked closer. "It can't be Kurtis from college. It looks like him, though."

Jake straightened and explained. "Dom and I met at Harvard. We planned Corisi Enterprises over pizza and some serious beer. But we weren't alone. Kurtis Vine was involved at first. At least at the very beginning, when we were still writing everything on napkins. He was brilliant and for a while we thought all three of us would take over the world together."

Marc asked, "What happened?"

Dominic frowned. "He and I didn't share the same vision."

Jake smiled. "You know, the one where Dominic gets all the glory and everyone else is grateful to go along for the ride."

Dominic glared at his friend. "You want to be the face of Corisi Enterprises, Jake, just say so. It comes with this great desk and all the blame for anything that ever goes wrong."

Jake raised his hands with a placating smile. "I'm perfectly happy to take the copilot seat."

Marc said, "But Kurtis wasn't. Why didn't you mention him last night when we were generating a list of possible suspects?"

Dominic shrugged. "It was a long time ago. When we split ways, all we had was a vague business plan written on napkins and scrap paper. He didn't contribute anything of value."

Jake continued. "We designed our first software interface after he left. We didn't screw him out of anything."

Marc turned the monitor around and did an Internet search. Failed company. Failed company. Then nothing. He dropped off the map just about the time Jack Mineoff was hired by Stephan. "Looks like he had some good ideas but couldn't pull them off. He failed at everything he's tried since college. He probably resents the fortune you've made, Dom. It has to be him. He disappeared from the record just about the time Jack was hired by Stephan."

Jeremy said, "He must hate you for doing so well when he hasn't."

Jake asked, "Enough to mastermind something like this? Why?"

Dominic's face darkened with memories of his own journey. "Revenge."

Alethea spun on her heel and said, "I'll be right back." She practically sprinted down the hallway to get out of earshot of the other women. Her first instinct was to race to the park herself, but it would take too much time—just as it would to convince Abby to have the kids brought back to the house.

Instead, she called Marc. When he picked up, she didn't give him time to speak. "Abby just received a photo of Rosella in the park with the kids. It came from Stephan's phone."

"Shit," Marc said. "I'll call my men. No one was supposed to go out today. They said they'd all be there with you. Hold on." He spoke rapidly into a small radio he always carried with him and instructed his men to get Rosella and the babies home. Immediately. He also instructed two men to do a perimeter sweep for anyone unusual. After a moment of listening to his men report back in he said, "Alethea, they're fine and en route back to Dominic's. You did the right thing by calling me. Was there a message with the photo?"

"No," Alethea said. "Just a photo of them walking. Marc, I'm worried. This is an escalation of the baby monitor. He wants us to know that he's watching—in person. Did Jeremy find anything? It's a warning."

"Don't worry, we're handling it. We believe we know who this guy is. I'll tell you more about it tonight when I see you. The important thing is that we keep this to ourselves. You can't tell anyone what you know, Alethea. It would only scare them unnecessarily."

When Alethea didn't answer, Marc said, "More importantly, it could jeopardize our ability to catch this guy. We need him to think we have no idea who he is. Can I trust you to do the right thing here?"

"Yes," Alethea said and hung up on him. *I probably should have warned him that we might have very different ideas about what that looks like.*

Lil was behind her when she turned. "Who are you talking to?"

Don't... don't do this, Lil. "Marc," Alethea said dismissively.

"Head of security Marc?" Lil asked, her voice rising an octave with concern.

I miss my old partner in crime. How did we get to a place where we are so outside of each other's lives that you don't know about me, Marc, and everything that's going on? I wouldn't even know how to start to fill you in. "Yes."

Lil threw a frustrated hand up in the air for emphasis. "Because Stephan sent a photo to Abby? You still think he's out to hurt the family, don't you?" She shook her head and her eyes flew heavenward as if seeking assistance. "Alethea, if you don't let this go, everything we achieved today is going to fall apart. All it will take is the mention of a concern about Stephan and Nicole will freak. Marie will jump to her defense. Abby won't want to, but she'll end up asking you to leave. You promised me that you wouldn't do this."

Something inside Alethea snapped. She shook with an anger that had been building over the past year—growing larger and larger until it had the power to destroy their friendship. "What did I promise not to do? Be myself? Because that's a horrible thing? It never used to be. Not before you and Abby made up. As long as I can remember it was you and me against the world. I had your back and you had mine. Now you want to be accepted by them so much that nothing else matters to you. I don't matter to you."

"That's not true." Lil went pale and reached for her, but Alethea stepped away from her with disgust.

Maybe every childhood friendship comes to this place—the awful day when you realize you no longer have anything in common. "Yes, Lil, it is. I didn't want to see it because I didn't want to believe that our friendship was ending. But I can't be who you want me to be. And I'm tired of trying."

Alethea pushed past Lil and strode back into the atrium. Just inside the door, she stopped and said, "Abby, Marie, Nicole... I have something I need to say."

They stood and gathered around her. Lil put a hand on her arm in caution, but Alethea shook her off without even sparing her a glance. She was angry. Angrier than she'd been in a very long time. And scared. Scared this was the last time she'd be welcomed in their home.

None of this matters in the end. Judy and Colby need to be kept safe. That's what's important. She looked around and knew she couldn't lead off her story with Stephan's involvement. That would end the conversation as soon as it started, and they wouldn't hear the important part of her message.

She heard Marc's voice in her head. *If they knew you, the real you...*

Raising her chin, Alethea said, "I don't see the world the way the rest of you do. I know that. I wish I could, but I can't. There was a time, when I was very young, that I thought nothing bad could ever happen to me or my family. I learned the truth the hard way. My father never told us that he was involved in something dangerous and, because of that, I failed to protect him the day he died. I let a man walk right into our house and take papers off his desk because I trusted him. I trusted everyone back then. He used that information to have my father killed. I played a role in my father's death and I've had to live with that."

Lil gasped.

Abby stepped closer, real sympathy showing in her eyes. "I'm sorry, Alethea. What a horrible thing to happen to you while you were so young. You have to know it wasn't your fault, though."

I don't want or need her sympathy. There is a very good chance that this is the last time I see any of these people anyway. "What I know is that lies hurt. The truth is all that matters. You can't protect yourself if you live in an illusion of safety."

Marie's expression became as concerned as Abby's. "I'm not sure why you're telling us this now, but it explains a lot. Bad things happen to good people every day, Alethea. You can't let the past have so much power over you. By holding onto it, you're not only hurting yourself, you're hurting everyone who loves you."

I'm hurting all of you? Me? Of course, this is still about me and how they think I should change.

Nicole hovered on the outside of the group. "Marie's right. Letting go is the only way to find happiness."

Lil took one of Alethea's hands in both of hers. "I didn't know about your father. Are you sure? Is there a chance that you were too young to understand the circumstances?"

Alethea pulled away from Lil in outrage. *I'm so done here.* "Misunderstood? Oh, there are things I've been wrong about in the past." She looked pointedly at her friend. "But I read the original 911 transcript. The backup copy they missed during their cover-up. My father was shot. The government did their best to hide how and why, but I know what really happened. Not that any of you care about the truth."

She turned to leave, but Abby rushed to block her way. "Why share that story now? Does it have something to do with the photo Stephan sent me? If you know something, tell us."

Alethea turned back and looked around. Lil was practically begging her to remain quiet. Nicole was pale and nervous. Marie appeared torn between concern and anger. *The moment I open my mouth, I lose. I lose Lil. I lose everyone in this room.*

Dominic will be furious.

And then I lose Marc.

But if I say nothing and something happens to one of them because I said nothing, I'd never forgive myself.

I'm sorry, Marc.

You were wrong, no one wants the real me.

Straightening her shoulders, Alethea looked Abby right in the eye and said, "That photo didn't come from Stephan. Someone has been hacking into his server and, now, apparently his phone. Someone wants to make it look like Stephan is doing this, but he isn't."

Marie put a hand over her heart in shock. "What are you saying?"

"Oh, my God," Abby said in growing horror, "are the kids in danger?"

Lil rushed closer and stood beside Abby. "If you think they are, why wouldn't you tell us?"

Alethea glared at her friend. Her voice was cold as ice as she said, "You're the one who keeps telling me not to say anything." The real fear in Abby's eyes softened her tone a bit. "Don't worry, I called Marc. Rosella and the kids are safe and on their way back."

A heavy silence hung over the group, and Alethea realized they still did not entirely believe her. "Wake up and see what's going on. You've all been kept in the dark from the real danger you're in. Abby, don't let anyone close to Judy. Lil, get yourself a bodyguard and don't let Colby out of your sight. Not until whoever is doing this is caught. When your men come home tonight, demand that they tell you everything they know. It's the only way you'll be able to protect yourselves against this guy."

"You're serious," Abby said, her face losing all color.

Give me strength.

"Always. This is real. And escalating."

Wrapping both arms around her waist protectively, Nicole asked quietly, "Why do you know and we don't?"

With a harshly expelled breath, Alethea growled, "Because I found the problem first. Because I look for problems even when I shouldn't. That's who I am. Love me. Hate me. I don't give a shit. But for God's sake, protect the kids."

Unable to contain her rising temper, Alethea turned and strode out of the house. Lil tried to stop her on the way, but her words were a blur as Alethea brushed her off. As she stepped out onto the stairs, the limo with Rosella and the children pulled up in front of the house.

Another limo pulled up and Dominic leapt out of it, rushing toward little Judy. Abby arrived at the vehicle just behind him, flanked by Lil. Jake ran to Lil's side. Marie hugged Rosella, who looked a bit confused by the commotion surrounding her return.

The normally calm Abby was clutching her baby to her chest and yelling at Dominic. Jake was being similarly cornered by a very angry Lil. Nicole stood off to the side, visibly shivering. Another car pulled up and she rushed into Stephan's arms. He held her, then walked her over to the others gathered around the children.

Even in a time of turmoil they were a family—*one that I'm not part of.*

Alethea looked down at the pavement and started walking away. Two black Rockport lace-up shoes blocked her path.

"You told them."

Alethea froze at Marc's cool tone. Instantly defensive, she said, "It was the right thing to do."

"That wasn't your decision to make. We were working on this together. All of us."

Still feeling raw, Alethea snapped, "Well, maybe I don't do teams. Or friendships." She stepped to one side, but he stepped with her and blocked her. "Or relationships. Some people are meant to be on their own, and I apparently am one of those people."

"Alethea—"

The emotion of the group behind her echoed across the distance, fanning Alethea's anger. "Don't 'Alethea' me. You say you want me to be myself, but you don't mean it. You and Lil have this image of who you want me to be, but it's not me. This is me."

Dominic called Marc over. He looked like he had more to say to Alethea, but when Dominic said his name again he took a step in his direction. "I have to talk to them right now, Alethea. But this conversation isn't over."

With a brittle smile, Alethea said, "Yes, it is. It's as over as we are. Goodbye, Marc."

She walked away, head held high, hating that she wished he would follow her, because she knew that he wouldn't.

CHAPTER *Sixteen*

AT MARC'S URGING, Dominic moved the discussion off the street and into his house. The group gathered in the hearth room. Abby and Lil stood beside each other, holding their children to them even as one squirmed to get down and the other cried loudly from the stress in the room. Dominic and Jake hovered beside their furious women, attempting to explain the unexplainable. Stephan was quietly holding Nicole in his embrace.

Marc used the time to coordinate his men. He increased the number of suited men in the house. He dispersed plainclothes men and women throughout the neighborhood. Autonomy was forgotten. Everyone was to check in on a rotating fifteen-minute schedule. His closest team would filter the information and report hourly.

Marc paused and met Jake's eyes across the room. He didn't need to ask the question. Nor did he require more than a nod to implement the same plan at Jake's house. Stephan shook his head, which made sense. He had his own team, and given the same situation, Marc would have chosen his own people over others' every time.

Abby's strained voice carried across the room. "Is there anything else you're holding back?" She pinned each of the men down with the fury of a protective lioness. "God help the one of you who thinks hiding something from me now is a good idea."

Jake made an uncomfortable face. "She sounds more like Dom every day."

Lil turned to Jake and, if looks could kill, an ambulance would have been needed at the very least. Her voice was equally high and emotional. "I know you use sarcasm when you don't feel comfortable, but I'm holding on to my sanity by a very thin thread, Jake. A very thin thread. You should have told us what was going on. Someone should have told us."

Marie said softly, "Someone did."

Alethea.

Although her name wasn't uttered, everyone got her reference.

Nicole pulled back a bit, looked up at Stephan, and said, "She tried to tell me that you were involved. Actually, she said your IP address was. I didn't believe her."

Marc stepped outside of his normal silent role to defend the woman he loved. *Loved.* No use denying the undeniable. He loved her. And so would these people if they began to see her as he did. "Alethea was trying to clear Stephan's name."

Tears welled in Nicole's eyes and she searched Stephan's face. She asked, "Is that true?"

Stephan nodded and addressed the others in the room. His face was twisted with torment. "Yes, someone hacked my server and now my phone. I had no idea. We know who's doing it. I hired him and gave him access to my systems and then to Dominic's. This is my fault, Nicole. All of it."

Ever the voice of reason, Jake interjected, "You had no idea he was planning this."

Stephan's face reddened and he asked angrily, "So, you knew I was innocent?" He looked across at Dominic. "Or did you instantly believe the worst of me? What do I need to do to prove to you that last year was a mistake I deeply regret?"

Nicole tried to reassure her fiancé. "They know that, Stephan." She left his side and crossed the room to her brother in quick strides. "Tell him, Dom. Tell him that you knew he was innocent," she pleaded.

Never one to lie, Dominic said nothing.

Lil pointed back and forth between the men. "It's sort of understandable. I mean, Stephan was out to get him for years."

Abby cautioned her sister softly. "Lil..."

Over the head of his sister, Dominic growled at Stephan, "I'm not doing this right now. Your feelings don't matter when I'm receiving texts like this." He held up his phone.

Abby read the message out loud. Her voice started strong, then tapered to a horrified whisper. "Next time, I'll take more than a photo."

She hugged Judy closer to her despite the baby's cries. "Oh, my God."

Dominic pulled both wife and child into his arms. "We're going to get this guy, Abby. It's an empty threat."

Marc crossed the room and looked at the text. "This was sent a few minutes after the photo. Still using Stephan's phone."

Lil put her daughter down and took out her phone. She whipped it open and removed the battery. "Alethea taught me that. She warned me to upload encryption software, but I didn't."

Stephan took out his phone to do the same, but Jake waved a hand at him and then motioned for him to hand it over. He took out his own phone, then held out his hand to collect everyone else's. Even Marc's. He walked out of the room and then returned without them.

Jake said, "Leave your phone on, Stephan. Jeremy and my parents can wipe ours clean and double-check our safeguards. They can also try to trace whatever virus was put into your phone. But Lil is right. Until we have this guy, we have to assume our phones can be used as listening devices."

Nicole put a shaky hand up to her mouth. "Is this about what happened last year?"

Marie put an arm around a sobbing Rosella. In a firm voice, she said, "Forget last year. We need to focus on what is happening right now. Not old wounds. We all just had a good scare. Take this as a reminder to never relax our guard. No one becomes successful without encountering people who want to take that success away. Life was easier when you all felt you had nothing to lose, but with happiness comes the responsibility of protecting it. So, I don't want to hear about last year, or five years ago. I want to know who this asshole is and how we are going to fucking get him." In the shocked silence that followed her tirade, she said, "I swore. Get over it. Someone threatened my babies today. I've never been this angry. I want this bastard found."

Dominic rubbed his forehead roughly. "Marc, how close are we to finding this guy?"

"Jeremy has his real name and is searching every legal databases, and some that are illegal, too. We'll have a breakthrough soon. Then it's just a matter of cornering the rat. This time we won't simply shut Sliver down—we'll drive him out of his hiding place."

Dominic walked to the corner of the room, picked up the landline, and dialed a number. He turned his back to the others in the room and said, "I'm calling in your debt." After listening to the reply, Dominic said, "Yes, and I need someone with political immunity to do it."

As he continued his conversation in a lower tone, Marie pried a crying Judy from Abby's arms. "Rosella and I will take the babies to the other room." When Abby moved to follow, Marie said, "Judy doesn't know what's going on. She'll be happy with a bottle and a nap. Stay with your husband. He needs you right now."

Abby nodded and went to Dominic's side, linking her hand with his. Her unspoken support for whatever he was planning was clear.

And the move touched Marc. They were a team. *Strong. Solid.*

That was love.

Alethea was the only woman he could picture having that with. More than just chemistry—she had the potential to be a real partner. He respected her intelligence, admired her spirit. Sexy as hell and passionate about the same things he was—she was his future. He'd never been as sure of anything as he was of that.

When Dominic hung up the phone and rejoined the group, Nicole looked around frantically and said, "Stephan's gone."

Jake rushed out of the room and then quickly returned. "He left his phone, but his car is gone."

Nicole went to the window. "He's going after Sliver himself."

Jake shook his head. "That's not wise. We don't know what Sliver is capable of. We don't even know where he is."

Marc added his thoughts from across the room. "Stephan has leads of his own. He might be following one of those. I'll see if Jeremy has found anything. I'm in radio contact with my men. If you want to send me a message, contact me that way. The line's encryption algorithm is changed daily so it should be secure."

Dominic said, "I'm coming with you."

"No," Marc answered firmly. "This is what you pay me to do."

"If you think I am going to sit here while..." His voice cracked with emotion. Abby tucked herself under Dominic's arm and hugged him.

Marc nodded toward Abby. "You need to be here in case Sliver tries anything else. I'll find Stephan and get this guy. You keep your family safe."

Jake pulled Lil closer. Marc completely understood. Risking their necks in foreign countries while completing dubious government deals had always been a thrill. Waiting for the next move of a sociopath who threatened the ones they loved—there was nothing exciting about that. That kind of threat was a game changer.

Nothing else mattered.

Not the financial empire they'd built.

Not their power or influence.

This was war.

Marc was headed toward the door when Lil called out his name. He stopped and turned. She said, "If I know Al, and I do, she's going after him, too. She may be angry with me, but she would never walk away while any of us were in trouble." Her eyes filled with tears. "I tried to text her right after she left, but she's not answering me. If your paths cross in this, tell her that I love her. And tell her to be careful."

With a nod, Marc turned and walked out. Behind the steering wheel of his Lexus, he confronted his greatest fear. *I might not be in time.* He had to get a step ahead of her before she faced Sliver alone. *This time I'm bringing everyone out alive.*

How would Alethea find Sliver?

Jeremy.

Back at Andrade Global, Stephan met with the team he'd assembled when he'd first learned that his server had been hacked. Only the most loyal to him had been informed of the threat, and even then they were not told the whole story. They were told a hacker was trying to sabotage Dominic's company and he was using his prior access to Andrade Global to do it.

"Do we have any new leads?" Stephan demanded loudly.

One of his men stepped forward with a folder. "We found a loft apartment in the Meat Packing District that Jack Mineoff bought under his real name. He still pays utilities there."

Stephan took the folder and looked over the photos and descriptions inside. *Sliver is smarter than this. It's almost as if he wants us to find him.* "I don't like it," he said. "It feels too easy."

His head of security shrugged. "Maybe he didn't consider that you'd become close enough to Dominic to be able to discover his real name."

"Maybe," Stephan said. "I still don't like it. We need to check out if he still lives in that loft. Two of you will come with me. The rest of you, I want you here digging up anything and everything you can on this guy. If he went to the dentist in the past few years, I want to know about it. Everything." Walking over to his desk, he said, "Meet me in the outer office in five minutes. I need to make a call before we go. Wear your tactical vests. This guy is dangerous."

The men nodded and left, closing the door behind them. He punched in an international number on his office landline and waited.

"Pronto!"

"Dad."

His father instantly switched over to English. "Are you all right? You sound upset. Has something happened?"

"Not yet, but I have something I need to ask you."

There was a short pause and then Victor said, "Anything. You know that."

He knew his father meant it, and if there was time he might have taken him up on his offer, but what he had to do couldn't wait for the time it would take his family to gather. "If anything ever happens to me, I need to know that you and the family will take care of Nicole."

He didn't try to hide the seriousness of the situation. Victor was the strongest man Stephan had ever met—a good man who deserved better than this from his only son.

"What's going on, Stephan?"

"I can't tell you, Dad. Just promise me that you'll be there for her. I don't want her to ever feel alone or afraid again."

"Are you in some sort of trouble?" Victor asked urgently. "Tell me what you need. We have friends who can help. Influential friends. Have you spoken to Dominic?"

"He's the one who needs the help this time, Dad, and it's because of what I did last year. I caused this problem and I'm going to eradicate it. I appreciate your offer, but I'll never be free from the past unless I face it myself. Don't worry, I have my own resources. I'm not alone."

"I can be back in New York by tonight."

"It'll be over by then, Dad. I'll call you this afternoon and hopefully have good news for you."

"And if you don't call?"

Stephan knew that if he met up with Sliver one of them wasn't coming back alive, and there would be consequences for the one who lived. "Just know that I love you."

Stephan hung up the receiver. He opened the bottom drawer of his desk, took out a loaded gun, and tucked it into the belt of his suit pants. He walked to the changing room where he kept extra suits and took out a Christmas gift from Lil's paranoid friend Alethea. A bullet-resistant suit jacket. After the fiasco at Abby's baby shower, Alethea had reached out to all of them in one way or another. He remembered laughing when he'd received it and wondering what sort of person would actually wear it.

He wasn't laughing anymore.

Alethea called Jeremy's office phone. It rang four times, then went to voice mail. Alethea called back. *Pick up. Pick up, Jeremy.*

"Hello?"

"Jeremy, it's Alethea. Don't hang up. Dominic asked me to call you for an update."

"Really? Do you think I don't know when you're lying?"

With a loud sigh, Alethea said, "Fine. I've just had a blowout fight with all of them. None of them will probably ever talk to me again, but that doesn't change what I need to do. I'm going to take this guy Sliver down, and you're going to help me."

Jeremy was not that easily convinced. "Jake told me to report whatever I found directly to him and only him."

Come on, Jeremy. I know you. I know you want to do this. "Jake handled it last time and look what happened. He didn't finish it. He has a family now and it's made him overly cautious. Something Sliver took advantage of."

"I want to say, yes, but I told Jeisa..."

"One more time, Jeremy. Just one more time. I'll never ask you for anything again. This isn't about me, it's about saving people who are also very important to you. Sometimes it doesn't matter how angry people get, what matters is that you do what has to be done. We can beat this guy, Jeremy. You know we can."

After a slight pause, Jeremy said, "I don't have anything more than Sliver's real name."

"Then hack into Stephan's server. He's had his men working on this. Maybe they have a lead."

"He has sewn his server up—it's airtight now."

Really, Jeremy? You forget how well I know you. "You went in with full access. Don't tell me you didn't create a back door just in case he ended up being involved after all. I won't believe it. No one changes that much."

With a guttural sound of frustration, Jeremy admitted, "Don't tell anyone. I wasn't planning to, but I couldn't trust him completely. Not with all that is at stake."

That's the man I know. "Your secret is safe with me. Now, what did they discover?"

Jeremy typed furiously for a moment, then said, "They went old-school and offline. Looks like one of his guys found something in the city records about a purchase of a loft in the Meat Packing District made under his real name a year ago. I should have thought of that. That's so simple I can't believe I missed it."

"Why would a man who doesn't want to be found buy property under his own name?"

"Either he's stupid or..."

"Or he wants us to find it."

"Like a trap?"

"Maybe. When was that file last opened?"

"About half an hour ago."

"That gives Stephan enough time to hear about it and head over there."

"Al, Sliver will be ready for him. If that's his lair, it's going to be well protected."

Alethea cornered her car decisively. "Send me every bit of information you can about the building his apartment is in. I want the layout, recent and old. Everything."

"On it."

Marc stormed into Jeremy's office a short time later. "Have you heard from Alethea?"

Jeremy didn't say anything, but he wouldn't meet Marc's eyes.

Marc walked over, laid both of his hands flat on Jeremy's desk, and leaned down so he was eye to eye with Jeremy. "I need to know what you told her."

Jeremy stood and met Marc's aggressive stance with his own. "To stop her? You can't, you know. I've never seen her as dead set on something as she is on this. You'd be better off staying out of the cross fire."

With a growl, Marc grabbed Jeremy by his shirt collar and hauled him halfway across the desk. "She is not going in alone." He let Jeremy go just as roughly.

Jeremy adjusted his shirt and stood tall. He'd need a good reason to betray his friend.

Marc played his last card. "I love her. We're a team, even if she can't see that yet. I will not let her get herself killed today."

With a slowly expelled breath, Jeremy said, "We found an apartment Sliver bought under his real name about a year ago. Stephan is headed there. Alethea is trying to get there before him, but he had a head start."

"How do you know where Stephan went?"

"Is this a trick question?"

"Just tell me. It may matter."

"I still have remote access to Stephan's server."

Marc frowned, but decided not to pursue that revelation at this time. "And?"

"And the address was in the last report his men pulled. It makes sense that he's headed there."

"I'll need that address and any other information you have. Now."

Jeremy hit a button to print out a shot of his screen. With some sarcasm he said, "I don't mind helping you people, but would a please or a thank you now and then kill you?"

Marc took the papers from Jeremy and shook his head as he focused on more serious matters. "What I don't get is if this guy, Sliver, is so smart, why wouldn't he start his own company instead of targeting Dominic's?"

Jeremy sat back down in his chair. "Intelligence doesn't ensure success, and revenge can become an addiction. Sliver wants to be important, but he chose a negative way to go about it. He tears things down instead of building anything of his own. It's a lifestyle that has become an obsession."

"Creating a man who is capable of anything," Marc said, as he built a mental profile of his target.

"Exactly."

Chapter *Seventeen*

STEPHAN AND HIS men did a second sweep of the loft apartment. It was devoid of furniture. A huge empty space filled with a disappointing amount of nothing. *If he doesn't live here, why buy the place?*

Had it been easy for us to find for the simple reason that it wasn't important?

Like the coding errors, is this place just another distraction?

He sent two of his men out. One to the roof. One to the street.

I'm here, Sliver. Just where you'd hoped someone would be. But why?

One of his men returned. "Nothing on the roof. Are we done here?"

Stephan nodded reluctantly. "I guess we are. Let's head back. Give the security guy downstairs another tip on our way out. We may need to come back. There has to be a reason Sliver bought this place and I intend to find out what that is."

The guard stepped through the door first. Before Stephan had time to react, it slammed shut behind the guard, trapping Stephan inside the apartment. A thick metal sheet slid across the door, locked into place, and beeped.

A man's voice spoke through an intercom from above. "Tell your men to leave the building. You didn't just hear an alarm arming. That was a remote-activated bomb—aka my insurance that you'll do as I tell you."

When his guard banged on the door, Stephan said loudly, "The door is rigged. Don't touch it."

"Now tell him to leave. Unless you want him to die with you. An unnecessary loss."

"Get out of here, Steve, and evacuate everyone you can."

"Uh, uh, uh. I wouldn't do that. That would bring the police. Warn anyone and I push the trigger now. How noble of you to want to save strangers along with your men. And you can save them. You can save them all. All you have to do is help me."

"Help you?" Stephan cased the loft with new motivation. There had to be another way out.

"Tell your men to go. Just your men. I'm watching every move you make so I'll know if you try to fool me. Send them out of the area and then we'll talk."

"Sliver? Or, more accurately, Kurtis."

No answer.

Stephan spoke to his men through the door. "I need you to pull back from the building. Both of you."

"Out of the area," Sliver warned. "It's an easy equation. I see them and you die."

Stephan slammed a fist into the wall beside him but said loudly, "Give this place a half-mile radius."

"What about—" Steve started to say, but Stephan cut him off.

"Do it."

"Yes, sir," Steve said, then asked, "Do you want me to call anyone?"

"No," Stephan ordered. "Wait for me to contact you. I don't want anyone else coming here until we know what we're dealing with."

"Yes, sir," Steve said and left.

Stephan paced the loft's entryway angrily.

"How touching. So concerned for others. A good man with a bad reputation. Another Corisi casualty." Sliver's voice dripped with sarcasm.

Stephan began searching the loft again for anything that would turn the tables in his favor. "I know who you are now. I know everything about you. You say Dominic stole your ideas and built his fortune with them. He didn't, you know. That's why you're so angry. Your contribution was a mediocre suggestion at best."

"Mediocre? I'm the one who suggested the future lay in interfacing technologies. I saw the trend. I knew where the money would be."

Yes, get angry. Give me something to use. "An insight they took advantage of, but they didn't throw you out, did they? Your mistake was thinking you could do better without them."

"And your mistake was switching sides at the last minute. I could have destroyed him last year in a cleaner fashion. No one had to die. You should have let me finish what we started. The bloodshed will be on your conscience. You pushed me to this."

Years of hating Dominic gave Stephan a sad and unique insight into Sliver's twisted thinking. Could he use that bond to gain Sliver's trust? "You don't have to do this. I know. I hated Dominic. I lost sight of who I was, and everything became about beating him. It almost cost me everything. My family. My future. Everything. You can stop before this goes any further. It's never too late to realize that revenge is a dark monster that destroys even its master."

"And what? We all become friends? How has that worked for you?"

Stephan didn't say anything. His words found a fresh wound Stephan didn't want to acknowledge. Dominic still thought the worst of him. There was a chance he always would. He hoped to God the love he shared with Nicole was strong enough to survive that truth.

Sliver continued. "Imagine your life without Dominic. Wouldn't it be wonderful? All you have to do is call him and tell him that you're here. Tell him how you tried to stop me but failed and need him. When he comes—leave. I'll give you time to save everyone else in the building. I believe there is a sweet woman living just below who has two young children. One is sick and home with her today. What a shame if you choose not to help me and they pay the price."

"You're a sick bastard."

"We can spin this scenario so you win. You get his sister without having to deal with him. The news will credit you for risking your life to save everyone in the building. Hell, you'll be a hero. So, what's it going to be? How much is your rival's life worth to you?"

Taking a deep breath, Stephan made one of the most difficult decisions of his life.

CHAPTER *Eighteen*

DRESSED IN A blonde wig, baggy jeans, and a sweatshirt, Alethea assessed the building Jeremy had directed her to. She stood at a safe enough distance that it was unlikely Sliver would use surveillance cameras where she was. Jeremy had given her the blueprints of the loft apartment building. She studied the surrounding area.

Why? Why this building? This area?

She was so engrossed she screamed when a hand closed over her arm. The sound was quickly silenced by a male hand over her mouth, and she was pulled backward off the street into an alley. Her heart pounded loudly in her chest.

Thankfully, she recognized that touch.

And the strong chest pressed against her back.

Marc.

He removed his hand and turned her. Without stopping to think, she threw her arms around his neck and met his mouth halfway. The kiss they shared was a declaration. An affirmation of what they both knew but hadn't yet vocalized.

He broke it off and hugged her to him.

"How did you find me?" she asked.

He kissed her forehead. "I talked to Jeremy. He told me you'd be here, so I had my men perform a shrinking sweep of the surrounding area."

She shook her head in self-disgust. "I should have been watching my back as well as doing reconnaissance. I know better."

He ran a hand down her back, cupping one of her ass cheeks possessively. "You don't have to watch your back. I'm more than happy to do it."

Heart still thudding in her chest, she rolled her eyes and asked, "Did you seriously just go there?"

He tapped her nose with one finger in reprimand. "Hey, no critiquing my sexual banter. I'm working the moment here." He kissed her deeply again and said, "Promise me one thing."

After a kiss like that—anything.

"Yes?" she asked huskily.

"Save that wig for later. I love it." The devilish grin he shot her sent a wave of desire through her.

"This is not helping," she said dryly, but in fact it was. *I'm not alone. He came.*

"Right." Marc shook his head as if to clear it. "Do you have anyone planted in the area?"

Alethea pointed westward. "I have a dog walker if I need him, but I didn't want to send him in until I knew what I was dealing with. I have a bad feeling about this. It was too easy to find him. He wanted to be found."

"I agree. Jeremy voiced the same concern. That's why we're sweeping inward. I'm treating this area like a minefield because it just may be." Marc turned his head away for a moment as he listened to his earpiece. "We just made contact with one of Stephan's men. They were inside the loft when they were separated and somehow Stephan got locked inside. They heard another man's voice and then Stephan told them to fall back and stay there until he contacts them."

Alethea leapt out of Marc's embrace. "Sliver has Stephan."

Tight-lipped, Marc nodded. "It looks that way. I have enough men to surround the building. And snipers. I can set up a perimeter that he can't escape and then we'll lure him out."

Alethea grabbed his arm. "No. Hang on. Why would Stephan send his men away?"

"Because someone has a gun to his head?"

No, that's not it. I am way too nauseated for it to be that simple. "A gun would be a direct attack. That's how you'd go after someone. Sliver is as much a coward as he is a genius. He's not in that building. He's nearby—watching. I know it."

Alethea was used to people dismissing her theories, but Marc nodded in full agreement. He rubbed his chin thoughtfully, then asked, "Does all that watching require something we could trace? Like an unusually high amount of electrical usage?"

A smile spread across Alethea's face. "You're a genius."

He shot her a humble smile. "No, but I've watched spy movies." Then he pulled her back into his arms. "We're going to get this bastard."

Alethea wasn't quite as confident. Having a hostage definitely gave Sliver an advantage. "What makes you so sure?"

The warm smile he gave her sent her heart beating wildly. "Because Sliver planned for Jeremy and Stephan. He even planned for me." He hugged her closer and nuzzled her neck. "But no one—no one can prepare for you."

She raised one eyebrow and leaned back. "I believe you just gave me a compliment." When he smiled down unabashedly at her, her confidence rose. *I hope to hell I'm half as good as he thinks I am.* She took out her phone and called Jeremy. "Jeremy, I need you to hack into Con Edison for me."

Jeremy instantly began typing. "We definitely need to start speaking in code. Okay, I'm in. What are we looking for?"

"Someone using enough electricity to power a command center in one of the nearby buildings."

"Gotcha. Brilliant."

Alethea looked up into a watchful pair of blue eyes. "It was Marc's idea."

Jeremy's typing didn't pause as he answered, "I like him."

"Me, too," Alethea said, then blushed when amusement filled Marc's eyes and she realized he'd heard Jeremy's comment.

"Found one," Jeremy said with enthusiasm. "It's across the street to the left. It has had at least two complaints from Con Edison regarding excessive usage."

"We've got him," Alethea said, and threw her arms triumphantly around Marc.

It took everything in Marc to resist picking Alethea up and carrying her as far away as he could from Sliver and the very real danger he posed. Over the years, Marc had stood proudly as the front line of Dominic's security. He'd faced rebels, foreign police forces, and hired assassins.

Negotiating the deals Dominic and Jake had made over the years had taken them all into dicey situations, where the fact that they'd survived, had often been an inexplicable miracle. It was how Dominic had made his fortune. There wasn't a country he wouldn't deal with. No toppling government was too dangerous to bargain with. They'd checked their morality at the door and done whatever was necessary—short of murder—to achieve their goals.

Marc didn't regret a moment of it. His loyalty to his boss had always come first. Without question. Without hesitation.

But he wasn't as generous when it came to Alethea's life. She had the heart of a Marine and the kick-ass attitude to be an honorary one, as far as he was concerned. He thought back to the men he had fought beside and lost, and closed his eyes briefly. He couldn't lose Alethea, too.

But he also knew she wouldn't leave, no matter what he said. She understood the risks and yet she wouldn't leave this battleground willingly. He held her closer and breathed in her perfume.

Sophisticated.
Bold.
Just like her.

Oblivious to Marc's inner turmoil, Alethea continued to direct Jeremy as she put him on speakerphone. "Are you able to cut off the electricity to that apartment? The one across the street?"

"I can shut off the whole building. The street, if you need it," Jeremy answered.

"Good. Marc has men in the area. We can surround him where he is and, if we take away his eyes and ears, Marc can extricate him. But we'll need to time this perfectly." She met Marc's eyes. "If Sliver has that loft rigged somehow, we'll have to make him believe that keeping Stephan alive is his bargaining chip."

Her eyes held the answer Marc feared. "While you...?"

Alethea met his eyes boldly. "I'm going to free Stephan. I've never met a security system I couldn't breach."

Except mine.

She flashed a smile at him, acknowledging that she knew exactly what he'd been thinking. "Honestly, I didn't try that hard with yours."

Jaw tight, Marc demanded what he knew she couldn't promise. "You get in. Get Stephan and get out." Then he surprised even himself by saying, "Because I won't lose you now. I have every intention of marrying you."

Alethea pulled back with irritation rather than the rosy, pleased flush he'd expected. "Marry? Are you seriously picking this moment to ask me?"

"Who said I'm asking? We belong together." His smile became more confident as he said it out loud.

"No."

His smile dimmed. "No?"

She put a hand on either hip. "This is not how you are going to propose to me. I want flowers. I want you down on your knee. All that hokey romantic stuff. And a ring. Something tasteful."

There's the woman I love. Tough as nails on the outside, but on the inside, wanting to be loved and cherished just as much as any other. It was a heady combination for him. She would indeed be a real partner to him in life, but she also needed him—just as much as he needed her.

Marc kissed her until the anger left her, and then teased, "How about I just toss you in my trunk, marry you quick, and make it up to you during our honeymoon?"

Before Alethea could answer, Jeremy's voice rang out from the phone she still held in one hand. "Uh, guys? I don't want to interrupt, but this is getting awkward. Do you want to call me back when you have a timetable?"

Back to business. Marc took the phone. "Jeremy, I may need a direct link to Sliver's phone, in case we need to negotiate with him." He quickly kissed Alethea's upturned nose, then set her back from him.

He'd said what he needed to say, and although she hadn't said yes, she'd given him an answer he could work with. "Once we do this, it has to go down fast. Sliver's too smart to be kept off balance long. We don't want to give him time to come up with plan B."

Jeremy said, "I can't imagine this failing. Not with the two of you working together. Is there anything else you need?"

Marc held out a hand to Alethea.

She placed her hand in his and wordlessly accepted the meaning behind his offer.

"I have what I need right here," Marc said, as he raised her hand to his mouth and kissed the back of it. "And we're going to kick some ass today."

After they outlined a plan to Jeremy, there was no time to second-guess it. Marc radioed his men and put everyone in position to move in once the electricity was cut. Alethea would use that brief chaos to free Stephan. Jeremy sent over the specs for both buildings.

Marc gave Alethea one final, deep kiss. When they separated, she said softly, "Don't you get killed, Marc. Don't you dare get killed. I didn't mean it when I said I don't need anyone."

He checked his watch, had Jeremy start the countdown to blackout, and said, "I'm not going anywhere. I have a proposal to plan."

She gave him a cheeky smile. "Go big or go home."

Jeremy interrupted their banter. "Blackout in ten minutes. Good luck guys."

Marc hung up the phone and walked out of the alley side by side with Alethea. After she crossed the street, he signaled his men to close in and then sprinted into the other building and up the stairway to the fourth floor where, if they were correct, he'd find the only man he'd ever looked forward to killing.

CHAPTER *Nineteen*

STEPHAN FLIPPED HIS wallet open and took out a small photo of Nicole. He remembered exactly when it had been taken. Last Christmas, at his uncle's home. They'd been opening Christmas presents in a large group and one of his young cousins had tackled Nicole to thank her. She'd rolled back onto the couch with him, laughing. Her eyes had sparkled with so much love and laughter when she'd righted herself, that he hadn't been able to resist snapping a photo. She'd never been more beautiful to him or more a part of his family.

He gave the photo one last look, then placed it in the pocket near his heart. *I'm sorry, Nicole. You deserve a better man than I am. I brought this on us and I wish there were a way I could spare you from what I have to do.*

Forgive me.

He cleared his throat and said, "Sliver, I've decided to take you up on your deal."

Sounding gleeful, Sliver answered, "Excellent. I knew you would. You win this way."

"Yes. I do. But I have one condition."

"You don't get to make conditions," Sliver protested angrily. "I'm in control here."

"Kurtis, we've worked together for a long time. You know how much I hate Dominic. But you also know that I need a guarantee that this will be clean. I won't make a phone call unless you clear this building of people. Tell them it's a gas leak."

"Why would I do that?"

"Because, just like me, you don't want witnesses. The more people involved, the more risk there is that the truth will come out. You kill them, you bring unwanted attention to both of us. Get rid of them and I'll make sure Dominic comes alone. You won't have to blow up the building. You can bide your time and pick him off with a sniper shot if you want. Clean. Or drug him and take him somewhere else to dispose of him. I don't care. But if you think I'm going to let this become an FBI investigation that lands me in prison, you're insane."

There was a long pause, then Sliver asked, "How do I know I can trust you to follow through if I clear the building?"

Stephan chose his words carefully. "You were right. I never stopped hating Dominic. My life will be better without him. My only regret is that you'll be the one who gets to kill him."

After another long pause, Sliver said, "I've just sent a message via the gas company's computer to the woman downstairs. Gas leak, just as you said. Immediate evacuation necessary."

Stephan heard the phone ring downstairs. Followed by a rustling, then a door slamming. Stephan watched from the window to ensure that she did indeed leave the building with her child. He let out a sigh of relief when he saw both enter a taxi moments later.

His relief was short-lived. "Now, make the call," Sliver demanded.

Stephan put a hand over the photo in his pocket and said, "Go to hell."

"But you said..."

Stephan laughed in triumph. "How can someone be so smart and remain so gullible? Dominic is my family and, to an Andrade, family is everything. I would never give him to you."

With a voice that held a hint of desperation, Sliver threatened, "You think I won't press the button? You think I won't blow you up? You're wrong. If you won't make the call, you're worthless to me. At least I can enjoy watching you die."

"Do it, you coward. If killing me gives Dominic a heads-up on where you are, then I die happy. Your plan for revenge has gotten sloppy, my friend. How does it feel to know that you won't live much longer than I will?"

CHAPTER *Twenty*

JEREMY'S PHONE CALL drained all color from Dominic's face. He looked across the room at his sister, who was sitting stiffly on the edge of a chair, watching him. Her expression turned hopeful when their eyes met.

I can't tell her what's really happening. I swore I would never be the reason she cried again.

Abby was at his side in a flash. "Who was that?"

Even though he wanted to, he couldn't lie to her. "Jeremy."

"What did he say?" She grabbed his arm desperately.

Dominic pulled her to him and just held her for a moment. Not since the birth of Judy had he felt so unsure of what to do. Stephan was wrong; Kurtis was not his fault. *I did this to my family. I let my anger divide us and gave Sliver the advantage.* "Jeremy is working with Alethea and Marc as we speak. They found Stephan. Sliver has him."

Nicole stood up and swayed. "What do you mean, Sliver has Stephan? Has him how? Has him where? Is he hurt?"

They were past sugarcoating the events. "Somehow Sliver locked Stephan in his loft apartment. Stephan ordered his men to fall back. Alethea and Marc think that means Sliver rigged the building to explode."

Abby wrapped her arms around Dominic's waist and hugged him tightly. The shiver he felt pass through her tore at him.

It should be me in that loft.

With tears in her eyes, Abby asked, "What does this guy want?"

Dominic looked down and tucked a stray hair tenderly behind one of her ears. *God, I love this woman. I know she won't want to hear what I have to say, and I hope she forgives me.* "Me. He wasn't expecting Stephan to show up."

Nicole rushed to her brother's side. "If he doesn't want him, he'll let him go, right?"

Dominic shook his head slowly.

Abby sensed a change in Dominic. She searched his face for confirmation of what she knew was coming. "Don't go, Dominic. Marc is already there. He won't let anything happen to Stephan."

Dominic slowly released Abby. "You know I have to do this," he said softly. "Jake, I need your helicopter."

Abby covered her face with both hands and started to cry.

Jake shook his head. "This is what he wants you to do, Dom. He wants to lure you out. This is a game to him."

Very gently, Dominic took Abby's hands in his and leaned down to kiss her wet cheek. "Abby, you came into my life and made me a better man. I know what's important now. I can't sit here while a member of my family is in danger." He turned and touched his sister's shoulder softly. "You will have your wedding day, Nicole. I'll make sure of it. And your husband will be my brother."

Nicole threw herself in her brother's arms and sobbed.

Fresh tears streamed down Abby's cheeks, but she met Dominic's eyes and nodded. She gripped her hands in front of her. "You get this guy, Dom, and you make sure he can never hurt us again."

Lil didn't try to stop Jake when he went to stand beside his business partner. Instead, she took her sister's hand in one of her own and Nicole's hand in her other. She said, "They aren't going in alone. Alethea is there and I've never seen her fail."

Abby hugged Lil and looked up at the ceiling. "I swear if no one dies today I am going to hug that woman until it gets embarrassingly awkward."

Dominic was suddenly all business. "Marc said they have the ground covered. I want to be in the air in case Sliver has an upward escape planned. We'll land on the roof."

Jake instructed one of the security men to relay a radio message to his pilot. "Are we taking anyone with us?"

Dominic named his elite team. They'd traveled with him around the globe and could be trusted with any situation that developed.

"Should we call the police for backup?" Jake asked.

Adrenaline rushed in and Dominic smiled. "No. When we catch this guy—and we will—he's not going to prison. Not an American one, anyway."

Poised just outside of street camera range, Alethea waited. Hopefully their plan would completely blind Sliver, but she couldn't count on that. In the event that it didn't, she would still have a limited window in which to move in while he was distracted by the surprise.

She'd joked with Marc that she was smarter than Sliver, but the last four minutes of waiting had been long enough for her to run a hundred worst-case scenarios through her head. What if he had a generator? What if he wasn't in the building she'd sent Marc to? What if basing her decisions on her instincts was foolhardy? They had no hard evidence of his exact location. She'd risked Marc's life as well as her own on a hunch.

She let out a long, calming breath.

Focus.

Focus on what you can control.

She checked her watch.

Two minutes until blackout.

A woman and a child came out of the building and hailed a taxi. The woman looked worriedly back at the building.

Is her exit a coincidence?

Had Sliver sent her out? Had Stephan? Why would they clear the building?

This is bad.

A quick flash of her life before her eyes brought her some pleasure and some shame. She glanced up at the clear sky above.

I haven't lived a perfect life.

I'm not always kind.

I tend to think my way is the only way.

If my life ends today, let it be for something. Help me beat this bastard.

She grimaced.

Sorry about the profanity.

Although, I'm sure your shockability has been tested by worse.

Anyway, if you can hear me, take care of Marc. He's a good man. Ideally, the one I'll marry and have kids with. I know, me with kids. Shocking, right? Well, it's your fault for giving women damn internal biological clocks.

She almost swore again, but caught herself.

No offense meant regarding the clock thing.

Listen, I'm not good at this, but I'd like to think you wouldn't show me all I could have just to take it away.

I'll make you a deal.

I'll stop reading erotica on the Internet if you let us all live through this.

Shit, I probably shouldn't have admitted I do that.

And what happens if I break that promise? I'm right in the middle of a series.

Stop. This isn't helping.

Note to self: Never pray under pressure.

She looked down at her watch again.

Thirty seconds.

One last glance upward.

Let's keep this simple.

I'll try to be a better person, and you do whatever you can today.

We'll figure the rest out later.

Her phone beeped softly and she took off across the street. She looked up at the window and saw Stephan. Or more importantly, he saw her. He tried to wave her away. She whipped her wig off, never so happy to have signature red hair.

The revelation of her identity didn't stop his frantic waving. He was pounding on the window, then bringing his hands together and outward repeatedly in a mime of an explosion. She nodded that she understood, then pointed to herself, then him.

He shook his head and banged on the window again. The sound of his pounding ended only when she entered the main lobby of the building. The lights were out. A security man at the front desk was trying to make a phone call, then put down the phone in frustration and picked up his cell phone instead. Alethea leaned over the desk, gave him a flirty smile, and grabbed his phone.

"What the hell?" he said, standing aggressively.

Her expression instantly turned serious. "Something sick is about to go down. Whatever they are paying you to work here is not worth it. I'm taking your phone as a favor. They can trace shit like this. If they know where you are, you won't get out of here alive."

A betraying sheen of sweat on the guard's forehead reflected the dim light coming through the entrance. "They? Is this about the guys who were here earlier? I let them upstairs, but they didn't really give me a choice."

"I'm not allowed to tell you more than that. This is a classified operation, but it's going bad—and fast. You can stay and die or run now. You decide." She held out his phone. "Want it back?"

He shook his head.

"Don't say a word to anyone. Right now you're off the radar. I'll tell them that you saw nothing. But if you call the police or tell anyone about today, you won't live to tell the story twice. They have people who clean up messes like that. You don't know who you're dealing with."

Reality didn't matter. People watched enough crazy crap on TV to believe even the most far-fetched scenario. Her lie would save his life, just not the way he thought. Either way, if the building blew he'd be out of it.

"Do you have any ID?" he asked, remaining skeptical a bit longer than most.

She lifted one side of her shirt and revealed her holster and gun.

He turned and ran.

Okay, that's one man to remember not to hire.

She used his phone to contact Jeremy. "The electricity is off, but that might not be enough. Stephan definitely thinks this place is about to blow. I'm at the security station downstairs and there's a computer."

He asked her for some information, then said, "I'm in. What am I looking for?"

"Work orders? Something electrical in nature? If Sliver was here installing something he had to have a cover for it."

"Got it. Trouble with a cable box on the same floor about a month ago. It required some external wiring."

"That's all you have?"

"So far. I'll keep looking."

"I hope that's it. Where is it?"

"Second floor. The loft is the first door on the right."

Alethea was already sprinting up the stairs. She called to Stephan through the door.

His answer was swift and authoritative. "Alethea, get out. The door is reinforced with a steel panel and Sliver is about to remote-blow this place. Go now."

Into the phone she said, "Jeremy, there is nothing on this side of the door. I don't see how he wired it."

"Is there something on the other side?" Jeremy asked.

Alethea finally answered the man she'd come to save. "Stephan, I'm not leaving without you, so forget it. How did you get locked in?"

"We came in. We didn't find anything and were leaving when the door slammed and locked. Sliver was keeping in contact via an intercom, but he fell silent a few minutes ago."

That means we have a chance. "Good. Look around the door. There has to be something that is concealing a control device."

"Not good," Stephan said roughly. "The last thing Sliver said was goodbye. He said he'd enjoy watching the fireworks."

Although her heart was thudding painfully in her chest and adrenaline was rushing through her veins, Alethea kept her calm. All that stood between her and her goal was one measly security system. "Stephan, focus. He may or may not be neutralized by now, but you can seriously increase the likelihood of us surviving by helping me here. Do you see a box near the door? An intercom? A security pad?"

Sounding calmer, Stephan said, "There is an intercom, but it's not what he was speaking through."

"Good. Open it."

There was a rustle and then Stephan said, "I had to get something to pry it with, but I opened it. There is a keypad behind it."

Yes. Yes. Yes. "Jeremy, we found a keypad near the door. It has to open it."

"Or it's rigged to the bomb," Jeremy said dryly.

She considered his warning, then dismissed it. "No, Sliver wouldn't need it. He has everything at the other place. He's not a self-destruct kind of guy. Rip out that panel, Stephan."

Stephan hesitated. "Are you sure? Jeremy could be right."

For once, just believe me. "I'm sure enough to be standing on the other side of the door while you do it. If I'm wrong, we both pay for the mistake. Rip it."

There was the sound of metal being bent. "Done. What do you want me to do?"

Let it be easy. Come on. "Turn the panel over. Is there a serial number? A brand? "

"Yes," Stephan said in surprise.

Perfect. "I need you to read off all the information. Jeremy, you may have to hack, or you may find the information on a help page. How do I reset this thing?"

Jeremy laughed a bit sarcastically. "He used a market model?"

"His laziness is our salvation."

Jeremy searched, then came back on the line. "There is a tiny button. Reset it with a clip or a pen. Then type in this reset code and it should work."

There was a momentary silence from Stephan, and then he responded, "Looks like my pen will fit. Will this work if there is no electricity? The panel is dark."

Oh, ye of little experience breaking into places. "Most security systems have a small battery installed as a backup. It gives you time in case of an outage. Often not enough juice to light the panel, but enough to surge and open the door."

Jeremy cleared his throat. "Hey, Alethea. Before you do that. I have something I need to say."

Alethea took a deep breath. *Please don't ask me to waste my last few moments on earth apologizing again for being bitchy to your girlfriend. I've said I'm sorry already.* "Yes?"

"If you survive this, you will always be welcomed in the home Jeisa and I make together. I see now that I was just as much at fault for what happened as you were."

He doesn't think this is going to work. He may be right. "I should have been a better friend to you, Jeremy. I should have been nicer to Jeisa. From now on, I'm going to be a better person. Marc is my chance to get it right."

Stephan cut in harshly. "Can we talk about all this after you tell me how to reset this thing? All this good-bye shit is freaking me out."

Jeremy guided Stephan through using the reset button and typing in the reset code, then told him to activate the door.

Alethea held her breath.

The door swung open.

Stephan was through it in a flash. He grabbed Alethea's arm and they ran together down the stairs all the way to the street. Once safe, he swung her in a grateful hug that drove all air out of her lungs. Over his shoulder, she saw Jake Walton's helicopter land on the building Marc had entered. Dominic.

Although Marc had her phone, she didn't contact him. She didn't know what his situation was and she could give his location away. She grabbed Stephan and pulled him out of sight in case Sliver saw them.

She dialed Dominic's cell number and prayed he had it on him. When he answered, she wasted no time with pleasantries. "I have Stephan. He's out. Marc's inside with a likely desperate Sliver."

"Get Stephan back to Nicole," Dominic ordered after a short pause.

"I'm not leaving Marc," she said in a rush.

In a steely tone, Dominic said, "You did your part. Let me do mine. Now, tell me what you know about what's going on inside."

She knew exactly how to make him understand her stance. "Could you leave if it were Abby up there?"

Dominic countered with a good argument. "What you're not seeing is that if Marc knows you're there, he'll feel he has to protect you, and that could get him killed."

No, we're different. We're equals in this. "I'll send Stephan back, but I'm not leaving. I'm in communication with Jeremy and there may be a way I can help." She motioned for one of Marc's security men to hand over his earpiece.

He shook his head. She waved the phone at him and pointed to the helicopter on the roof. "Trust me, your boss wants me to have it."

Dominic's voice boomed out of the phone. "Give it to her before she takes it from you. We need everyone we have right now."

Alethea slid the earpiece in and said, "I'll be your eyes down here."

The guard looked at her as if to ask, "And what was I?"
She shrugged.

The building was evacuated. Marc's men had used the power outage to their advantage, claiming it was tied into a larger grid problem that could reverse-surge and potentially explode. They'd warned everyone to leave the area.

He heard the helicopter land on the roof. He and several of his men were on the floor where they suspected Sliver was. He wanted to rush forward through the door that separated him from his target, but first he needed to know who the helicopter was backup for. He fell back around the corner and pressed a button on his earpiece. "Dominic?"

"Yes."

Thank God.

Dominic said, "Stephan is out. Alethea is your eyes on the ground. She has an earpiece now. Closed channel nine three seven. Don't let her distract you."

Relief flooded through Marc. *She did it.* He hadn't doubted that she could, but now he could breathe again. Marc thought about the strong woman he loved and said, "This guy is not getting away, Dom. We have him pinned."

Dominic was quiet a moment, then said, "Bring him to me alive."

"Yes, sir," Marc said, and switched over to the channel Alethea was on. "Alethea?"

"Yes," she answered with an emotional burst. "I'm right here, Marc."

"Good work next door."

"I didn't do it alone."

"I told you being part of a team was better."

"I still don't take orders well. Dominic tried to send me back with Stephan."

Marc chuckled. "I can imagine how that went."

RUTH CARDELLO

"He did make a valid point. I don't want to divide your attention. I'm down on the street. Safe. Just close enough if you need me."

"Oh, I will need you... all night. As often and as creatively as my stamina allows. This may require revisiting our bunker," he said suggestively.

He heard the smile in her voice. "Seriously? That's what you're thinking about right now?"

"Imagining you beneath me, above me, crying out my name as I come inside you. It's my happy place. Are you saying you didn't think about me before you rushed into that building to get Stephan?"

"I did," she admitted. "I also did a little bargaining with God. You might want to try it."

"What did you offer to give up?"

"Erotica."

With a judgmental hiss, Marc said, "That's a shame, but I'll do my best to replace your smutty literature."

He imagined her stance, hand on hip, rolling her eyes. "Hurry up and get this guy. Then we'll see if you can live up to all that talk."

"Oh, I can."

In a more serious tone, Alethea asked, "If you have to switch back to the other channel, I'll understand. I can radio them if I see anything."

"No," Marc said. "Stay with me through this, Alethea. You're not my distraction. You're my strength."

"I will kill you if you die today," Alethea said seriously.

Marc laughed and signaled his men to surround the door. "I'm not going anywhere. I finally have something to live for."

From below, Alethea could hear what was going on, even if she couldn't see it. She heard the crash of the door as they broke it in. She heard the light footsteps of the men as they likely dispersed through the apartment. She held her breath.

BREACHING THE BILLIONAIRE: ALETHEA'S REDEMPTION

Marc's voice rang out, "Sliver. The game is over. You might as well come out. There is no escape route we haven't covered. Unless you decide to jump to your death out a window, and even then, I have someone to catch you, because we'd want you alive."

Marc was brilliant.

A promise like that always lured a cockroach out.

A second later a nervous male voice said, "I have your friend trapped next door. All I have to do is touch this button and he and half that building are gone. Tell your men to put down their weapons."

Marc laughed harshly. "The only reason you didn't just get a bullet through your head is because Stephan is long gone. So go nuts. Click away."

"How—" He stopped, then said, "Luckily I have this building rigged as well. Was that Dominic's helicopter that landed above? He's here, isn't he? Probably just outside the door. Too afraid to confront me himself. That's fine. All I have to do is press this button. If you shoot me, I'll still have the chance to take you all with me. You lose."

Alethea spoke spontaneously. "He's bluffing." Then her stomach flipped painfully. It was one thing to risk her own life on a hunch, but this was Marc. What if I'm wrong? She'd never played it safe in the past. Never. But she suddenly understood why people surrendered. The life of someone you loved resting on your decision was a terrifying responsibility. She wanted to tell him to give Sliver whatever he wanted. Let him by. Let him have the helicopter. Do anything it takes to get out of there alive.

But that wasn't an alternative she could live with either.

None of them would ever be safe. He'd come back stronger, nastier, and better prepared now that he saw how they worked together.

No, it ends today.

Alethea said, "He's a coward, not the type to kill himself. And he never thought we'd get this far. He didn't plan for this."

Marc said, "Understood."

And that was it.

He trusts me.

Oh, God, don't let me be wrong.

I can't lose Marc.

I love him.

If you spare him, I'll...

I'll...

She looked down at her feet and imagined her extensive collection of stilettos. "I'll wear flats from now on," she whispered aloud. *There. It may not be much, but if there is a God, He'll understand what it means to me.*

Marc asked, "What did you say?"

Sliver repeated his threat. "I said, have them drop their weapons or I'll blow us all up."

"Not you," Marc said impatiently. "Alethea?"

Alethea said, "I love you, Marc. I thought I didn't need anyone, but I need you. I want to go to sleep next to you. I want to wake up to your overly happy morning personality. Come back to me. Marry me. Today. Tomorrow. Just don't leave me."

Clearing his throat, Marc said, "I'm sorry, but no."

"No?"

"No, you don't get to propose to me. I have the whole thing planned out in my head."

Marc waved a finger in a circle and then pointed to Sliver. Men from both sides moved in. Sliver dropped the remote and tried to run, but there was nowhere to go. They pulled his arms behind him and raised him up onto his tiptoes. With a grimace, Marc watched a wet area spread down the man's cargo pants.

Sliver said, "This isn't over. It'll never be over. Even prisons have Internet—and something beautiful called parole."

Marc leaned in and snarled, "Oh, how cute. You think we called the police? I almost feel bad for you. You'll soon wish you had rigged this place. You don't fuck with a man's family. You don't threaten his children."

Sliver went to say something else but Marc instructed someone to stuff something in his mouth. Whatever he had to say, there wasn't a man there who wanted to hear it.

He was half hauled, half carried to the roof of the building. Jake took one look at his soiled pants and said, "Do we have to use my helicopter?"

Dominic glared at his friend. "I'll buy you a new one."

Jake shook his head sadly. "This one has good memories, but whatever. I guess we have to do what we have to do."

Sliver was pushed into the helicopter.

As they watched him being taken away, Jake said, "I feel like we should say something to him."

"What the hell would we say?" Dominic growled.

Jake shrugged. "I don't know. In the movies there is always a parting remark. Maybe you should punch him or something."

Dominic raised an eyebrow and shook his head. "I wouldn't be able to stop, and I told Abby I don't kill people."

Nodding in understanding, Jake asked, "So, what are you going to do with him? We can't take this to the police."

"I called Rachid. I told him we were overnighting a package to him. He said Najriad has a wonderful penal system. There is a plane gassed and ready to take Sliver there now. He's going to the same place Rachid sent his brother's shooter."

Jake frowned pensively. "I can't imagine that man is still alive."

Dominic shrugged. "Plausible deniability. What happens in Najriad stays in Najriad." He nodded at the pilot and they backed away from the wind of the rotors.

Once the roof was quiet again, Jake said, "I don't think you have to worry about Abby with this one. She'll be glad it's over."

Dominic closed his eyes for a moment. When they opened, they were shiny with emotion. He turned to Marc and held out his hand. "Thank you, Marc. I owe you for this. You tell me what you need and I'll make it happen."

Out of the corner of his eye Marc saw a blur of red hair rush him. He braced himself, but still had to take a stabilizing step back when Alethea launched herself at him, wrapping her legs around his waist and kissing him wildly. For a few moments Marc forgot where he was and simply savored the shared passion. Finally he broke from the kiss, not putting Alethea down, and said to Dominic, "I'm taking a short vacation. You won't hear from me for a couple of days. I'll write up a report when I come back. Mind if I borrow one of your toys?"

Dominic and Jake exchanged a look and Jake shrugged. "At least he asks."

"Fine," Dominic said gruffly. "Call Marie, but I don't want to know the details."

A siren in the distance warned that someone might have seen the commotion and called the police. Dominic and Jake left the roof with the rest of their security.

Marc and Alethea stayed for one more long kiss, leaving at the last moment before the police arrived. Hand in hand they bolted down the stairs, out of the building, and to a town car and driver he had waiting near the rear exit.

Once inside the vehicle, Marc took out his phone and Alethea stopped him by laying a hand over his phone. "Don't call Marie."

"She's the gatekeeper to his three-hundred-ninety-foot yacht. Have you ever seen it? We could take it out to his private island or wherever you want to go."

"It doesn't feel right."

His stomach clenched painfully. In the thick of the danger, had she spoken hastily of feelings she didn't really have for him? He'd seen that in the thick of war. People clung to each other while fighting for survival, but that bond was situational and often didn't hold up in the calm that followed. All he knew for sure was the depth of his love for her. If she needed more time, he could give her that. It wouldn't be easy, but her happiness was what mattered to him. "Which are you uncomfortable with? The yacht, or running off with me?"

"Involving Marie," Alethea said, and looked away. "The ladies and I didn't exactly part on good terms. It's time for me to admit that Lil and I are living very different lives now. I don't fit into hers any more than she wants to be a part of mine. I didn't want to see it, but maybe it's time to let that friendship go."

Marc hugged her to his side. He felt her pain and sought the words that would show her how wrong she was. "After today, I'm sure those women would forgive you anything. You saved Stephan and very likely the lives of whoever was next on his list. They'll love you."

Alethea shook her head. "No, they'll be grateful. They may even be nice to me for a short time because of this, but then we'll go right back to where we were before. Because at the end of the day, they can't accept me as I am. I can continue to fight with them, or I can accept the reality of the situation and focus on those who do." She laid a hand on his cheek and brought his mouth down to hers. "You."

Her kiss held a sweet desperation that tore as his heart. Who wouldn't want to be the center of this woman's universe? Not sharing her was tempting, but she wouldn't be happy if she walked away from the people who had become her family. "You sure about the yacht?"

She smiled, a mix of love and sadness in her eyes. "Don't you have any toys of your own?"

"Of course, but nothing as impressive."

"I'm not with you for the size of your... um... boat," she teased.

"I have a better idea where to take you." When she pulled back a bit cautiously, he laughed. "If you keep looking at me like that, we won't make it out of the back of this car, and I want to show you my place up on a small island off the coast of Massachusetts. It's not fancy—no underwater bedroom—but it has a private beach, and we could make love to the sound of the waves crashing in the background."

"That sounds perfect," Alethea said, then murmured against his lips, "Although that dividing window is tinted, and it's a thirty-minute drive back to my place."

Hauling her onto his lap, Marc growled, "I love the way you think."

A plan was forming in his head for a surprise for her when they returned from Massachusetts, but for now, all he could think about was how she felt against him. He wasn't one who usually employed a private driver, but he could now see the perks of having one.

Abby met Dominic halfway down the stairs of their house and flew into his arms. "You're back!"

He hugged her to him and buried his face in her hair. "It's over." The deep kiss they shared melted away her fear. For a moment she forgot everything beyond the feel of his lips on hers and the strength in the arms that held her to him. Relief came with a release of emotion, and she started crying even as their kiss continued.

With a hand on either side of her face, he broke off the kiss and wiped away her tears gently with his thumbs. "Don't, Abby. It's done. He'll never bother us again."

She searched his face desperately. "Are you sure?"

He nodded.

"Jake?"

Dominic looked over his shoulder and Abby stood on her tiptoes to do the same. She laughed when she saw Jake and Lil in a similar embrace a few steps below them. Jake was reassuring her sister between kisses.

Abby looked up into Dominic's loving eyes again. "Alethea? Marc? Are they both okay? Stephan is inside with Nicole. He said he left as soon as he knew you had Sliver. He said no one was hurt. Was he right?"

Lil overheard her question and added one of her own. "Why didn't Alethea come back with you?"

From the open door behind them, Marie called out, "Come on in, ladies—let your men catch their breath so they can fill us all in."

Lil's voice went up a few octaves when she asked, "She's okay, right? If something happened to her, just say it."

Jake kissed her on the forehead. "She's fine," he said, and smiled down at his worried fiancée. "She and Marc wanted some time alone."

Abby cocked her head to the side at the revelation. "Alethea and Marc? Really?"

Dominic frowned. "I thought you ladies told each other everything."

"We used to," Lil said, so sadly, that Abby elbowed Dominic to stop him from inquiring further.

"Marie's right. Let's talk about this inside," Abby said and wasn't surprised when Dominic appeared to have no idea what he'd said wrong. As they walked in, she whispered to him, "Things have been rocky between Lil and Alethea lately." As they crossed the foyer, Abby stopped suddenly. *I'm blaming someone else for something that's at least partly my fault.* She took Dominic's hand in hers and looked up into the eyes of the man she knew would love her no matter what she confessed to him. "And I haven't helped the situation. I couldn't let go of old insecurities. I wanted Lil to choose me over Alethea. She risked her life today for us, all of us. How petty am I that it took all that for me to forgive her for doing nothing more than loving Lil?"

Dominic raised her hand to his lips and kissed the inside of her wrist. "Before you bestow sainthood on her, wasn't Alethea the one who told Lil that curfews were made to be challenged?"

"Yes."

"Did you, or did you not, tell me that she was the one who encouraged Lil to take your car out the night she totaled it—a car you'd just paid off?"

219

Some of Abby's tension dissolved and she started to laugh. Memories that used to be painful were now humorous when relived in the arms of her loving husband. "Oh yeah, that was her. Lil wanted to get her license, but I didn't have the money to add her to my insurance so I asked her to wait one more year. Alethea thought taking the car would change my mind." And in that humor she found the strength to face the heart of her problem with Alethea. "The more I tried to protect Lil, the more Alethea encouraged her to challenge me."

"So you were both wrong," Dominic proclaimed and smiled with encouragement. "You can fix this. Someone once told me that all you have to do to stop being an asshole is to remember that every word you say, every action you take, defines you. Was that you who said it, or Jake?"

Turning slowly, Abby put both hands on her hips and said quietly, "Did you just call me an asshole?"

Jake's deep laugh boomed through the room. "Back away, Dominic. Don't say another word. Run for flowers."

Lil stepped in with advice where few would dare to tread. "Abby, I'm sure what Dominic was trying to say was..."

Marie followed suit, hoping to smooth the situation over, "It's been an emotional day for everyone..."

Abby put up a hand to silence them. She stood before her husband, glaring up at him, and demanded, "No, I want to know what he meant. He's a big boy. He can speak for himself."

Dominic hauled her to him, and right in front of everyone said, "You were wrong about Alethea, Abby. You held a grudge too long. You're flawed just like the rest of us, and I love you more every day because of it. I wouldn't change a thing about you, Abby. No, you're not perfect, and you don't have to be, because you're perfect for me."

With a sniff, she threw her arms around Dominic's neck and kissed him.

Standing beside Lil, Jake said sarcastically, "She let him off too easy."

Lil laughed at him, and with a hug said, "I think it was sweet."

He raised one eyebrow doubtfully. "And if I told you that you had flaws?"

"You'd sleep on the couch for a week," Lil said, but hopped onto her tiptoes to kiss him impishly.

He deepened the kiss, reminding her of all the reasons why that would be a difficult stand for either of them to take.

Clearing her throat loudly behind them, Marie said, "Nicole and Stephan are waiting for all of you in the atrium."

Reluctantly, the two couples separated and followed her down the hall. Rosella met them with little Judy in her arms as Colby toddled along next to her, holding onto her leg. Nicole was seated on the couch beside Stephan.

They both stood as the others entered the room. Dominic approached his sister and her fiancé. "Stephan..."

Abby put a hand on her husband's arm in caution. "Dominic, are you sure now is the time?"

Nicole took a defensive stance between them, but Stephan gently pulled her back beside him. "You don't need to protect me, Nicole. I know that I'm ultimately responsible for what happened today. Without me, Sliver would have never gotten as close as he did."

Shaking, Nicole glared at her brother. "That's not true. He used you, but if it hadn't been you he would have used someone else. I won't let Dominic pin all the blame on you—"

"Enough, Nicole." Dominic's voice boomed through the otherwise silent room.

Stephan straightened to his full height. In a soft but deadly tone, he said, "I don't care if she is your sister. The next words you say to her in that tone will be your last."

Dominic's eyes flew to Nicole, and when he saw how he had indeed upset her, he reached out to her. She took a step back, shaking her head. He threw his hands up in the air. "Why does everyone assume I'm going to say something awful?"

Abby slid beneath her husband's arm and hugged him. "Because you're yelling? And people do that when they're angry."

Dominic swore. Continuing on in an aggressive tone, he said, "I am angry—with myself. Sliver thought he could divide and demolish us, and he almost won because I let my temper get the better of me and cloud my judgment." He held out his hand to Stephan. "I appreciate what you did today."

No one moved.

The air crackled with tension.

Stephan smiled tenderly down at Nicole, then shook his future brother-in-law's hand. "I didn't do it for you, Dominic."

Jake lightened the mood with a bit of humor. "That's as close to an apology and an acceptance of one as we're going to get. Am I the only one who needs a stiff drink?"

"Here, this is better for you." Marie handed him a squirming Colby, who grabbed his face between her hands and said, "Daddy. Daddy."

Jake laughed, and without looking away from his giggling daughter, asked, "Does anyone know why her hands are sticky?" Amusement bubbled within those around him and spread until everyone was laughing.

The home phone rang and everyone froze, still off balance from the earlier events. Marie answered it, then said, "It's Marc." When Dominic made a move to the phone, she shook her head and said, "He wants to talk to Lil."

Lil took the cordless phone from Marie and asked, "Is Alethea with you?"

She nodded once. Nodded twice. Then she said, "If you're sure that's for the best." She seemed to agree with whatever Marc was saying and then her face lit up in a huge smile. "Really? Oh, my God, I would love to do that. I'm sure everyone else would, too. No, leave it all to me. I'll organize it. Great. See you Thursday night. I'll text you the location."

After Lil hung up, Abby asked, "What would we all love to do?"

Suddenly unsure, Lil looked around the room hopefully. "Throw a surprise engagement party for Alethea and Marc when they return on Thursday. He wants to ask her to marry him in front of all of us."

Abby put an arm around her sister's waist and said, "Let's do it."

Tears filled Lil's eyes. "You mean it?"

"Absolutely."

Biting her lip, Lil said, "Marc said she can't face us yet. He said we need to show her that we care."

That glimpse of vulnerability in Alethea fanned Abby's determination to make things right between them. "Then let's make this the best damn party New York has ever seen."

Nicole stepped closer, her voice growing stronger as she spoke. "I want to help you plan it. She believed in Stephan all along, and she's the reason he came home to me. I don't know how to begin to thank her for that."

Marie joined them, smoothing her hair with determination. "I am meticulous with details. I would love to help, also."

Rosella handed baby Judy to Dominic and joined the conversation. "A celebration will be good for all of us. How many people do you think we'll invite?"

Abby pondered it for a moment, then said, "At least fifty."

Nicole clapped her hands together in excitement. "We have to include the Andrades. They love stuff like this."

"Maddy will lose her mind when she hears what we're doing," Lil said, a huge grin lighting her face.

"So we'll plan for a hundred," Abby said. The group was buzzing with excitement over possible locations and details. With everyone temporarily occupied, Abby laced her fingers with Dominic's and gave his hand a small tug. He took the hint and bent an ear in her direction. "I will never take what we have for granted again. I'll never complain about the security you employ. I am so grateful that everyone came home safely. I don't know what I would have done if I'd lost you."

His hand tightened on hers. "I'm not going anywhere."

"I know," she whispered. Looking up into her husband's loving eyes, Abby fell in love with him all over again. Better not to spoil him, though. "But don't think this gets you out of midnight feedings," she teased.

He groaned but hugged her to him with a chuckle. "As long as I can wake you when I'm done." As he always did.

Abby winked and hugged him. *Should I tell him that's why I send him?*

Nah, he's a big boy. He'll figure it out.

It was well past midnight when Alethea slid out from beneath Marc's arm, wrapped a blanket around herself, and stepped out onto the deck of his small beach house. The cool night air carried the rhythmic sound of waves crashing in the distance, reminding her how she and Marc had made love their first night right there on the deck, in the glow of the moonlight.

And on the beach the next day.

Then in the shower.

Then gently the next morning when they'd woken.

Leaning against the railing, Alethea hugged the blanket tighter. Marc was more than she'd ever dared hope for. Passionate. Intelligent. Brave. Consistently better than a vibrator—and that wasn't something she could say about every man she'd been with.

He would have laughed at that joke if she'd said it to him, and then he likely would have tackled her and made her pay for it in some delicious way. She smiled into the darkness and acknowledged to herself how well they fit—in and out of the bedroom.

She didn't normally do long-term relationships. Friends with benefits was more her style. But Marc was different. Just the thought of him set her heart pounding and she started imagining how forever with him would be. He'd want children. A house they'd make into a home. There would be birthday parties, shared holidays. Family things.

Am I ready for that kind of life change?

I'd have to give up... traveling alone, eating alone, celebrating every accomplishment alone. Not that she couldn't find male companionship whenever she wanted it, but she was discovering that if you're not with someone who genuinely cares about you, it is possible to be with someone and still be alone.

I want a real life partner.

One who makes me feel like a valuable part of his team.

A treasured piece of his life.

Someone like Marc.

Unless I'm wrong about him.

She'd expected him to propose sometime during their last few days together, but he hadn't. Was he regretting his declaration of love? Dangerous situations heightened emotions, and all his talk of wanting to marry her may have faded away once things calmed down.

Not something that would be easy to tell a woman.

Is that why we're here? One hot fling before he breaks it to me that he doesn't see how things between us could actually work?

He's probably in there right now, rehearsing how to let me down easy on the flight home tomorrow. I should ask him to do it now while I'm still numb from the fact that I haven't heard from Lil or anyone in the Corisi compound.

No "Glad you made it out alive" text.

No "Thank you for the heads-up" phone call.

What did I expect?

Nicole to thank me for freeing Stephan?

Lil said it's not what I do that they find offensive but how I do it. I don't know how I offended them this time, but I'm sure I don't care anymore.

If I'm not good enough for them as I am, it is time to let them go.

"Hey, what are you doing out here?" Marc asked from behind, sliding his arms around her and resting his cheek against her hair.

"I needed some air," she said, continuing to look out into the darkness.

"Are you thinking about your friends back in New York?"

"No," she said too quickly.

He turned her in his arms and tipped her face up toward his. "I know when you're lying."

She refused to meet his eyes, snapping in response to feeling cornered, "What do you want me to say?"

Instead of reacting defensively to her tone, he continued to hold her, just hold her until she looked up at him. She saw love and acceptance in those deep blue eyes, and it shook her. Could he love her just the way she was? Could anyone?

"The truth. Nothing more. Nothing less. Don't pretty it up. Don't choose your words carefully. Not with me."

Still pushing him away when she really wanted to hold him closer, she said, "And what if the truth is ugly? People always say they want to know, but they don't. Not really."

He caressed one of her cheeks with the back of his hand. "I'm not most people. I thought you knew that by now."

Alethea turned away from him. "Why? Because we said some ridiculous things in the heat of the moment? Because the sex is good between us?"

Marc sighed behind her. "I didn't say a single thing I didn't mean. You can second-guess every moment we've spent together and twist it up into God-knows-what in that pretty little head of yours, or you can believe me. Love is a leap of faith. It doesn't come with a guarantee, and no one can convince you it's there if you don't want to see it." He stepped back and away from her. "I'm going back to bed."

Alethea didn't move even as she heard the door open and close behind her. She wanted to turn and run after him, but she didn't.

She gripped the railing in front of her.

Am I really this much of a coward?

I'm going to throw away an incredible man now because I'm afraid he'll leave me later?

Firming her lips into a line of determination, Alethea turned and walked into the beach house. She didn't stop until she was standing angrily at the end of the bed, resenting that he looked like he'd been about to fall asleep again.

Staring down at him, she put a hand on one hip and said, "I hate not knowing what's going on between us. I'm terrified that you're going to wake up and realize that you can't spend the rest of your life with someone like me."

"Come here," he said softly.

"No, I have to say this. You want to know the truth? I can't change who I am. I've tried. I don't know how I do it, but eventually I drive everyone I love away from me. It's only a matter of time before you decide I'm not worth the trouble. We should end this now."

There's your chance, Marc.

Break it to me gently or say it flat out.

Just do it.

With cat-like speed, Marc sat up, grabbed one of her arms, and dragged her down on top of him. "I'm not going anywhere," he said and rolled her beneath him.

"Everyone says that," Alethea said, blinking back tears that suddenly threatened. "But no one stays."

Marc bent and kissed her lightly. "That's not true, Alethea, and I will show you how untrue, but not tonight." He hugged her closer. "I know you're scared, but I need you to trust me one more time."

She hit him angrily in the chest, then nodded. He kissed her again and she met his lips eagerly, desperately, as if this might be their last night together.

Just in case it was.

Later, Marc stared at the ceiling, long after he'd heard Alethea's breathing deepen and felt her relax against him. He could have told her about his conversation with Lil, but it may or may not have made her feel better. She would have instantly begun to question why they'd agreed to host the party and might have even requested for it not to happen.

Knowing ahead of time would only lessen the effect.

Alethea needed to see love in the eyes of the people she'd risked so much of herself to save—and he was going to give her that. Even if it meant showboating their proposal, something he would have preferred to keep a private affair.

She'd get her proof.

It hadn't been easy to sneak away from Alethea long enough to coordinate the details with Lil, but he'd done it. Now all he had to do was convince her that she wanted to spend their first evening back in New York double-checking the existing security system of a building he would tell her he'd been hired to upgrade.

Although this time the request was a ruse, working together in that fashion made sense. Every system needed to be tested, and no one was better at finding a weakness than Alethea. She could enjoy the excitement of a challenge without also risking her life.

She sighed in her sleep and snuggled closer. He closed his eyes and rested his head against hers.

Tomorrow she'll see that she's not alone.

And she never was.

CHAPTER *Twenty-One*

"WHAT ARE YOU wearing?" Marc asked, when he returned to Alethea's apartment to pick her up and found her dressed from head to toe in a reflective, metallic jumpsuit with matching hood. It fit her snuggly in all the right places, sending his blood rushing downward and his thoughts toward activities that would make them very late.

"It's the newest in Stealth Wear. Isn't it amazing? It reduces my thermal footprint and reflects light in random patterns that blur my outline, making it harder for the naked eye to see me in a video." She flipped the hoodie up and over her long braid. "When up, my face will be blurred to cameras by blinking LED lights. So even if someone took a picture of me, my features would be indistinguishable." She twirled before him, giving him a brief view of how the material clung to her delicious ass. "The material looks smooth, but it actually has sections with prototype setules."

I'm not going to be able to get her into a dress easily, am I?

"With what?" he asked and loosened the bow on his tux absently. The temptation to remove it, along with all of his clothing, was strong.

"You know, setules—the tiny triangular hairs spiders use to climb walls." She lifted an arm to give him a closer view.

Temporarily fascinated, he ran his hand down her arm, but not because he cared about the suit's texture. He wanted the woman inside the suit. Now. The properties she'd listed gave him some creative ideas on how to test it. His hand stopped on her elbow, where the material felt rougher than the rest. "If you can climb the walls in this thing, I can think of an immediate application for it right now."

She swatted at his hand and lowered her hood. "The technology hasn't advanced that far, but it does provide better grip when I'm climbing through an air duct, or anywhere else with a smooth surface." She put her hands on her hips, looking glorious. "So keep it in your pants for now—I can't hang from the ceiling."

Damn. He leaned down and kissed her deeply. "How did you know what I was thinking?"

"It's what you're always thinking." She laughed and kissed him, not seeming the least bit bothered by it.

He smiled against her lips. "A fact that is entirely your fault. Now, go change into something appropriate for a formal business dinner. I spoke to my client and he wants to meet with us first before showing us around. If you showed up looking like you do now, he wouldn't be able to concentrate long enough to explain what he needs."

Her disappointment was clear in her expression. "A guided tour? You have to be kidding." She turned away and began to unzip her jumpsuit. "I wouldn't have said yes if I'd known."

He gulped as she eased the jumpsuit down over her bare shoulder, revealing the curve of her back and then her lace thong. When she stepped out of the suit, Marc's resolve fell to the floor with it.

"I need you," he said from just behind her, loosening the tie from around his neck.

"Earlier you said we had to be there by a certain time." She took two dresses out of her closet. Her high, pert breasts bounced slightly as she walked past him and held the dresses out to her sides.

He'd lost the ability to breathe.

"I'm sure I can find something you'll like." She returned the dresses to the closet, then bent before him to pick up a pair of simple black flats.

He couldn't move.

Couldn't speak.

The smile she flashed over her shoulder revealed she knew exactly what she was doing to him. He closed the distance between them and cupped her ass with both of his hands, loving how the string of her thong concealed nothing from his touch. "This works," he said huskily.

She straightened and turned, running her hands under the jacket of his tux and up to caress his chest. "We'll be late."

"I don't care," he growled, and swung her up into his arms and carried her to her bed.

Well over an hour later, Alethea stepped out of Marc's Lexus and walked with him toward the uptown office building, leaving their vehicle for valet parking. Her body was still humming from Marc's touch. He knew exactly how to bring her to orgasm again and again while somehow leaving her craving more.

Dressed in a sleek blue dress that Marc had convinced her was necessary, Alethea couldn't help but wonder about the man they were going to meet. He must be someone important if Marc was this concerned about impressing him. Marc didn't need the money. He was well paid by Dominic, and his side business of designing bunkers for the wealthy must have brought him a fair amount of additional income. So why the concern over this one side job?

Something didn't make sense.

Looking up, Alethea noted the entire top floor of the building was lit and that many people were visible in the windows. "You didn't tell me they had an event scheduled."

He shrugged. "It's a private affair. He uses a separate security service for events. Washington-based. Ex–Secret Service. They've never had a problem with it, so it's not part of what I was hired for."

Ex–Secret Service and he won't tell me who we're meeting. Now a party that should be, but probably wasn't, secured. "We should crash it."

Marc guided her into the building and hedged, "I don't know. I really want this job. Is it worth the risk?"

A month ago, Alethea would have said yes without giving it a second thought. She always rolled the dice and took her chances, sometimes winning, sometimes losing. The outcome had never mattered to her until she thought of it in terms of how it would affect someone she cared about. "You're right. We should ask your client if he wants it tested."

Marc stopped and looked down at her in surprise. "Won't that take the thrill out of it for you?"

Strangely, no. She wanted to see Marc get the contract more than she wanted to prove she was better than the Secret Service. The revelation was freeing. *I'm good at what I do. Marc knows how good I am. I don't need to prove myself to either of us anymore.* She went up on her tiptoes and kissed him impulsively on the lips. "I want you to get this job. Helping you do that will make me happier than breaking in ever would have."

A small frown darkened his handsome face. "You don't have to change for me."

She put a hand on his now tense jaw. "I am changing, but not *for* you—*because* of you. Thank you for asking me to come with you tonight. It means a lot to me that you want to work with me. You were right. It all comes down to trust."

She hadn't expected her comment to make him look even less happy. He shifted uncomfortably and said, "Alethea, I have something to tell you..."

"Yes?"

He looked torn, then seemed to come to a decision. "Let's walk straight into that party like we belong there. Let's just do it and see what happens."

"Are you sure?" *Now I really am confused.*

"I'm going to trust my gut on this one. Yes."

Hand in hand, they took an elevator to the top floor of the building. Way too easy. The security on the main floor had been expecting them, but what would happen when they reached the floor of the event? So far she hadn't seen anyone who looked liked they were ex–Secret Service.

Just before they reached the top, Marc said, "Whatever happens, remember I love you."

Alethea didn't have time to ask him why he was worried before the elevator door opened directly onto the party—a party where she recognized every formally dressed person in attendance.

Marc urged her to step out of the elevator, something she would have done naturally if her feet had not been frozen in shock. Lil, Jake, Abby, Dominic, Nicole, Stephan—they were all standing there in a semicircle with huge smiles on their faces. Marie stood off to one side with Jeremy and Jeisa. A young child ran around the room with his mother in quick pursuit behind him, which could only mean that, yes, Stephan had brought his whole clan with him.

Speechless, Alethea scanned the crowd. The faces were all familiar to her. She'd worked with each of them in the recent past.

Lil rushed forward and gave her a bone-crushing hug. "We were starting to worry that you weren't going to show up to your own—"

Marc intervened quickly. "She doesn't know yet."

Instantly on alert, Alethea pulled back from her friend and asked, "My own what?"

With a painful shrug, Lil said, "Surprise party?" She waved her hands in the air comically. "Surprise!"

Looking up at Marc, Alethea asked, "Tonight was about a party? So, there's no job here? You weren't asking me to work with you?"

Marc reached for her, but she backed away. "Not exactly..."

"You lied to me..."

"Technically, yes..."

Alethea wasn't sure what to think. All eyes were on her, and she knew they were expecting her to smile, but the mix of emotions rushing through her was overwhelming. *What is this? Why did you gather all these people together?*

Alethea's arms. "Don't be upset. He wanted you to have everyone who loves you around when he—"

Marc took Lil's hand off Alethea's arm, gave her a gentle push in Jake's direction, and said, "I'll handle it from here."

The lights around them dimmed, leaving the two of them lit by a spotlight. Marc reached into his jacket pocket and took out a box. He dropped to one knee before her and said, "Alethea Niarchos, you have driven me crazy since the first time I laid eyes on you. Every day with you since then has been an adventure, and one I don't want to end." He opened the velvet box and revealed a simple, deeply set, one-carat diamond solitaire. "I asked the jeweler what kind of ring could be worn while scaling down the side of a building and this is what he suggested." He held her left hand in one of his and the ring in his other. "You once told me to go big or go home. I plan to go home, Alethea, but home for me is wherever you are. Will you marry me?"

Looking down into his loving eyes, Alethea felt the last of her fear drop away. Tears began to run down her face and she said, "Hell, yes."

He slid the ring on, stood, and kissed her soundly. The sound of applause was deafening. Alethea pulled back, wiped the tears off her cheeks, and said, "You're crazy."

He bent and growled into her ear, "Only for you."

From a short distance away, Lil said, "Now can we hug her?"

Marc laughed into Alethea's ear and said, "You know she loves you."

Alethea glanced over her shoulder, then looked up at Marc again. "Do you mind?"

He shook his head and released her.

Alethea and Lil met each other halfway, laughing and crying. They started to apologize at the same time, neither of them caring they had become the focal point of the party.

Lil gushed, "I shouldn't have doubted you. And I shouldn't have asked you to change. I love you the way you are."

Alethea hugged Lil, not caring that her tears were likely smearing her makeup. "And I shouldn't have asked you to keep any secrets from your family."

Dominic's voice boomed above the music. "All right, everyone back to their tables so we can celebrate with a toast." The authoritative tone he used didn't leave room for question, and almost everyone returned to their tables, where flutes of champagne were being served.

Abby touched Alethea's arm gently. "I don't even know how to begin to thank you for what you did for us."

Nicole stepped forward also. "Alethea, we owe you more than we could ever repay. Stephan told me how you didn't leave him even when it could have cost you your life." She wiped a tear away. "Thank you for believing in him."

From just behind her, Marie said, "It's not easy for me to see that, even at my age, I still have a lot to learn. I'm sorry I misjudged you."

Alethea nodded, still feeling overwhelmed by the turn of events. Marc took her hand in his. She smiled up at him through her tears. She thought about the conversation they'd had on the way over and how it applied to those around her. She conceded, "I'm not the easiest person to get to know. Sometimes I charge forward without thinking of the effect my decisions will have on others." When no one said anything, Alethea shrugged and smiled. "I'll work on it."

Her humor spread through the group of women and Marc hugged her, smiling down with approval.

Lil laughed and hugged Abby. "See? She'll work on it. Problem solved. Now I can have my wedding."

Looking serious for a moment, Abby said, "I won't be offended if you choose her to be your maid of honor. I can't believe I'm saying this, but it's really good to see the two of you together again."

It was the first time that Alethea had ever felt truly accepted by Abby. It brought another layer of joy to the day. "Abby, I hear that married women are matrons of honor and that some brides have both."

Abby teared up and covered her mouth with one hand as she nodded.

Dominic took his place at Abby's side and said, "You know, we could use someone like Alethea on our payroll. Marc says his bunkers are impenetrable, but there's only one way to know for sure."

Jake interjected, "They've already been tested—from the inside, anyway."

Lil asked, "We have a bunker? Like one of those underground bomb shelters? How come I don't know about this?" When everyone looked away, she said, "I can keep a secret."

Alethea started laughing, and everyone else followed suit.

All except Lil, who put her hands on her hips and protested, "I can."

It was wonderful to realize that no matter how much things changed, some things stayed the same. In the face of the continued amusement of those around her, Lil took a page out of Alethea's book. She shrugged and said, "I'll work on it."

Abby shook her head and laughed. "Let's go get some champagne."

As the group headed off to the main area of the party, Marc whispered in Alethea's ear, "This is what I wanted you to see. Yes, you fight with them, but these people are your family and they love you. As I do."

Alethea tightened her arm around Marc's waist and whispered back, "I love you so much, Marc Stone. I can't believe you did this for me."

"Wait until you see how we get home. Jake bought us a helicopter."

"A what?"

"You heard me. It's our engagement present."

"They are over the top."

Kissing her neck, Marc said, "I hear it's better than any backseat ever could be."

Alethea threw back her head and laughed. "You would think like that."

He growled against her neck. "Always."

"Excuse me," a female voice said from beside them. Alethea turned to find Jeremy standing there with his provocatively dressed Brazilian fiancée, Jeisa. "Do you have a moment?"

It was probably too much to expect the entire evening to be without drama. Here it comes. Stay away from my man. How dare you include him in something dangerous? It doesn't matter what she says, nothing can ruin tonight.

She has a right to her residual anger.

I didn't exactly help her engagement go smoothly.

Breathe and smile.

"Jeisa, what a surprise," Alethea said, hoping she sounded happy. Marc's hand tightened on her waist in silent warning.

I know, I know. Play nice.

Jeremy said, "I told Jeisa about everything that went down with Sliver. She flew in just to see you."

Lucky me.

Jeisa stepped forward and took both of Alethea's hands in hers. "I am so happy for you, Alethea. You are glowing tonight. You and I had a bumpy start, but that is in the past now. I hear people say you were not a good friend to Jeremy, but I wanted you to know I think they are wrong. Look at him today. No, you were not a love match for him, but you gave him something to hope for when he had nothing else. He is an amazing man, and part of the man I love came from his friendship with you. After hearing what you did for Stephan, I knew I had to come and tell you something. I spent a good part of my life trying to avoid unpleasant situations, but it was only by facing them that I was able to move past them. You grab ugly by the horns and ride it out. You inspire me. Jeremy is lucky to have a friend like you. I hope that we can be friends, too, as we move forward, Alethea."

Looking from Jeisa to Jeremy and back, Alethea pulled Jeisa into a hug. "I would like that. I would really like that."

She met Jeremy's eyes over Jeisa's shoulder and saw her old friend smiling back at her from beneath his buffed businessman exterior.

He looked over at Marc and said, "If you ever hurt her, you'll have to deal with me." When Jeisa returned to his side, he added, "And worse—Jeisa. I can empty your bank accounts and send the funds overseas, but you do not want to incur the Brazilian wrath. There isn't a bunker, not even one you've built, that could save you from that."

Marc accepted the warning with a smile. "Understood." He took Alethea's left hand in his and raised it to his lips. "Your friends are as protective of you as you are of them, Alethea." He sighed as if in pain. "Looks like you're stuck with me."

"Looks that way," Alethea agreed with a huge, giddy smile. She looked across the room to where Lil had taken the microphone and was standing on a small stage beside the live band. "We'd better get our champagne. It looks like Lil is going to make a speech, whether we're ready or not."

In her ear, Marc said softly, "I've been ready for this since the first moment I saw you across the room."

CHAPTER *Twenty-Two*

"WHERE DID I put my vows? I can't find my vows." Lil frantically searched the room, her long wedding dress and veil whipping wildly behind her in the bridal suite of the small Manhattan church. "I put them right there near my makeup bag and they're gone."

Dressed in a floor-length silk off-the-shoulder gown, Abby held up a white silk satchel. "They're in your bag so you won't forget them. Exactly where you told me to put them."

Snatching the bag from her sister, Lil let out a relieved breath when she opened it and pulled out a paper. "I should have printed this in bigger font. What if I start crying and can't read it?"

"As long as you speak from your heart, Lil, it doesn't matter what you say up there. What matters is you and Jake will finally be married. That's the most important part of today," Abby said.

"Is Alethea back yet?" Lil asked in a worried tone.

"She's talking to King Rachid's Royal Guardsmen—probably telling them how to do their jobs," Abby said with some irony. "Zhang said she and Marc offered to coordinate security for today. I'm not sure Zhang thought it was necessary, but I told her to just be grateful Alethea asked. Don't tell Alethea, but I feel better knowing she's involved. I still worry whenever I leave Judy, even though I know she's perfectly safe with Marie."

"It's been two months, Abby. Sliver isn't coming back."

"I know. Rachid told Dominic he handled it. I don't know what that means exactly, and I'm not normally one who advocates that kind of justice, but I've never been so afraid in my life."

"You're freaking me out, Abby. Can I go back to worrying if the boutonnieres have arrived?"

Wise enough to know that her sister was serious, Abby said, "So, what mischief have you planned for today? At my wedding, you dared Zhang to kiss a sheikh. For Zhang's wedding you had all of us belly dancing the night before. Your own wedding can't go on without a dare or a surprise."

Alethea jumped into the conversation. "Don't worry, I have that covered."

"Al!" Lil hopped with excitement at the return of her friend. "What did you do?"

Dressed in a similar but edgier version of Abby's dress, Alethea walked over and joined her friend near the makeup table. "Nothing yet. It's just an idea. Have you seen Stephan's cousins? The ones he flew in? I don't think there is a woman here who won't appreciate how Stephan's near-death experience prompted him to reach out to them."

"That's awful," Abby said, but her tone held no bite.

Lil paused and laughed. "Maybe, but they're gorgeous."

Chiding gently, Abby said, "Aren't you getting married in a few minutes?"

Lil smiled shamelessly. "Marriage does not make you blind."

Giving up, Abby laughed. "Okay, I've seen them, too, and they represent the Andrades well. What a gene pool. I'm afraid to ask, but what's your idea?"

"A friendly competition. We'll call it, 'Who's the best matchmaker?'"

Lil said, "Hands down, Maddy is."

Alethea looked across at Abby slyly. "You think she's better than you?"

Abby adjusted her long gown. "Maybe... maybe not. I know I'm better than you."

Alethea's eyes narrowed at the challenge. There would always be an edge of competition between them, but they had both acknowledged the fact and even laughed about it. The future might still hold a few bumps for them, but the core of their relationship had changed. They'd discovered that when it mattered, they had more in common than they'd thought: loyalty to family. Everything else could be worked out. "A hundred dollars says you're not."

"Ooooooh..." Abby drew the word out for emphasis. "You are so on."

Lifting and dropping the large skirt of her custom-made, fairy-tale-style white wedding dress, Lil looked over her shoulder at the two women and said, "I'm in, too. Are we calling the win at an engagement or a wedding?"

"Engagement," Abby and Alethea said in unison, then both smiled.

Lil clapped with excitement. "I love it, Al. This is going to be so much fun. Are there any rules?"

"They can't know what we're doing, and none of you can whine when I win," Alethea said, with a flip of her long red mane.

Abby added, "Stephan told me he used to be close to these cousins until something happened between his father and their mother. Stephan really does want to bring them back into the fold. Whatever we do can't jeopardize that."

Maddy walked into the room with a tray of champagne. "Look what I found out in the hall." As each woman took a glass, Maddy asked, "What can we not jeopardize?"

Entering the room behind her, Queen Zhang refused a glass. "I see nothing has changed. Who are you daring today, Lil?"

Lil rushed over to hug the friend who lived too far away for her liking. "I didn't start this one. Alethea did."

Maddy's eyes rounded. "We're not going to do anything illegal, are we?"

Alethea shrugged a shoulder carelessly. "Is it illegal if you don't get caught?"

If possible, Maddy's eyes grew even wider.

Abby intervened, "She's joking, Maddy. She has a funny sense of humor. You'll get used to it." She softened her words with a smile and a wink at Alethea. "Eventually, you'll even like it."

Zhang looked around, a pleased smile on her face. "It's nice to see everyone getting along. Now back to what I missed."

Nicole rushed in. "I'm so sorry. There were a few people Stephan wanted me to meet, but it should have waited until after the ceremony. I forget how many Andrades there are. They flew in from everywhere for today. It's crazy out there. Lil, thank you for inviting them. I know they aren't technically your family, but it means a lot to Stephan that they're welcome here."

Lil walked over and hugged Nicole. "You're my family and, through you, so are they. I always used to wonder what it would be like to come from a big family with aunts and uncles and crazy family gatherings. Victor and Katrine opened their home to me the first time I met them. We're happy to have them here."

Turning to Alethea, Nicole said, "Speaking of Stephan's parents, they haven't stopped talking about how happy they were to meet you. They want you to come over for dinner again soon."

Alethea smiled. "I may have to do just that. I need to dig up whatever I can on Stephan's first cousins: George, Luke, Nick, and Max. I intend to win."

Lil turned to Maddy with excitement. "We're taking bets on which one of us is the best matchmaker, and we're going to prove ourselves with them. There are four of them, right? We have to be able to marry one of them off."

Instead of showing excitement, as Lil had expected, Maddy's expression fell a bit at the mention of her cousins. "I'm very close to the rest of my family, but my aunt moved her children away from us after a falling-out with Uncle Vic. We may not see them again after today. I helped Stephan convince them to come, but it wasn't easy. I think a couple of them came just to meet Dominic."

"We don't have to do this if you don't want us to," Abby said gently.

Alethea added, "Sure, if you don't like a challenge. What better way to get to know them than to dabble in their business a bit?"

Chewing her lip, Maddy looked uncharacteristically unsure of herself. "You think?"

Zhang smiled. "And so it begins..."

The wedding planner stuck her head in the door and said, "Are you ready?"

Lil took Abby's hand in one of hers and Alethea's in the other, then gave them both a squeeze. "You're right, Abby. There is nothing to be nervous about. This is already the best day of my life."

As they walked out the door, Abby held the back of Lil's dress off the floor and whispered to Alethea, "That was perfectly timed. She was getting really worked up. Now she has something fun to focus on instead of how everyone will be watching her. Genius."

"You can butter me up all you want, Abby, but I'm going to prove to you there is a science to this."

Without missing a step, Abby answered just as softly, "And strategy. I call Marie for my team."

"Ooh, that's cheating," Alethea said under her breath.

Lil stopped and looked over her shoulder. "Are you two getting along?"

They both smiled sweetly at her and, in unison, said, "Of course."

Alethea whispered, "The one we have to watch out for is Maddy. She has inside information, and that gives her an advantage."

"She's pregnant again. That'll slow her down," Abby said.

With admiration, Alethea said, "Who knew you were this competitive? I like you more the better I get to know you."

Abby nodded in agreement. "I know exactly what you mean. I just hope you handle it well when you lose."

The wedding planner led the way out of the suite and down the hall to the room where all the guests were gathered. Colby was waiting with Marie, dressed in a lavender flower-girl dress. She ran to her mother as soon as she saw her. "Mommy, Mommy, up, up."

Marie tried to redirect her. "Colby, you're the flower girl. You walk in first and throw the flowers. Remember what we practiced?"

A young lip protruded and tears threatened. "Mommy?"

Lil reached down, lifted her daughter onto her hip and said, "We can throw them together."

Marie hovered. "Are you sure? Maybe she wants to walk with Auntie Abby?"

Colby shook her head and buried her face in her mother's silk bodice. Lil hugged her tightly and said to her daughter, "You can walk with me if you want, Colby. It's like Auntie Abby says—we're always better together."

Colby raised her face and smiled, allowing Lil to lower her onto her feet beside her. Holding her mother's hand, Colby said, "Togedder."

Lil straightened from her daughter and looked at her sister and best friend standing side by side. A huge smile spread across her face. "Best wedding present ever."

Jake resisted adjusting the bow tie on his tuxedo as he stood in front of a white rose-covered altar with the minister. Dominic, Jeremy, Stephan, Rachid, and Richard stood in a line off to the side of him. Although he and Lil had lived together for almost a year, his stomach was still doing crazy flips in anticipation of seeing her walk down the aisle to him.

He spared a glance at the men on his side. Time had tested each of their friendships and they were stronger because of it. He couldn't imagine what his life would have been like if he'd never met Dominic. Jeremy had become the younger brother he'd never known he wanted but now couldn't imagine not having. Rachid had stepped out of his life for nearly a decade, and his return had been chaotic, but having him there felt right. Stephan and Richard represented half of the people in attendance—the Andrade family, people Jake couldn't imagine marrying Lil without. He saw a bit of himself and Dominic in Alessandro and Victor and hoped to one day have a legacy as large and loving as theirs.

Marc met his eyes from over the heads of the seated guests. He'd told Marc that he didn't have to work that day, but like Alethea, Marc couldn't turn off his inner watchdog.

Music began to play, and the guests fell silent.

The door at the end of the aisle opened, catching the women a bit unaware, still smiling and laughing over some private joke.

Under his breath Richard asked, "I wonder what they're plotting today."

Dominic said firmly, "Let's not go looking for trouble."

Richard answered with humor, "No need to look for it. It's dressed and walking this way."

"Stop before you make me laugh. Lil will kill me," Jake muttered.

Stephan interjected, "They definitely look too happy."

Rachid added with royal confidence, "Women are always happy at weddings."

"Mark my words," Richard said, "something is brewing."

Jake muttered, "Will you all just shut up? You're making me nervous."

Dominic chuckled. "You have nothing to worry about unless you forget your vows or step on Lil's veil. Whatever you do, don't accidentally call her the wrong name."

"You're such an ass, Dom," Jake growled without taking his eyes off the procession of women walking down the aisle.

Jeremy burst out with a laugh that had all of the guests looking forward at the men instead of back at the bridesmaids. "Sorry. I just pictured Lil's face if Jake called her the wrong name."

With a forced smile, Jake said, "You'll be where I am soon enough, Jeremy. Remember that payback is sweet."

Jeremy gulped and kept his next thought to himself.

Dom flexed his shoulders and bragged, "Luckily, I'm safe."

Jake said, "Oh, no, Dom, you have an upcoming baptism. Push me and I'll use that event to tell Abby that you said you're ready to start on your second child."

Dominic fell silent after a muttered curse.

Stephan laughed.

Dominic glared at him.

Further teasing would have been wasted; the moment Lil stepped out from behind the door and started down the aisle, Jake's attention was riveted on his bride. She walked toward them slowly, handing a now happy Colby off to Abby, and joined Jake in front of the minister.

The minister started the ceremony with the usual formality. "We are gathered here today to celebrate the union—"

Lil burst out, "I do."

A chuckle echoed through the church. The minister said, "We're not at that part yet."

Flushing a deep red, Lil said hastily, "I didn't mean to say that out loud. Just keep going. I guess I'm nervous." She looked across at Jake apologetically. "And now I'm babbling."

"I do, too," Jake said with quiet dignity, as if it were perfectly appropriate. Then he winked down at his bride.

Lil's eyes filled with happy tears. "You do?" she asked.

Jake nodded solemnly and held out a hand to her. "Today. Tomorrow. Forever. I promise you, Colby, and the family we'll make together that I will be there for you. Always."

The minister closed his book in resignation and waited.

With a huge smile, Lil took Jake's hand. "I promise you the same. Today. Tomorrow. Forever. I will be there for you—always."

Rolling with the impromptu change in script, the minister asked, "Do you have the rings?"

Jake slid Lil's on. Lil slid Jake's on. She burst into happy tears and he pulled her to him for a deep kiss.

The minister coughed. "Okay, it looks like we're kissing the bride now. With the power invested in me by the state of New York, I now pronounce you husband and wife." He cleared his throat loudly again. "What God has brought together today, let no one separate." As their kiss continued, the minister smacked Jake on the shoulder lightly with his Bible. "A little separation is necessary sometimes."

With a laugh, Jake and Lil ended their kiss and turned to the people gathered.

The minister said, "I now present, for the first time, Mr. and Mrs. Jake Walton."

Lil held out her hand to Colby, who was straining to leave Abby. She came running across the altar to them. Jake gathered up his adopted daughter and held her with one hand as he took Lil's hand in his other and they walked down the aisle together.

Dominic held out an arm to Abby. She took it and, even as she smiled, said, "Don't think we didn't hear you guys laughing. You're wearing microphones, you know."

With a half smile, Dominic threw his friend under the bus. "Richard started it. He said you ladies are plotting something."

Abby smiled. "We are."

"Should I worry?"

"Maddy, Lil, Alethea, and I have a bet going. First one to marry off an Andrade cousin wins."

"Good luck with that," Dominic said. "Victor says those boys have had a rough time."

Abby said smugly, "I don't need luck. I have Marie."

"You included Alethea in on this?" Dominic whistled softly. "You'd better hope that Stephan's family doesn't have any skeletons in their closet."

Abby covered her mouth with a worried hand. "I never thought of that."

Dominic shrugged, bent, and kissed his wife's cheek. "What's the worst thing she could find?"

The *End*

Don't miss out on any of Ruth's books!

Go to RuthCardello.com and add your email to the mailing list.

We'll send you an email as soon as
A new book *is released!*

Made in the USA
San Bernardino, CA
19 May 2020

72083614R00144